NOTH.

By Kris Tualla:

Loving the Norseman
Loving the Knight
In the Norseman's House

A Nordic Knight in Henry's Court
A Nordic Knight of the Golden Fleece
A Nordic Knight and his Spanish Wife

A Discreet Gentleman of Discovery
A Discreet Gentleman of Matrimony
A Discreet Gentleman of Consequence
A Discreet Gentleman of Intrigue
A Discreet Gentleman of Mystery
A Discreet Gentleman's Legacy (2019)

Leaving Norway
Finding Sovereignty
Kirsten's Journal

A Woman of Choice
A Prince of Norway
A Matter of Principle

The Norsemen's War: Enemies and Traitors
The Norsemen's War: Battles Abroad
The Norsemen's War: Finding Norway

Sempre Avanti: Always Forward (with Thomas Duhs)
Ice and Granite: The Snow Soldiers of Riva Ridge (with TD)
Viking Spy (2019)

An Unexpected Viking
A Restored Viking
A Modern Viking

*****

A Primer for Beginning Authors
Becoming an Authorpreneur

Camp Hale Series: Book Two

Ice and Granite
The Snow Soldiers of Riva Ridge

Kris Tualla
with Thomas Duhs

"Ice and Granite - The Snow Soldiers of Riva Ridge" is a work of fiction. Names, characters, places and incidents are products of the author's imagination or are used fictitiously and are not to be construed as real. Any resemblance to actual events, locales, organizations, or persons, living or dead, is entirely coincidental.

© 2018 by Kris Tualla and Thomas Duhs

ALL RIGHTS RESERVED. No part of this book may be used or reproduced in any form or by any means without the prior written consent of the Publisher.

ISBN-13: 978-1720918110
ISBN-10: 1720918112

*We dedicate this book to the
Tenth Mountain Division soldiers in World War II
and the legacy they left behind.*

And to those who won't let them be forgotten.

Chapter One

January 11, 1943
Camp Hale, Colorado

"Geez, it's freezing!"

Lucas Hansen tugged his Army-issued wool coat tighter around his neck as he stepped out of the overheated train along with hundreds of other new recruits. Hit by a glacial Arctic blast on the crowded wooden platform at tiny Pando Station, high in the Rocky Mountains, he wondered if he'd made a terrible mistake.

But whatever he was, he wasn't a quitter.

And it's time to get back in the game.

Lucas hefted his tightly packed duffel bag onto his shoulder and trudged after the line of men who got off the train before him. Their heavy-soled Army boots thudded loud and hollow against the platform's boards in the otherwise quiet morning. He assumed someone in front of the line knew where they were supposed to go.

When the group came to a halt, he pulled a deep, frigid

lungful of the thin mountain air and lifted his eyes to the surrounding snow-covered peaks, pink-topped in the sunrise.

For a guy who grew up his whole life in the flatlands of rural Kansas, the Rocky Mountains of Colorado were astonishing. It took all night for their train from Denver to climb the Tennessee Pass and ease down the other side into the high valley where Camp Hale was situated.

Now here he stood, utterly amazed by all that he saw.

"Over here, privates!" A sergeant in a line of sergeants waved a clipboard. "Check in with one of us."

Lucas stepped forward.

A red-cheeked sergeant squinted up at him and blew a frosty breath. "Name?"

"Lucas Thor Hansen."

The man awkwardly flipped a couple pages with glove-clad hands before he spoke. "Eighty-Seventh Regiment, Second Battalion, E Company." He tipped his head to the right. "That way. Your platoon sergeant is holding a sign."

Lucas nodded.

87th, 2nd, E.

Should be easy enough to remember.

He joined a small group of men, counting them out of habit. Eleven plus himself.

An extra man on the field.

Lucas grimaced. Six years after walking off the football field at the end of his final state championship game he still felt the sting of the touchdown called back for having an extra player on the field. At least they won the title, thanks to a two-point safety in the fourth quarter.

"Welcome, privates. I'm Sergeant John Simpson, your platoon sergeant." A muscular man with brown eyes and thick black hair grinned at them without joy. "Welcome to Camp Hell."

Lucas glanced at the men standing with him trying to discern

Ice and Granite: The Snow Soldiers of Riva Ridge

if the sergeant was making a joke. They looked as confused as he was.

"We are standing at nine-thousand and four-hundred feet of elevation. The air here is thin. Altitude sickness is real," Sergeant Simpson continued. He gave each one of them a stern look. "Your first goal is to become accustomed to the conditions here at camp, because they only get worse from here on out. Got it?"

The men nodded.

"The correct response is *yes, sir!* Got it?"

"Yes, sir!" Lucas barked.

Simpson shot him an evaluative glance. "Good. Follow me."

The sergeant led his silent platoon of strangers through the huge, flat-bottomed valley filled with hundreds of two-story, whitewashed wooden barracks hunkered in straight rows along paved and plowed roads.

The air above the camp was hazy and stunk from the coal smoke belching from both the train and the smoke stacks on the camp's perimeter. Everything they walked past was covered with soot, even the snow.

Maybe hell was an accurate description after all.

Sergeant Simpson led them to one of the barracks and opened the wide front door. "Welcome home, boys."

Lucas climbed the steps and entered the heated building. His chilled cheeks stung from the sudden change in temperature.

"Take any bunk you want that's empty," Sergeant Simpson instructed. "Breakfast's at eight in the mess hall. Don't be late."

Lucas hurried forward to grab a bottom bunk.

"Mind if I take the top?"

Lucas turned to face a lanky private with shockingly red hair. "No. Go ahead."

"Thanks." The private threw his duffel on the top bunk and then extended his right hand. "David Fraser."

Lucas shook his hand. "Lucas Hansen. Pleased to meet you."

"Hansen? That's Norwegian, right?"

Lucas grinned. "Yeah."

Fraser smirked. "Explains the blond hair and blue eyes. You speak Norwegian?"

"Nah." Lucas waved a dismissive hand. "My father's ancestor settled in Boston not long before the Revolutionary War, so it's been a few generations. Why?"

Fraser stuffed his cold-reddened hands into his pockets. "I heard a group of guys who speak the language are training here at Hale. The Ninety-ninth. They call themselves the Viking Battalion."

"Yeah, I heard about them. That's what got me thinking about joining up in the first place." Lucas shrugged. "But like I said, I don't qualify."

Fraser looked confused. "So what drew you here?"

Lucas pulled a breath while he thought about how to put his feelings into words. "I wanted to be part of something… special. Not just another regular soldier, you know?"

"So you're a skier, then."

Lucas chuckled and wagged his head. "No. I'm from Kansas, near the Nebraska border. Never been on skis a day in my life. You?"

"Yeah. The Smoky Mountains in North Carolina." Fraser frowned a little. "How'd you get into the Ski Troops?"

Lucas shrugged. "I went to the recruiting station and signed up. Why?"

"Because…" Fraser glanced around the room of recruits settling in. "The guy who started this whole program, Minnie Dole, insisted on personally vetting every man who was assigned here."

That was news to Lucas. "Really?"

"Yep. He asked for three letters of recommendation and an application from everyone wanting to join the Ski Troops."

Lucas sank slowly onto the bottom bunk. "The recruiters didn't mention anything like that. They just assigned me here when I asked for it."

Several of the other men gathered around Lucas and David Fraser, obviously drawn by their conversation.

"I don't ski, either," one of them said. "And nobody at the recruitment office said anything to me about it being required."

"Same here." The stocky brunette who spoke looked around the group. "But the office in San Diego was really crowded and they were trying to process guys through as quick as they could."

Lucas returned his attention to Fraser. "I guess we all had the same idea. Once the Japs bombed Pearl Harbor we knew it was just a matter of time until we joined up. And when the Ski Troops came around it sounded like a great opportunity."

Fraser looked resigned. "I guess they'll have to teach you all, now that you're here."

"Guess so." Lucas grinned again. "But I'm sure I'll catch on. I'm really good at physical things."

Fraser, who was a couple inches shorter than Lucas, swept him with an evaluative gaze. "I believe you."

Lucas looked at his watch and stood. "It's almost eight. Let's go find the mess hall."

The men left the heated barracks and once again faced icy winds and soot-filled air as they headed across camp toward the mess hall. Conversations floated back to Lucas on the thin breeze as the soldiers began the process of getting to know their new brothers in arms.

In spite of the obvious challenges ahead, Lucas felt a surge of belonging that had been missing from his life for the last six years. This was where he should be, where he would thrive.

This is my team now.

*****

After breakfast the platoon gathered in the Field House while Sergeant Simpson began the tedious process of familiarizing them with their winter gear. Stacked on the platform in front of the bleachers were gloves and mittens, snow pants, snow jackets, knit caps, helmets, and goggles. Off to the side were seven-foot-long skis, poles, and snow shoes in two sizes.

And all of the gear was white.

"Camouflage in the snow," the sergeant explained as each man claimed his items from every pile. "Being a dark target against a white background is signing your own death certificate."

That made sense.

Lucas stood next to David Fraser. The stocky brunette from San Diego—whose name was Xavier Martinez—stood on his other side.

"Take off your boots!" Simpson ordered. "The snow pants go on over your fatigues. Put them on."

Simpson waited while the men donned the snow pants then held up a jacket. "The coats are reversible. White on one side and olive drab on the other, for when you're mountain climbing in areas where there is no snow."

"We're going to learn mountain climbing, too?" Martinez shuddered as he slid his arms into the coat. "I'm really afraid of heights."

"I've never seen anyone climb anything taller than a silo," Lucas admitted as he put the coat on white side out.

"This is definitely warm enough," Fraser swiped the heel of his hand across his brow. "I'm beginning to sweat."

Simpson picked up one of Lucas's size twelve Army boots and addressed the soldiers. "See this groove on the back of the heel of your boots? It's for the ski-binding cable. Put your boots back on."

Lucas donned his boots while Simpson crossed to the stack of skis leaning against the wall. "Hansen, step forward."

He did.

The sergeant bent down and fastened a ski to Lucas's left

Ice and Granite: The Snow Soldiers of Riva Ridge 7

boot. "This is how you loop the cable for cross-country skiing. It allows the heel to lift during the stride."

Then he fastened a ski to Lucas's right boot, running the cable differently. "And this secures the heel for downhill skiing."

Simpson straightened. "Any questions?"

"No, sir," the group chorused.

"All right. Fasten your own." Sergeant Simpson bent down and loosened Lucas's cables. "Now do it for yourself, Private."

He got it right on the first try.

"This." Simpson held up the larger snow shoe. "This bear paw is for regular use in situations where skis aren't appropriate."

He handed it to Fraser who figured out how to put it on—it was even easier than the skis.

"And this is for emergencies." The instructor waggled the smaller snow shoe in the air before handing it to Martinez. "Now take off the skis and put on the bear paws."

Simpson went down the line of twelve men assuring each one had his equipment correctly in place. "When you're done, put on your cap, goggles, helmet, and mittens."

Lucas moaned. Sweat was dripping into his eyes and running down the groove in his back.

Simpson stopped in front of him. "Are you warm enough, Private?"

"Yes, sir," Lucas replied. "Warm as a black snake on a flat rock in August,"

Simpson chuckled and immediately coughed into his fist to hide it. "Good."

Then he addressed the platoon. "When you men are properly outfitted, we expect you'll be both warm and invisible to enemy lookouts."

"Yes, sir," the group chorused.

"All right. Take off your gear, return to your barracks, and stow it properly. Grab a pair of skis and poles on your way out.

Your ski training starts tomorrow." Simpson looked at his watch. "Take the next couple of hours to get yourselves settled in. Lunch is at noon. We'll head for the Transition Range after that."

He looked up, seeming malevolently pleased. "Dismissed."

*****

Lucas wasn't sure what he expected the Transition Range to be, but it certainly wasn't this.

"The object is to simulate battle conditions," Sergeant Simpson explained to the freshly-outfitted platoon wearing their new white uniforms. "You men will crawl through the snow under barbed wire while machine guns fire over your heads."

He chuckled a little. "And yes. The ammunition is live."

Lucas's eyes rounded. *Oh, hell no.*

Certainly they wouldn't risk killing their recruits.

Would they?

Lucas looked at Fraser and Martinez and saw the same shock on both of their faces that was chewing a hole in his gut.

"They won't kill us, right?" Martinez said with a confidence that didn't match his expression. "That would be stupid."

"Right. It would be." Fraser stepped forward. "Might as well get this over with, then."

When Lucas's turn came he dropped to his belly and scrambled like a mouse being chased by a barn cat. The packed snow beneath the barbed wire had turned to ice—slick, rough-ridged, and freezing cold.

Lucas couldn't hear anything but the irregular bursts of machine gun fire behind him. He felt the guns' concussive punches against his back and hoped the sensation of bullets flying by him was his imagination. He closed his eyes.

It's just conditioning, he told himself.

Do the drill.

Lucas emerged from under the barbed wire and rolled

sideways to get out of the machine guns' line of fire. He clambered shakily to his feet and brushed the snow and ice off his pants so he didn't have to stand up straight away.

Okay. Survived that.

Once every man in the platoon went through the course, Sergeant Simpson made a note on his clipboard before delivering the news. "Congratulations. Most of you made it through under the maximum time. Now we're going to repeat this exercise until *all* of you do. Go back to the starting line."

*****

After a quick shower, Lucas stretched out on his bunk at the end of his first day in the United States Army's Ski Troops. His feet dangled off the end of the bed as he expected them to, since he was three inches longer than the six-foot standard cot. But that was the only thing about today that did not surprise him.

The dry, dirty air trapped in the valley where Camp Hale was built was the first thing that caught him off guard. He thought mountain air was supposed to be the purest kind of air, not like this.

The cold was expected—winters on the plains of Kansas could be brutal as well. But there was an underlying quality to the cold here that he could only attribute to being surrounded by huge mountains of solidly frozen granite. That and the thin high-altitude air which could not hold heat.

Speaking of thin air, the fact that he got out of breath just walking to the mess hall at his regular pace was deeply unsettling to Lucas. Besides football, basketball, and baseball training throughout his teen years, he was in very good physical condition as a result of working his parents' farm for all his life.

Lucas knew he couldn't go easy on himself if he wanted to rapidly adjust to these conditions. Starting tomorrow he would push himself as far as he could—and then one step farther. That's what he was good at.

He didn't have a great education to fall back on. He knew that, in spite of difficulties on his part, he'd skated through his high school classes because he was the varsity quarterback of a championship team. Plus he reached that coveted pinnacle as a sophomore. He was the town hero for three glorious years.

That all ended six years ago, and he'd felt lost ever since.

Now, with the escalating World War affecting every single American's life, he was determined to be a different kind of hero. To make his father proud of him for achieving something on his own, without any special help or consideration. Whatever it took, Lucas was determined to come out of this experience, and this war, having become the best man that he could possibly be.

And hopefully he would figure out what to do with the rest of his life in the process. His glory days couldn't all be behind him…

Thinking of his father shot a shard of jagged guilt through his chest. He resolved to write his father a letter the next day.

I'll tell him that I enlisted.
And where I've gone.

Chapter Two

Lucas woke up at five-thirty the next morning—it was already six-thirty in Kansas and he hadn't had time for his body to adjust. He rolled out of his bunk and dug paper and a pencil out of his footlocker, then padded barefoot into the latrine where the light was always on.

For the next hour he struggled with what to tell his family and how to say it, until he had two solid pages of words he believed he could trust to convey his situation. Then he sealed the letter, washed up, and got dressed.

Reveille sounded at sunrise.

Fraser sat up on the top bunk and rubbed his eyes. "You already up?"

"Yeah. I wanted to write a letter to my folks, let them know I made it here safely." Lucas held up the envelope. "I'm heading over to the E Company office to mail it. I'll see you in the mess hall."

The frozen snow layer on the narrow plowed street crunched under his boots as Lucas strode past three other barracks to reach the office. The morning air was just like yesterday's: cold, dry, and dirty. The sky was overcast however, and Lucas wondered if snow clouds in the mountains looked like the snow clouds over the plains of Kansas.

A bleary-eyed private, just finishing his twenty-four-hour duty, looked up from the crossword puzzle on the desk.

"Can I help you?"

Lucas held out the letter. "I just want to mail this."

The private shook his head. "It can't be sealed. Censors have to read it before it goes out."

Lucas pulled his hand back. "I didn't know that."

"Standard procedure." The man yawned. "You'll need a new envelope."

Lucas looked around the office, making an uncomfortable but necessary decision. "Is there a phone where I can make a collect call?"

The private gestured to a door behind the desk. "Yeah. In the back. Help yourself."

*****

Lucas's legs bounced nervously and his fingers drummed the top of the metal table in the starkly furnished back room while he waited for the operator to come back on the line. It was eight-thirty at home by now. His dad should be back from milking the cows and be sitting down to breakfast.

"Luke? Is that you?" his father's terse voice broke the silence. "Where are you? Your mother is worried sick!"

"Dad, I'm fine. And I'm sorry." Lucas heard the soft snick of the extension being picked up. "I made a decision and decided to act on it before I changed my mind."

"What decision?"

Lucas drew a steadying breath and pressed the heavy black receiver to his ear so he could hear clearly. "I enlisted in the Army. In the Ski Troops. I'm in Colorado."

Static crackling quietly on the phone line underscored his parents' stunned silence.

"Why?" his mother demanded. "You're our only son! You weren't going to be drafted."

"I know, Mom." Lucas fell back on the written words he worked so hard to craft. "But I need to do something—something that makes my life important."

"Working the farm is important!" his father countered. "This place will be yours someday!"

Lucas was prepared for that argument and he spoke quickly so his parents couldn't interrupt. "Dad—Mary's husband is working the farm, and you know Dan loves our land as if it was his. And that Ag Major at the university is following Suzanne around like she hung the moon. They'll probably be engaged by Christmas. Then you'll have both the brawn and the brains. You don't need me."

"Are you saying…" His mother's breath caught. "You don't ever want to come back?"

"No, I'm *not* saying that, Mom." Lucas pulled another deep breath, summoning the courage to be honest about the reality of his life. "But I've felt lost lately. And this war is important. I need to prove myself. To prove I'm more than just a washed-up quarterback."

"Luke. Son." His father's voice thickened. "You *are* more. You always have been."

Lucas rubbed his suddenly damp eyes, glad that his parents couldn't see him at that moment. "It doesn't feel that way, Dad."

"You're a smart guy. And a fast learner. By the time you were twelve you knew as much about farming as I did." His dad sniffed and cleared his throat. "And by the time you finished high school, you knew more."

"I know, but—"

"No buts, son! I know it's been hard—"

Lucas grabbed that straw before it slipped away. "That's the point, Dad. Here, in the Army, I can use my strength, my coordination, my ability as a leader, and all for a good cause. To defend my country."

"But the Ski Troops?" his mom interrupted. "You don't know how to ski!"

Lucas un-fisted his free hand, unaware it was clenched this whole time. His mother's question showed a very welcome shift in their conversation.

"I'll learn, Mom. You know I will. That's what I'm good at."

Another brief moment of static-filled silence passed before his mother spoke again. "You must promise to write to us. Every single week."

"Mom, they read and censor all the letters before they mail them."

"I don't care—do you hear me? Promise me you *will* write. Those censors don't matter, Luke. Not one bit."

"I... uh... sure," Lucas conceded.

"We just can't afford to have you call us every week," his father said carefully. "Maybe once a month, tops."

"Even that's expensive," his mom added.

Lucas winced.

They're right.

"Okay. I'll mail you a letter tomorrow."

"We love you, Luke." His father's deep voice washed over Lucas like a warm wave. "And we're proud of you. We always have been. And always will be."

"Thanks, Dad. I love you guys, too."

When he hung up the phone, Lucas sat in the chair for several long minutes just staring at the wall. He accomplished what he needed to this morning: his fate was set, his parents informed, and their begrudging acceptance secured.

Now I just need to learn how to ski.

*****

The first day of ski training was held in a field on the south edge of the camp. The snow was at least three feet deep and there was only a slight breeze on this bright but still gray day. Simpson's snow-uniformed platoon marched out there in formation, with skis and poles angling upward from their left shoulders.

All of the new recruits recently added to E Company were being divided up according to the skiing experience of each soldier.

Lucas was in the beginner group, as was Xavier Martinez. David Fraser opted to stay with them as an unofficial instructor.

"Thanks, Fraser." Lucas smiled. "I expect I'll pick this up pretty fast, but having an experienced skier to coach us along will sure speed up the process."

Fraser flashed a modest grin. "Glad to help."

"Strap your skis onto your boots for cross-country!" the second lieutenant who was instructing the beginners barked. "We all have to walk before we can run."

Lucas did as he was ordered, remembering where to loop the cable so his heel lifted. He straightened and dug his poles into the snow, staring down at the white strips of wood which were nearly a foot longer than he was tall. Having his feet anchored like this unexpectedly made him feel trapped. He was unable to move or maneuver in the ways he was accustomed to.

His heart rate jumped and he felt a surge of panic.

Stop it. Get a grip.

Once every man was strapped and standing, they were given the order to, "March!"

The soldiers in front of him looked like wobbly toddlers, all trying to move forward but unsure how.

Fraser appeared between Lucas and Martinez. "Have you guys ever ice skated?"

Both men shook their heads.

"Okay, it's like walking but on your toes, not your heels.

Slide one foot forward." Fraser did so. "Your other heel will lift, see? You push off with that foot."

Lucas imitated Fraser's motion.

"Then, you slide the other foot forward like this, and do the same thing." Fraser made it look easy. "The key is the push-off."

Martinez made a valiant attempt but his front leg slipped out in front of him and he went down like a flailing newborn colt.

Fraser helped him up. "Lean forward, Xavier. Not back. Keep your weight on the front foot. Use the poles for balance."

Lean forward.

Carry the ball.

Lucas slid his right leg forward, bent his knee, shifted his weight, and gripped both poles.

"Good," Fraser encouraged. "Now slide your left leg forward."

He did. He was still standing.

Do it again.

With an athlete's focus Lucas moved methodically forward, concentrating on the contraction and extension of the muscles in his legs and his core. He adjusted as needed, and though his thighs and calves burned, he was still vertical and moving forward.

"Show off," Martinez grumbled, struggling to keep up.

"Fraser's right," Lucas replied. "Keep your weight forward and your knees bent."

The initial lesson lasted an hour, but it felt like five. Lucas was panting and sweating heavily despite the cold, and his body ached with the exertion. He couldn't remember any practice session he'd ever been in which had demanded so much of him.

This was immeasurably harder than running, because every push to move forward was thwarted by the fact that the waxed skis moved backward just as readily as they moved forward. Somehow he needed to control that backward thrust, but he had no idea how.

Yet.

"All right, men. Ten minute break," the instructor shouted.

Lucas dropped to his bottom and lay back along the length of the skis with his bent knees in the air. He took gulping breaths and tried to slow his racing heart.

Martinez was moaning beside him. "What have we done?"

Lucas had no good answer at the moment.

"Honestly, this is the hardest part." Fraser sat between them. "Going downhill will be a breeze."

"When do we get to do that?" Lucas asked.

Fraser snickered. "After you learn to go up."

*****

The camp's official training plan called for forty half-days of ski instruction, with the other half spent in a new theater watching training films.

The films addressed the care of equipment, methods of waxing their skis, judging which wax was appropriate for their conditions, ways to fix broken bindings, and general skiing vocabulary. That afternoon Lucas watched the film with half of his mind replaying the morning's activities.

He knew he would be sore, but there wasn't any sort of treatment available for that. His best bet was to keep stretching and flexing his legs to alleviate some of the stiffness before it all took a debilitating hold. But he couldn't stretch fully in the theater seats, as much as he tried.

Simpson glared at him. "Hansen. Sit still."

"Permission to stand, sir?" Lucas asked.

The sergeant hesitated before grumbling, "In the back."

Lucas stood and slid past the other men in the row, and then walked to the back. Even that amount of movement helped. He continued to flex and stretch, but now he was also able to give more of his attention to the instructional films. After the one on equipment finished, the next one explained various skiing techniques.

Lucas watched intently and analytically as the soldiers on the screen demonstrated how to sidestep and herringbone uphill, and then snowplow down to control their speed and direction. He hadn't ever considered how a person could ski uphill, against gravity and on slippery strips of waxed wood to boot, but the movements all made sense to him. He nodded thoughtfully as he watched.

I can do this.

*****

Over the next three weeks the recruits' training intensified until the men were ski marching alongside the road up to Cooper Hill—about six miles from Camp Hale—while wearing ninety-pound rucksacks packed with enough gear to spend a month in the rough.

Lucas breathed in through his nose, and out through his mouth, his breath forming wispy clouds in front of his face as he and the other men skied up to Cooper Hill at a solid pace.

When they reached the hill, the soldiers were able to remove their packs before they rode the T-Bar to the top. The newly installed contraption was reputed to be one of the most efficient and powerful ski lifts in the entire world.

"Seven miles an hour," Sergeant Simpson bragged. "Takes two men at a time up the mile-and-a-quarter slope to the top."

"How high is the top?" Martinez asked the first time they were there, clearly nervous about the height.

"Eleven thousand feet. Almost two thousand above where we are now."

Martinez blanched.

Lucas watched in fascination as two men at a time sat on the inverted metal Ts and slid on their skis up the snowy slope and out of sight.

He slapped Martinez on the back. "What goes up, must come down."

"That's what I'm afraid of." Martinez swallowed thickly. "Please tell my family that I loved them."

The first trip down was taken slowly, with the soldiers instructed to snowplow the entire way. Most complied, though a few of the men risked pulling the backs of their skis closer in and picking up speed over the snow-packed mountainside.

Lucas was one of them.

Fraser was right—coming down was a much easier skill to master than skiing across flat ground. Gravity was on his side now. But Lucas thought cross country skiing felt like running through thick mud with bricks strapped to his ankles, and their overland marches left him sweating and out of breath.

But it was better now than when he first arrived.

Lucas realized last week that he was no longer panting as he jogged to the mess hall or to E Company Office to mail a letter. That was a relief. He had managed to avoid altitude sickness so far, and after watching instructional films about the dizziness, headache, muscle aches, and nausea it caused, he was extremely thankful.

Most of his platoon was adjusting to the below-freezing temperatures, high altitudes, and low oxygen, but one of the guys had pulled out and asked for a transfer to a flatland unit.

Lucas tried not to display his disgust and disappointment in the man he thought of as a quitter.

"Not everyone can adjust," Fraser reminded him.

"But we did," Lucas countered. "You, me, and Martinez—we're three strands in a very strong rope."

When they finished the day's training at Cooper Hill, Lucas shouldered his rucksack for the march back to camp, looking forward to a hot shower and a friendly game of cards with the guys in the barracks. Above him the sun sent streaks of silvery pinks and oranges over the treeless tops of the majestic granite mountains, setting the pale blue winter sky afire.

He smiled to himself, completely content at the moment with his choices. Then he fell in with Fraser and Martinez, and the trio of friends headed back to Hale.

Chapter Three

February 2, 1943

"It's called the Homestake Maneuvers, because this two-week field exercise will take place on Homestake Mountain, twelve miles southwest of this camp," their E Company commanding officer told the forty assembled soldiers. "It's the first regimental-sized high-altitude winter maneuver ever attempted by the United States Army."

He paused to let that tidbit sink in before he continued. "Brigadier General Rolfe has selected a combat team of about nine-hundred soldiers, comprised of Second Battalion of the Eighty-Seventh and supported by Norwegian guys in the Ninety-ninth Battalion's Artillery."

Lucas frowned. "We're only halfway through our initial training, right?" he murmured to Fraser.

Fraser's brow lowered as well. "Right."

Martinez leaned over and spoke past Lucas to the Scot. "So why are *we* involved?"

He shrugged. "Beats me."

"Because the higher-ups aren't fully on board with this whole elite ski troops idea," Sergeant Simpson admitted later in an uncharacteristic display of candor. "Minnie Dole's been fighting Army Ground for the formation of mountain troops since the start of the war in Europe. The Germans have them but we don't."

"So what are we supposed to do?" Lucas asked.

The sergeant sighed and rubbed his forehead. "Tomorrow you'll be issued your outdoor gear: tents, sleeping bags, stoves and such, before we head for Cooper Hill. The next day, we march to Homestake."

That night before lights out Lucas pulled Fraser and Martinez aside. "What do you think's going to happen with this Homestake thing?"

Fraser looked more hopeful than Martinez did. "There'll be nine hundred of us up there on that mountain. They won't risk losing an entire battalion to the elements for the sake of maneuvers."

Martinez's expression brightened. "Sarge said it's the first winter maneuver ever attempted. So, if things don't work out they'll have to call a halt and bring us back. Right?"

"I hope so." Lucas felt less optimistic than his friend. "I just know we're not ready for anything like this. We've only been training for three weeks."

Fraser rested a hand on the other two men's shoulders. "A strand of three is not easily broken. We'll get through it together."

The next afternoon, armed with the fresh gear which none of the new recruits had any chance to try out, E Company was trucked up Cooper Hill to spend an uncomfortably crowded night in the ski instructors' barracks. In the morning they would set out on skis with full field packs, and most of them armed with as-yet unused weapons.

This couldn't end well.

Lucas hadn't been in the Army long, but he knew something about planning ahead and preparing your men for the task at hand, whether that task involved a goal line or a military objective. All he could do at this point was try to ensure that he and his buddies made it through without any serious injuries.

Fraser kept a speculative eye on the mountain sky throughout the day, warning their officers that a storm was imminent. That warning had no impact on the Army's plans however. This morning they awoke to blizzards blowing horizontal snow and temperatures which were recorded at a bone-chilling forty-eight degrees below zero.

Carrying their ninety-pound packs, the men moved out on snowshoes at a brutal pace, trying to outrun the storm. Their route led downhill a thousand feet to Tennessee Creek, and then climbed back up an old logging road toward their assigned camp site at over eleven thousand feet elevation.

Lucas thought their training had been rigorous, but this march under these severe conditions made the past three weeks look like a Sunday picnic. He panted heavily, gasping for oxygen in the thin air and sucking in lungfuls of dry snowflakes in the process. His core perspired with the demands of the march, while his face, fingers, and toes grew numb with the extreme cold.

Thankfully the officers called for a ten-minute break every half hour. Lucas spent that time trying to get feeling back in his extremities while tamping down the urge to vomit. He refused to succumb to altitude sickness at this stage.

After each break, Lucas, Fraser, and Martinez pulled each other to their feet, pounded each other on the back, and headed off together. All three were determined to help their new brothers succeed. Not one of them would be left behind, no matter how hard the task became.

A few hours into the march some of the soldiers on the trail stopped getting up after their break. They just sat in the snow, resting against their packs while those soldiers still on the move passed them by.

"What are they doing?" Lucas managed against his own

exhaustion.

"Giving up." Martinez sounded angry. "But if a Mexican from San Diego can do this, then they can, too."

"They're probably the newest guys," Fraser posited. "A bunch of recruits arrived last week."

"Last week?" Lucas was so horrified he almost stopped his forward momentum. "There's no way they could adjust to the altitude in such a short time. They can't survive this!"

Poor bastards.

It was obvious now that a substantial number of the men were being felled by exhaustion, altitude sickness, and frostbite. They were never going to reach the relative safety of their assigned bivouac location. So the E Company commander separated out the skiers with more skill and experience.

"You men go on ahead and set up camp at the designated site," he instructed them. "We'll catch up."

Lucas watched those men ski off and felt a stab of anger. He felt like his pride was on the line—he was never the weaker man, never the one who needed rescuing when physical prowess was involved.

I should be as good as they are.

"Now all we have to worry about is finding them." Martinez climbed to his feet and held out his hand. "You coming?"

"Hell yes," Lucas growled and grabbed the man's hand.

Once again, the trio set out on the uphill climb. As the blinding blizzard conditions gradually eased up and the afternoon grew dark, some members of the group that had skied ahead returned to assist their comrades. They helped sick and weary soldiers to their feet and shouldered their rucksacks for them so the men could continue unencumbered.

When one offered to take Lucas's pack he angrily shoved the man's arm away. "I've got it."

Fraser shot him an intense look but said nothing. Both he and Martinez also refused help, which gave Lucas pause. Had his friends turned down assistance they might have welcomed because his own stubborn pride made him do so?

Lucas put his head down and strode doggedly forward calling on every ounce of strength he had left in his body so he wouldn't have to think about that. By the time they reached the *E Company Bivouac* sign, his legs trembled and his lungs burned. He couldn't feel his toes or his fingers.

The sun had dipped behind the mountain and the moon was rising in the east, but they still needed to pitch their tents, start a fire, and cook their dinner.

Lucas seriously considered not eating.

"Let's pitch our tents under that outcropping," Fraser suggested. "Use it as a wind break."

Lucas and Martinez followed Fraser to the spot. Fraser was Lucas's tent mate, but Martinez's guy was nowhere to be seen.

"Do you think he's one of the guys that quit?" Lucas asked him.

Martinez shrugged. "Don't know. But I'm not going to wait on him." He set his pack down and pulled out the brand new tent. "Let's see if I can figure this out."

It took the men an hour in the swirling, blowing snow to get the two tents set up securely in the protection of the rock. Lucas elbowed Fraser and pointed at some of the more experienced guys who packed snow around their tents.

"Why are they doing that?" he asked.

"Windbreak. Of course." Fraser heaved a tired sigh. "Let's do the same, guys."

Lucas's stomach rumbled loudly.

Martinez flashed a crooked grin. "How about we eat first?"

"I'm good with that." Lucas pulled his rations from his pack and pointed downhill with his head. "Looks like it's a shared fire."

About twenty yards away the men had built a growing bonfire and were circling around its warmth. Most of them had pried open their tin cans with their bayonets and set them near the flames to heat them up.

Lucas, Fraser, and Martinez claimed a space on the far edge of the fire ring and did the same. While they waited for their food to unfreeze and take on some semblance of warmth, Lucas pulled off his boots and rubbed his feet to restore circulation to his toes. True frostbite was dangerous. It could result in gangrenous and amputated toes followed by a medical discharge.

Out before I'm fully in.

And crippled for the rest of his life as a reminder that he failed. He could not let that happen.

As much as the heat of the flames stung, Lucas massaged his appendages until his fingers and toes lost their waxy look and glowed pink once again.

Sergeant Simpson approached. "You men seen Johnstone or Gordon?"

Martinez shook his head. "No. But Gordon's supposed to be my tent mate."

Simpson looked grim. "Looks like you're bunking alone. He doesn't seem to have made it up."

"How many are we missing?" Lucas risked asking.

"Our platoon is just missing those two. But on the radio they're saying at least a quarter of the men have already become casualties of the cold and altitude." Simpson sniffed and ran his mitten under his reddened nose. "They're currently being rescued."

The trio exchanged concerned looks.

"At any rate, the maneuver judges called tomorrow a 'day of rest' while they regroup and reconsider. So settle in."

As Simpson turned around and headed back to wherever it was that he came from, Lucas stared into the fire.

"We're supposed to be up here for two weeks." Fraser's tone was almost a question.

Lucas didn't have anything to say to that. He methodically

put his fire-warmed socks and boots back on before he retrieved his tin of little sausages from the fire's edge.

"I guess that'll give us time to see if we have what it takes to be ski troopers," Martinez offered.

Lucas slid a hard glance in his friend's direction. "There is no *if*, Xavier. There is only success."

"Um—yeah." The dark-haired man grabbed his own tin of food. "The strong rope right? We can do this."

Fraser nodded his determination. "Damn straight."

The three ate in silence as the snow began to fall once more.

*****

During their designated day of rest, new assignments were given to the platoon leaders.

"The tasks have been adjusted for the 'startling loss in numbers' and the 'unanticipated struggles'—" Sergeant Simpson read to his platoon, his sarcasm unmistakable. The following words were clearly embellished by his own opinion, "—which were caused by careening at unreasonably high speeds through mountains, in sub-zero blizzards, and with ninety pounds of equipment weighing the soldiers down."

A laugh burst from Lucas, muffled only slightly by the scarf wrapped across his face. Fraser elbowed him and he put up his mittened hands in contrite apology.

Simpson glared at him unconvincingly. "We are ordered to ski up to the eastern ridge of Homestake Peak tomorrow as a test of our equipment and readiness. We'll stay on the mountain overnight."

Lucas nodded, his expression neutral, and not daring to reveal any of his skeptical reaction to their new orders.

"The next day, after we return, the Ninety-Ninth will launch an artillery assault on the eastern ridge's snow pack to see if causing a controlled avalanche is possible."

"They *will* wait to make sure we're back—right? Before they shoot up there?" Martinez loudly blurted exactly what Lucas was thinking.

Simpson's shoulders drooped. "Yes, Private. We'll be in radio contact the entire time."

Martinez nodded muttering, "Geez. Just making sure…"

The next morning, after spending a second cold night on the windy peak and sleeping in tiny tents with their sleeping bags laid out on top of the snow, the E Company soldiers downed a hasty breakfast of frozen rations before setting out on their skis for the base of the eastern ridge.

Their going was relatively easy at first, traversing across what Lucas had come to recognize as typical Colorado terrain—slopes scattered with snow-covered spruce trees and blanketed with a foot of fresh powder from the recent storm.

As they steadily gained elevation, the company skied above the timberline and onto a treeless and rugged ridge. The ridge soon became a cliff, forcing the soldiers to ski single-file until they reached its rocky eastern side.

Behind Lucas, Martinez hummed and whistled constantly as they skied along the cliff, in spite of the physical exertion the treacherous path required.

"What are you doing?" Lucas called back to him.

"You know I don't like heights!" he bellowed back. "So I'm singing Benny Goodman songs to myself as a distraction."

Lucas stopped and looked back at his friend. "Is it helping?"

"Nope." Martinez glared at him. "And thanks for bringing *that* to my attention."

Thankfully they didn't need to go much further before the cliff sloped back and the soldiers reached Homestake's broad eastern shoulder. While the skiing might be less precarious here, the wind at this altitude was brutal, yanking viciously at the soldiers' wind-proof parkas, and catching and lifting the curved front of the men's seven-foot skis.

As if this wasn't already hard enough, now Lucas had to deal with keeping his skis from taking flight and throwing him down the mountainside.

"Take ten minutes!" Sergeant Simpson barked.

Lucas sank to the snow, grateful for the respite no matter how brief. He pulled his canteen from inside his coat—where his body heat meant the water wouldn't freeze—and drank deeply. Martinez and Fraser flanked him, but none of them spoke. If they felt as wrung out as Lucas did, they were just trying to keep moving forward. No other effort was worth the expenditure of energy.

When the brief break ended, the soldiers helped each other regain their upright stance on their skis. As they skied west along the edge of the high ridge, the ski troopers leaned into the headwind and tried to keep their footing on the hardened snow crust.

Just when Lucas believed he had reached the end of his strength, the company's forward movement stopped. E Company had arrived at the snow packed eastern summit of Homestake Mountain.

"Look down," Fraser said over the wind.

"No. Huh uh. No way." Martinez shook his head and kept his forward gaze level. "Not until we're headed in that direction.

Lucas turned around and looked back.

So far below that they looked like miniscule drab green ants, four teams of soldiers were maneuvering their canons into position on the far side of the frozen Slide Lake.

"They think they can knock the snow off this mountain with those big guns, huh?" Lucas pondered that idea as he turned back to Fraser. "It'd have to be pretty solidly packed, wouldn't it?"

"I would think so. But that's not my concern." Fraser shifted his attention from the scene below to Lucas. "You've never been in an avalanche, Hansen, but they are fast, quiet, and scary as hell. What I can't figure out is how they think they can control how much snow falls, and where it goes when it does."

Fraser looked concerned enough that Lucas's heartbeat stuttered. "I sure hope we're out of the way before they shoot."

"We've reached the top, like they ordered us to." Sergeant Simpson interrupted the conversation and waved his arm over his head. "Now let's go back down, men."

As always, down was easier than up. The men snowplowed to avoid gaining any unwanted speed that might inadvertently toss them off the edge of the ridge to their plummeting death. When the ridge broadened again, they picked up the pace and continued until they reached the timberline once again.

"We'll camp here tonight," Simpson told his platoon. "Get yourselves settled."

Like they had before, the soldiers gathered fallen wood from beneath the snow and built a communal fire. Lucas pried open a couple of his ration tins and set them next to the blaze before removing his boots and socks and setting them there as well.

His toes hurt more this time when they were exposed to the warmth of the flames. He rubbed them vigorously, willing the blood flow back into his frost-nipped feet. Only after they turned pink again was he willing to re-dress them with the fire-warmed socks and boots.

He claimed his rations and leaned against his pack to eat, keeping the soles of his boots close to the fire.

Chapter Four

Lucas curled inside his sleeping bag, his back pressed against Fraser's in a desperate attempt to share their body heat.

It wasn't working.

He wondered what it felt like to freeze to death. In their training classes they were told that their bodies would trick them and they would start to feel warm right before they died.

I guess I should be glad my ass is still freezing.

Lucas shifted, tucking into a tighter arc. Slight movements inside his clothes seemed to generate a little heat, or at least expose his skin to new bits of body-warmed fabric, creating that illusion.

He flexed and wiggled his toes to encourage circulation. He kept his hands tucked in his armpits. He used his breath to warm the tip of his nose under his scarf.

Making everything in his situation worse was the growing pounding in his head. Lucas knew it was altitude sickness. He'd been fighting the nausea all day.

Tomorrow they would descend once again, and that was the only cure. He just needed to rest enough that he could make the downhill march without help. Without showing weakness in front of his buddies.

Lucas closed his eyes and focused on breathing in, then out, then in again, using the slow, steady rhythm to remain calm and focused on staying alive—until the sky finally lightened and signaled the approaching end to his torture.

*****

Slide Lake sat in a glacier-cut natural basin directly below Homestake Peak's eastern ridge. After a two-and-a-half hour downhill march that commenced as soon as the sun was up, an out-of-breath E Company reached the lake's south edge.

Lucas tried to think of words that could adequately describe to his parents his relief at being able to once again breathe in air with measurable oxygen levels. His headache and nausea had eased with every thousand feet of his descent, until he now stood beside the solidly-frozen lake and felt confident that he was not going to die today.

Fraser and Martinez stood with him, all three stamping their feet to keep the circulation in their toes moving and staring up at Homestake Mountain's east ridge—where they spent the last two days—and where the high and ever-present winds had deposited a massive cornice of packed snow.

Martinez blew a low whistle. "I can't believe we were up there last night. I'm glad I didn't know how high we were."

"Xavier. You joined the *ski troops*." Fraser shook his head and flashed Martinez a disbelieving smile. "Didn't it ever occur to you that you'd be at the top of mountains?"

Martinez looked indignant. "The mountains by San Diego aren't like this. How could I know?"

Lucas chuckled. "Fair enough."

All around them the Ninety-Ninth Battalion's artillery guys were adjusting the seventy-five millimeter howitzers, aiming them sharply upward toward the cornice, and chattering in Norwegian on the radios. Eventually the Army brass and civilian engineers who were evaluating the experiment arrived. Once they were settled in place on a hastily built reviewing stand, the order to start the experiment was given.

Startled by the thunderous concussive blasts, Lucas clapped his hands over his ears and crumpled into a ball at the body-vibrating roar of the four nearby canons, which echoed and re-echoed in the natural amphitheater. Fraser and Martinez dropped to the ground beside him.

Lucas shot his friends a horrified gaze.

Damn!

After the first four rounds, the second four blasts assaulted the mountain and the men anew. Lucas stayed in his crouched position, palms pressed hard against the sides of his head, and squinted up at the target above them.

Four spouts of snow erupted horizontally just under the lip of the snow pack. For a moment, nothing moved.

Then the bank of snow shivered. Cracks splintered its frozen face. Chunks of snow the size of houses started sliding downward.

The artillery guys cheered, joined by the officers and guests and E company.

"Damn, that's impressive!" Lucas shouted over the ruckus.

"Hell, yeah!" Martinez agreed.

The ponderous mass of loosened snow gained headway on the way down. When the avalanche hit the slope at the base of the ridge, directly across Slide Lake from the observers' position, a blinding cloud of powdered snow exploded and raced across the surface of the frozen lake toward the spectators.

Lucas and his buddies were enveloped in an impenetrable and terrifying swirl of snow that obscured the world with a thick, icy fog. He didn't move because he couldn't see where to go.

As the thrown-up snow began to settle and their visibility

increased a bit, someone hollered, "The ice! The lake ice is moving!"

Deep cracking and grinding sounds of the unsettled ice, dislodged by the immeasurable weight of the loosened snow on the lake's opposite bank, sent icy fingers of fear up Lucas's spine. In an unexpected and terrifying consequence of the man-made avalanche, the heavy snow was actually shoving the lake's ice covering off the water and onto the opposite shore.

The gathered spectators in front of E Company, who watched the experiment from Slide Lake's shore, were directly in the path of the surging plate of thick ice. Realizing the looming danger, the panicked crowd leapt from the bleachers and ran for their lives.

Lucas turned and ran as well, flanked by Fraser and Martinez. They headed up the slope on the far side of the bowl-like valley, with the rest of E Company, scrambling to be faster than the sliding sheet of ice. The spectators were right behind them.

Panting and visibly shaken, the escapees stopped once they reached safety on the basin's slope opposite Homestake Mountain. Shocked glances bounced through the stunned crowd. No one spoke as they waited for the enveloping cloud of snow to clear and the echoes of falling rocks and grinding ice to fade.

When it did, they all stumbled back toward the lake to see the results.

Lucas's jaw dropped. "Holy hell. You ever see such a thing?"

A crumbled sheet of blue-green ice, thicker than a man was tall and wide as the lake was long, had settled solidly where the decimated reviewing stand recently stood.

Martinez stared at the unbelievable sight. "Nope."

Fraser walked forward. "Me neither. Geez, this is incredible."

"Look up," Lucas prompted.

Above them the recently snow-shrouded face of the eastern ridge was nearly bare, its rocky vertical cliffs now exposed.

"Well the idea of shooting down snow works, that much is clear," Martinez observed.

"True." Fraser walked close enough to the now unmoving ice sheet to touch it. "The question is, can it be controlled?"

Lucas shuddered. "I don't think it's worth the risk of finding out."

February 13, 1943

Nine days after marching up Homestake Mountain, and five days sooner than originally planned, E Company ski-marched back into Camp Hale. When they stopped at the edge of the camp to remove their skis, Lucas looked around the group of weary soldiers. Their rough, unshaven faces were all weathered by the sun, wind, and unrelenting cold of the mountaintop.

"We're a pretty sorry-looking bunch," Lucas admitted. He looked past Fraser at a couple dozen E Company guys who weren't headed toward their barracks. "Where are those guys going?"

"Hospital, I think." Fraser watched the men depart. "Just because we survived doesn't mean we're in good shape."

"Let's go." Martinez hefted his skis onto his shoulder. "I need a hot shower and I want to get one before we run out of hot water."

The trio trudged through camp toward their barracks and Lucas was startled to see that the line outside the camp's hospital stretched farther than the length of a football field. He pressed his lips together as the grim reality settled in his thoughts.

We really weren't ready.

Lucas, however, staunchly refused to go in for any sort of treatment. Though his extremities were frost-nipped, he managed to keep his fingers and toes from actually freezing. Plus his altitude sickness symptoms had lessened since descending to

Slide Lake's basin. He was determined to wait it out. To remain strong. Not to crumble.

And—more importantly—to figure out what he needed to learn from the harsh and harrowing experience that had very nearly bested him.

After showering and shaving for the first time in ten days, Lucas felt human again. He donned clean clothes and took to his bunk, intending to spend his day off building a solid game plan.

His team was the Ski Troops. More specifically, the guys of E Company. And his platoon members were the players on the field at the moment.

How can I make sure we beat the competition?

Knowing what they were up against was the key in planning any strategy. So what were they actually facing?

A third of the soldiers sent out on the Homestake Maneuvers immediately succumbed to exhaustion, frostbite, and altitude sickness, so the tactical part of the test had to be cancelled.

It was guys like Lucas and Martinez who suffered. The ones who were new to skiing, so just trying to keep up with the experts required double the effort. Compounding the maneuver's failure were the new arrivals who hadn't had time to become conditioned to the altitude. Not to mention the excessive loads they were all expected to carry.

Lucas had made it through for only one reason: he hadn't given up. He could have allowed himself to be helped, or even quit the maneuvers altogether and be rescued. But that wasn't how a quarterback won any game.

Winning was everything. Quitters didn't win, and winners didn't quit. If he wanted to lead men, he had to press forward, even when his head hurt like someone was pounding it with Thor's own hammer and he was afraid his toes would freeze and fall right off.

But, the guys who went through the ski troops' application process did fine.

Why? Because those guys already had plenty of ski and cold-weather experience. They knew the tricks—like packing snow around a tent to hold in body heat and protect the guys inside from wind, or sharing one big communal fire instead of trying to build dozens of small ones.

With a constriction in his chest, Lucas realized his crucial mistake. "I didn't understand the severity of the situation that I've put myself in," he whispered to the bottom of Fraser's bunk. "And neither did Xavier."

He knew right then that he had to train even harder. He'd push Martinez to do the same, and together they'd push Fraser to take them further. They would rise to the top of the platoon, then to the top of the company.

Together they would best the opponents they currently faced: the nearly uninhabitable sky-high terrain and its unrelenting and severe weather.

We can do this.
I can lead the way.
And I'll become a better man in the process.

*****

Lucas carried his unsealed letter to E Company's office. He hadn't written to his parents since talking to them on the phone, despite his promise to his mother. He kept meaning to, but he was always too tired or otherwise occupied at the end of a long day of training.

Plus, he wasn't sure what he was allowed to say. Their instructions were vague, and the rules seemed to leave a lot to the individual censor's interpretation.

He wanted to tell them about his last two weeks, but figured he had to be as vague as the rules. He settled for describing his initial experience on skis in a humorous way before he described the staggering cold conditions atop the mountain he did not name. Last of all he told them about the falling pack of snow that pushed the top six feet or so of a lake right off its surface and onto land.

That is true, he added. *I swear.*

Lucas opened the office door and walked up to the private on duty. He held out the addressed, stamped, and unsealed letter. "I want to mail this."

The private nodded, accepted the envelope, and dropped it in a wire basket. "It should go out the day after tomorrow. The censors are done for today."

Lucas's gut clenched at the thought of a stranger reading his personal letters to his folks, but he knew he had to get used to it. There was no other choice since phone calls cost three dollars a minute. His parents couldn't afford that on a regular basis any more than he could on his private's pay.

Besides, the chances of a random censor ever meeting him and knowing who he was, was improbable.

Nothing to worry about.

*****

The high number of injuries during the Homestake catastrophe led to the medical discharge of over two hundred soldiers. Another hundred or so requested transfers out of Camp Hale. As a result the number of soldiers remaining in the three Army regiments at Camp Hale—the Eighty-Fifth, Eighty-Sixth, and Eighty-Seventh—were completely out of balance.

Reassignments came the next week.

Lucas was moved to the Eighty-Sixth Regiment, First Battalion, A Company under the leadership of First Lieutenant James Loose. In a gift from God, Martinez and Fraser were moved with him. Lucas said a sincere prayer of thanks—he didn't know what he would have done without the two of them.

With new resolve, the trio resumed their interrupted training schedule with their new platoon. In contrast, after climbing and traversing Homestake Mountain, skiing down the main slope at Cooper Hill was a piece of cake. Even learning how to fall down without hurting himself was something Lucas had worked out on his own during the nine-day trial.

At the end of their interrupted six weeks, which after Homestake now included ski-marching cross-country up to thirty miles a day loaded with a rifle and a ninety-pound rucksack, each skier was required to take a skiing proficiency test at Cooper Hill. Flags marked out the three-mile course, and numerous strategically placed obstacles created a hazardous run that was intentionally tough and physically exhausting.

Because of his intense post-Homestake determination, Lucas passed the proficiency test with ease. And because he'd pushed Martinez daily, his southern Californian beach buddy flew through the test as well. Fraser's skills were never a concern.

The three men celebrated together in Camp Hale's Servicemen's Center.

Fraser lifted his beer, his grin wide and his eyes twinkling. "To flatlanders learning to ski!"

Martinez clinked his glass against Fraser's. "To the rope!"

Lucas tapped both their glasses with his. "And to whatever obstacles we face next."

Chapter Five

June 1943

Women's Army Auxiliary Corps Second Lieutenant Parker Williams stepped down from the train at Pando Station and got her first look at Camp Hale.

Her gaze passed over row on row of white-washed barracks, narrow paved roads, and scattered larger buildings resting in the mountain-fenced valley under a sunny sky. Tens of thousands of olive-drab uniformed soldiers hurried from building to building, or marched in groups of forty in tight formation.

A pretty blonde stepped out of the train and stood next to her, shading her eyes in the bright morning sun. "Will you just look at that view?"

Parker smiled. Growing up in Denver, the Rockies were an accustomed daily sight. It was nice to appreciate their majesty from a newcomer's point of view.

"Yep. Our home away from home."

"Follow me, ladies." A uniformed WAAC captain, who

appeared a few years younger than Parker's twenty-five years, strode to the end of the platform and joined a middle-aged Army captain waiting there.

She turned around and addressed the ninety-five women on today's train.

"I am Captain Martha Grayson, your commanding officer. This is Captain Myron Thayer, to whom I report." Captain Grayson paused. "As explained during your boot camp training, you will address WAAC officers as *ma'am* and Army officers as *sir*. You will salute us at the beginning and end of any interaction."

Captain Thayer touched his hat. "Welcome to Camp Hale, ladies. We are very glad to have your help."

Hearing the word *help* sent a surge of satisfaction through Parker's frame. After three miserable years spent teaching English Literature in a Denver high school, she joined the WAACs to do something—anything—that would provide a needed service to her country, which was currently at war in both hemispheres.

"We'll be replacing soldiers in non-combat-related areas such as administration and nursing, thereby freeing the men up for training and deployment," Captain Grayson continued, her expression stern. "Please keep in mind that as women in uniform, we are a novelty in general. And of course, we are the first women to be stationed at Camp Hale specifically."

"Once you all arrive, there will be just two hundred of you," Captain Thayer stated. "And twelve thousand of them."

"I love those odds," the blonde murmured. "Any gal who can't snag a husband here just isn't trying."

Parker smiled again, this time out of politeness. She enlisted to help the war effort as soon as the Army allowed women to do so. If a husband was all she wanted, she could have been married half a dozen times by now.

"Grab your duffel bags, privates. Our first stop is your

barracks. After that, we'll take you on a tour of the camp."

Parker slung the strap of her tightly-packed bag over her shoulder and followed the captains.

The blonde fell in step with her. "I can't get over these mountains. I've never seen anything like them in all my born days. I'm Emily Black, by the way."

"Parker Williams."

Emily smiled and her cheeks dimpled. "I'm pleased to make your acquaintance."

"Where are you from?" Parker asked.

"Atlanta, Georgia."

Parker chuckled. "That explains the accent. So why did you enlist? It doesn't seem like the type of thing a good Southern girl would do."

"It's not." Emily shrugged. "But my daddy only had girls and I think it was killing him not to have a son who could join and fight. At least I could do this much." She glanced sideways at Parker. "He fought in the Great War, you see."

"My dad did, too." Parker shifted the weight of the bag to her other shoulder. "And I have a younger brother who enlisted in the navy after Pearl Harbor."

Emily's brows pulled together. "So, why'd you enlist?"

I felt useless.

"After I graduated college I was a high school English teacher for three years." Parker wrinkled her nose. "But I wasn't cut out for it. So when I found out I could enlist, I did."

"Got yourself out of an unhappy situation," Emily observed sagely. "But instead of just quitting, you did something patriotic instead."

Parker looked at her new friend, impressed. "Yes. Exactly."

"Well, I went to college, too. Got a degree in mathematics."

Parker was even more impressed. "You did?"

Emily nodded, her expression somber. "I wanted to be a civil engineer, but my application to graduate school was denied because I'm a girl."

Parker wasn't surprised. "Maybe you can do something like that in the WAACs."

"We'll see, I suppose." Emily's buoyant expression returned. "I'll have a better chance here than in Atlanta, that's for darn sure."

The group came to a halt in front of one of the white two-story buildings.

"This is your barracks, ladies." Captain Grayson turned to the side and pointed across the paved road. "The hospital is that large building over there with the red cross on its side." She swiveled and pointed in the opposite direction. "And that stone-bottomed building down there is Camp Hale's headquarters. Most of you will be working in one of those two places."

"Most of us?" one woman ventured.

Captain Thayer fielded the question. "A small group of you will be in supplies, repairing equipment and uniforms."

Jeez I hope that's not me.

Parker was a disaster with needle and thread and had no patience for sewing. She'd rather wash dishes any day if it came to that.

"Go inside, claim a bunk, and leave your duffel on top of it." Grayson looked at her watch. "I'll give you ten minutes to freshen up, and then we'll start your tour."

Parker hurried inside and grabbed a bottom bunk. Emily took the bottom bunk next to her. Then both women joined the crowd in the latrine.

"Who here is a nurse?" one gal asked. Several gals waved their hands and moved toward each other.

"How'd you both get to be second lieutenants already?" someone asked Parker.

She answered for Emily as well, who was currently brushing her teeth. "We both have college degrees." That sounded snooty, but it was the truth.

The gal lifted one brow. "Well, lah-de-dah."

A tall brunette also wearing second lieutenant's stripes sidled over to Parker and Emily and smiled softly.

She held out one hand. "Sofia Romano."

"Parker Williams." She shook Sofia's hand. "This is Emily Black."

Emily wiped her mouth on a white Army-issued towel and shook Sofia's hand. "It's a pleasure to meet you. That's an Italian name, isn't it?"

Sofia nodded. "I was born in New Jersey, but I speak Italian fluently. I'm hoping the Army will make use of that."

"What was your major in college?" Parker asked.

"European History."

Impressive.

And useful at this particular time.

Parker looked at the two women in front of her. "I wasn't sure who I'd be serving with when I enlisted," she admitted. "But I'd have to say at this point, I believe we are definitely an extraordinary group of women."

Emily smiled in the way Southern girls did—sweet sugar covering a sharp thrust of truth. "Let's all hope that the Army agrees."

*****

The pace Captain Thayer set as the women were led around the massive grounds at Camp Hale wasn't rushed, but neither was it leisurely. It left Parker panting, which surprised her since she grew up in a mile-high city.

When they stopped in front of the rifle range, Emily wiped sweat from her forehead. "I can't catch my breath."

"It's the altitude," Parker said. "If you start to get a headache or feel nauseous be sure to tell Captain Grayson."

Sofia rested her hands on her hips and drew several deep

breaths. "Will we get used to this?"

Parker lifted one shoulder in an apologetic shrug. "Yes. But it might take a week or two."

The group of WAACs resumed their tour. The late-morning heat of the sun was trapped in the valley by the surrounding peaks and made the day warmer than Parker expected. A struggling breeze tried to move through the camp with little success.

Parker was glad for her green Army-issued sunglasses but wished the brim on her hat was a little larger. She was certain that her face would be sunburned before lunch at this rate.

Emily took her hat off and fanned herself with it. "It might be warm, but at least it's not humid. That's the only thing I hate about Georgia. Well, that and the bugs."

Captain Thayer stopped the group at the base of a forty-foot granite wall on the western edge of the camp. The nearly-vertical face was currently covered with dozens of drab-green-uniformed soldiers in climbing gear.

"In the winter the men train up in the mountains on skis and snowshoes," Captain Thayer explained to the women. "But when the snow melts, they train in orienteering and mountain climbing."

Parker watched the men in fascination, some ascending and some descending. Several men were shouting instructions or adjusting the ropes and clips of their gear.

"Martinez, just imagine there's a woman waiting for you at the top!"

Parker looked for the source of the deep and clearly amused voice. About halfway up a tall, neatly-muscled blond private was hanging on the side of the cliff and looking down. Even from below she could see the bright blue of his eyes.

"You can't fall, Xavier," he continued. "You're tied to a mountain and it's not going anywhere, I promise you."

A broad dark-haired man squinted up at the soldier. "I can

too fall. I'm skilled like that."

The blond chuckled. "Come on. I'll wait for you. We'll go up together."

Parker watched the dark-haired man painstakingly move up the rock face while the blond above him kept up his encouragement.

"Now that's what I call a real man."

Parker turned to Emily. "Which one?"

"That Nordic god up there. The blond with the blue eyes." Emily sighed. "I'd climb *him*."

Parker coughed a laugh. "What if your mama heard you talking like that?"

Emily winked at her. "My mama taught me to talk like that."

Sofia had been standing beside them, her eyes also focused on the soldiers "You think he'll make it?"

Both women looked at Sofia.

"Who?" Parker asked. "The guy with the black hair?"

"Xavier Martinez," Sofia murmured. "I heard the Nordic god say his name."

Parker bit back a grin.

So his nickname is now official.

Parker returned her attention to the soldiers. The trio remained in place, watching Martinez struggle and silently rooting him on.

Captain Grayson spoke from behind them. "It's time to go, ladies. Lunch will be served in ten minutes."

Parker wanted to ask if she could stay and watch the training but quickly reminded herself that she was in the Army now—well, sort of. In any case, her time was not hers. But as the three women joined the group and walked toward the mess hall, she kept looking back over her shoulder.

*****

Lunch in the huge, crowded, smelly, and stuffy mess hall proved basic but palatable. The WAACS were given a designated corner, separate from the soldiers, and they filled the ten tables allotted to their group.

"We'll eat in two shifts when the other half of our number arrives," Captain Grayson informed them. "For now, you all are assigned to the noon shift. I'll let you know when that changes."

Parker carried her finished tray to the kitchen drop-off point, keenly aware that since walking into the building, she and the other women had been under the grinning scrutiny of a couple thousand curious men. Parker dropped her silverware into the receptacles and set her plate and tray on the appropriate stacks, while trying not to make eye contact with any of them.

She had not enlisted in the WAACs to find any sort of romantic entanglement. She was here as a soldier for her country. Even if she was designated as 'auxiliary' personnel, she would still have to contend with the altitude and the weather, the same as the men. And she still would be keeping up her physical training.

The main difference was that women were not issued any weapons. That bothered Parker a little, but they certainly weren't going to encounter either enemy here in Camp Hale's remote location. Guns were one less thing for the women to worry about training for.

When everyone had put away their trays, the women were split up and taken to their assignments. Parker was very glad to see Emily and Sofia in her group. Then she noticed that everyone in her group was a second lieutenant. That was interesting.

We all went to college.
That must be relevant to our jobs.

Captain Thayer led the group down the road to the Camp Hale Headquarters building. At the reception desk he retrieved a stack of identity cards from the corporal working there.

"Keep these cards with you, and present them every time you

come to work. No exceptions," he ordered. "Anderson."

One woman stepped forward and accepted her card. Thayer called another name and then another, in alphabetical order, until all thirty-six of the women had their cards. Williams was the final one called.

As usual.

While the group of WAACs claimed their identity cards, a major came down the stairs and stood by the captain, waiting until they were finished. No one had dared to ask what sort of work they were going to be doing yet. They just glanced at each other, wide-eyed and curious, and waited.

The major murmured something in Captain Thayer's ear. He nodded, and then addressed the group.

"Lieutenant Romano?"

Sofia stepped forward. "Yes, sir?"

"Go with Major Schultz. He'll give you your assignment."

"Yes, sir." Sofia shot Parker a quick and enigmatic glance before joining the major.

"The rest of you, follow me."

Parker and Emily exchanged puzzled looks as Major Schultz led Sofia in the opposite direction.

"What do you think that means?" Emily whispered.

Parker shrugged and whispered back, "Maybe it's because she speaks Italian?"

Captain Thayer led the women up a wide staircase. The uneven cadence of Army-issued leather soles scratching against the wooden steps was the only sound the women made as they followed him to the second floor. He walked across a landing to a set of heavy double doors. A placard fixed on each shouted CENSORS.

"This is where you all will be working." The captain opened the doors.

Parker stepped inside.

The huge room had eight rows of oak desks, each with two

wire baskets on opposite corners. One was marked IN, and one was marked OUT.

"We have room for fifty WAACS with college degrees to act as censors for the soldiers' mail," Grayson explained. "Each of you will have your own desk, and will be expected to read up to fifty letters a day, five days a week."

"Will there *be* two thousand letters mailed a day, sir?" Parker risked asking.

The captain's eyes met hers. "Yes, if each man stationed at Camp Hale writes just once a week, that's forty-eight thousand letters every month. Some write less, but some write more. We'll have to adjust your hours if you can't keep up."

Parker nodded her understanding and kept her expression carefully blank.

"Captain Thayer, sir, if I may?" Emily's soft accent made everything she said seem genteel. "There are less than fifty of us here…"

"You'll work side-by-side with the men who are still waiting to be relieved, until the rest of you WAACs arrive." Thayer's gaze moved over the assembled women. "Are there any other questions?"

When no one spoke up, he bounced a quick nod. "Good. Now take a seat. Your training will commence immediately."

Chapter Six

Parker turned off the lukewarm shower with one towel wrapped around her head and wrapped another around her body. She gathered her clothes and stepped out from behind the privacy curtain.

"Next!" she quipped. "The water is... refreshing."

I hope it's actually hot when winter comes.

She walked to her bunk and slipped her nightgown over her head as the towel around her body fell to the floor. She picked it up and hung it at the foot of the bunk along with the second towel, and then sat on her mattress to comb out her wet hair.

Today's training had been both unsettling and eye-opening.

Parker obviously understood the reason for censoring the soldier's letters. Information that seemed harmless—like specifics about their weapons or artillery—could be used by enemies against the American Army if the letters were ever intercepted.

What was presented today that she had *not* thought about before was the possibility that a soldier might be sending information to someone—say a new girlfriend—who was actually mining him for details which she could then trade for favors.

When a country as big as the United States was at war on multiple continents, and had thousands of miles of open and unguarded borders, it would be a simple matter for an enemy spy to slip across one and start cultivating those sorts of relationships.

Especially with someone from the first generation families who emigrated from any of the countries who were currently fighting or occupied.

Sadly, Parker had been caught in a few situations concerning the parents of her students where she did not feel the parent was trustworthy. If that parent had a German name, or perhaps Asian heritage, she supposed the government had a right to be careful about what those people knew.

Just in case.

Each of the WAACs assigned to the censor's office had been issued a rubber stamp today that said *Passed by Army Examiner*, and that message was to be placed at the lower left corner of every page of the soldiers' letters once all the offending words or phrases were blacked out with India ink. The censors were also instructed to sign their names across the stamp.

Parker felt the seriousness of her new responsibility, and weighed it against the speed with which they were expected to read and redact the letters. To be honest, the task ahead of her made her nervous.

What have I gotten myself into?

*****

At the end of their first week, Parker, Emily, and Sofia headed to the Servicemen's Center after supper for a little rest and recuperation. On the way, Sofia told her new friends about her assignment.

"I'm not allowed to tell you anything specific, of course. You both know that as censors," she cautioned. "But I can tell you that the Army is doing detailed background checks of my family, and if all goes well I'll be working in Intelligence."

"Because you are fluent in Italian," Parker stated the obvious.

Sofia's smile was puckish. "I can neither confirm nor deny your statement, Lieutenant."

"Well done," Emily observed, grinning.

"What about you two?" Sofia asked. "How was your first week?"

"The responsibility is intense." Parker heaved a sigh. "We have to be so careful."

"And we're each supposed to read and redact fifty letters a day," Emily added.

Sofia's eyes rounded. "Is that possible?"

"Turns out it is," Parker said. "Letters can only be written on one side of the paper, so a lot of the guys only write one page."

Sofia chuckled. "Well, that part's not surprising, considering they're all men after all."

The sounds of conversation and music inside the club spilled out under the dusky sky and into the cooling mountain air every time the front doors opened. Soldiers came and went in a constant stream and every single one of them stared at the trio of WAACs daring to approach.

Several wolf-whistled.

After the fifth one did, Emily put two fingers in her mouth and whistled back. The sharp, shrill sound made Parker's ears ring and the southern belle's cheekiness surprised her once again.

"Emily!" she yelped.

"What?" Emily looked quite pleased with herself. "Stick with me, ladies. Us southern girls know how to take care of ourselves."

Parker laughed. Emily's puckish personality, tempered by her refined southern drawl, was irresistible.

"That's comforting to know, thank you." Parker stopped before opening the door. "So are you ladies ready to face the horde?"

Emily elbowed Sofia. "The real question is, are they ready for us?"

*****

Once inside the heavily alcohol and cigarette smoke scented building, the three friends went straight to the bar and stood in line to order their drinks. When he saw them, the bartender called them all to the front of the line.

"Ladies first," he quipped. "What can I get you?"

Parker raised her voice to be heard over the din of hundreds of male voices and the jaunty popular music blaring from a jukebox. "I'll have a beer."

"Make it two, please," Emily chimed in.

Sofia held up three fingers.

The bartender nodded. He filled three glasses at the tap and set them on the bar. "Welcome to Camp Hale, Lieutenants. Ladies drink free here."

"Why thank you, sir," Emily cooed and flashed her dimples. "You soldiers are such gentlemen."

Parker pressed back a laugh and smiled her thanks. Then the three women turned around to search for a table in the crowded club.

Parker noticed three soldiers sharing a table—a blond, a brunette, and a redhead. Her first thought was there had to be a punch line involved somehow, but then she realized the brunette's profile was familiar.

She nudged Sofia. "Isn't that—"

"Xavier Martinez." Sofia's smile was positively dreamy. "From the climbing exercise."

If that's Martinez, then the blond guy is...

Before Parker had the chance to say anything else Sofia cut a path straight through the crowd to their table. Parker and Emily scurried after her like a pair of obedient baby ducklings.

"Good evening, gentlemen."

The three men stood when Sofia spoke and Parker found herself staring up into the same blue eyes that she noticed on her first day at Camp Hale. The Norse god had to be at least six-foot-two. Or three. Maybe four.

"May we offer you our table?" he asked in the same deep, clear voice that she heard from the bottom of the mountainside.

She opened her mouth to accept, but Emily cut her off.

"Only if you three stay here to protect us." Her friend's cheeks dimpled adorably once again. "We are new here and don't yet know how to tell the wolves from the sheepdogs."

The redhead leaned forward with a mischievous grin. "What if we're the wolves?"

Emily flipped a flirtatious hand and winked. "We'll take our chances."

As the women claimed three of the four chairs at the table, Martinez and the Norse god found two more. Once the six were settled, Emily began the introductions.

"I'm Emily Black and this is my friend, Parker Williams. We work in the Censors Office."

The blond's gaze shot to Parker's. "The Censors Office?"

"Yes, indeed. We get to read all the fascinating details that you guys write home about." Parker giggled. "Or *not* so fascinating, as it turns out."

"Whose letters do *you* read?" he pressed.

"We're each assigned to a regiment and battalion first off, so we can spot trends if someone is constantly needing to be censored." Parker lifted one shoulder. "After that, we help anyone who is getting behind."

"What's your assignment?"

Parker thought it was odd that he kept pressing the point but she answered anyway. Was he worried about something in *his* letters? "Eighty-Sixth Regiment, First Battalion. Why?"

"That's ours." The redhead held out his hand. "I'm David Fraser from North Carolina. And this big lunk head who's giving you the third degree is—"

"Call me Thunder." The Norse god held out his hand as well. "It's my nickname."

David looked confused. "It is?"

"Yes. My middle name is Thor because I was born during a massive mid-western thunderstorm." Thunder flashed a broad grin. "So I was called Thunder all through school."

Parker gripped Thunder's hand and shook it tentatively. "Okay, Thunder." She read the patch on his chest. "Thunder Hansen."

Emily grabbed David's hand and looked into his eyes. "I'm from Georgia. We're practically neighbors."

Thunder looked at Parker, his blue eyes pinched at the corners by a very engaging smile. "Kansas. You?"

"Colorado. We *are* neighbors."

All this while, Sofia and Martinez were sending shy glances in each other's direction. "I'm Sofia Romano, from New Jersey."

"Xavier Martinez. San Diego, California." He chuckled. "We are definitely *not* neighbors. Are you a censor, too?"

She shook her head. "Army Intelligence."

"Oh, great." He heaved a resigned sigh. "So everything we say or write can be held against us. Proves my luck with women."

David laughed at that. "From my perspective, your luck is about to change, my friend."

Sofia blushed and took a sip of her beer.

"How long have you been in the Auxiliary Corps?" Thunder asked.

"We're all new recruits," Parker answered for the three of them. "We were assigned to Camp Hale after we finished boot camp. We met a week ago, when we came in on the same train."

Thunder pointed at her gold bars. "So how'd you become second lieutenants already?"

"College graduates are automatically entered as second lieutenants."

He looked inexplicably uncomfortable. "You went to college?"

Parker nodded. "English major. Taught high school for three years—and hated it. So I enlisted as soon as the opportunity presented itself."

Emily smiled across the table at David. "Math major. I want to be a civil engineer someday."

Sofia raised one hand and wiggled her fingers. "European History."

The three men exchanged shocked glances.

"Don't worry about it. Our rank doesn't matter." Parker laid her hand in the center of the table and met each man's eyes. "We are here to serve our country. Not to find husbands."

"Speak for yourself," Emily murmured into her glass.

David looked pleased.

Parker scowled at her. "What I *mean* is we can all be friends without having to worry about the whole courtship thing."

Sofia looked at Xavier. "Friends?"

He lifted his glass in toast and grinned at her. "Yes, ma'am."

Parker lifted her glass as well. "To friends and neighbors, then."

Thunder touched his glass to hers and his smile returned. "And may we all live long enough to tell very embarrassing stories about each other someday!"

*****

"Damn!" Lucas blurted as the trio headed back to their barracks hours later. The night sky was filled with more stars than he could count and the day's warmth had been chased off by chilly mountain air. "Two censors and Army Intelligence."

Fraser stopped walking and faced him. "*Thunder?*"

Lucas wagged a finger in his face. "Don't mock me. I'm the only one of us smart enough to disguise my identity. If she reads my letters, she won't know they're from me."

Fraser's jaw dropped.

"Hansen's a common enough name, after all," Lucas continued. "Especially with all the Norwegian guys here with the Ninety-Ninth."

"You're right," Fraser huffed. "Damn you."

"I don't have anything to worry about," Martinez boasted.

Lucas shrugged and started walking again. "Not unless she thinks you're a spy."

"Aw, *shit*."

"You know, once we're deployed and using radios, we all have to have nicknames anyway," Lucas pointed out. "I'm just ahead of the game."

"That's a good point," Martinez admitted. He looked at Fraser. "What will your name be?"

Fraser thought a minute. "I'll use Smoky. In honor of the Great Smoky Mountains back home. What about you?"

"Diego," he answered with enthusiasm. "Representing us California beach boys."

"Beach boys in the ski troops and college graduates in the WAACs." Lucas wagged his head. "Who ever expected that?"

July 1943

United States Army Headquarters made the well-received announcement that the Eighty-Fifth, Eighty-Sixth, and Eighty-Seventh Regiments stationed at Camp Hale would no longer be called either Ski Troops or Mountain Troops. On July fifteenth they were all officially joined together to form the Tenth Light Division, Alpine.

"Alpine, boys! That's where we're headed!" Fraser did a little highland jig. "It's only a matter of time until we make those signs at the camp's entrance a reality!"

Lucas chuckled. The trio had made it a ritual to punch the two caricatures of Adolf Hitler on the wooden boards every time they passed them.

One depicted a huge fist labeled *Camp Hale* knocking the Fuhrer backwards into Japan's Hideki Tojo.

The other declared, *We've got a date with this sonofabitch. Let's be on time!*

Lucas could hardly wait.

So when all three battalions of the Eighty-Seventh Regiment, which Lucas, Fraser and Martinez were originally part of, were sent to Fort Ord in California for amphibious exercises, Lucas was stunned.

"Amphibious exercises?" Lucas was incredulous. "Why on earth are they sending an 'Alpine' regiment to do *water* exercises?"

Fraser looked as perplexed as he was. "They didn't say why."

"I bet they're headed for the Pacific Theater," Martinez guessed soberly. "That's the only thing that makes sense."

"Does it make sense?" Lucas challenged. "They've been doing mountain climbing and high altitude ski training for months. How does that translate to maneuvering through sea-level jungles?"

"Don't ask me," Martinez grumbled. "It wasn't my decision."

Lucas angrily wiped sweat off his brow with his sleeve. The three men had just reached the top of one of the climbing walls around the edges of Camp Hale and were taking a water break before rappelling back down.

Martinez sat on the ground, far away from the edge.

"Why do they get deployed and not us?" Lucas knew he was whining but didn't care. "Damn it. If we hadn't been moved to the Eighty-Sixth, then we'd be the ones shipping out!"

"Well..." Martinez looked up at him. "There's no skiing in the Pacific. So maybe they seemed the least prepared *for* the Alpine stuff."

Lucas took a long drink from his canteen and considered that explanation. Partially mollified by the suggestion, he jammed his canteen back into its holster on his belt.

"I'll see you guys at the bottom."

As he backed over the edge of the cliff, Lucas knew his boiling anger wasn't justified. But damn it, he deserved a chance to fight.

He'd never worked at anything so hard in his entire life. Not even football. But to be truthful, there was no comparison—what he was doing now was immeasurably harder.

Football was played on carefully leveled ground covered in grass, not steep, rocky inclines and cliffs dangerously slippery with snow and ice. In football his pads were the heaviest thing he had to carry, not a ninety-pound rucksack. And in football, no one shot at him with live ammunition.

Lucas had seriously underestimated what signing up for the ski troops—the *Tenth Light* Division—actually meant when he made his impulsive decision. In the past five months since arriving at Camp Hale, he had been challenged and stretched to his limit far more times than any point in his life before this.

But he rose to every challenge he faced and conquered every task he was given, no matter how difficult they proved to be. So he'd better get the chance to show that to the world someday, or else none of his personal triumph would count for anything.

And nothing about his unremarkable life back at home on his family's Kansas farm would change.

Ever.

*****

Parker stared at the letter in her hand. It was almost illegible. Not because of the handwriting itself, but because the spelling was, well, creative at best. Not only that, but some of the actual letters were written backwards.

How did this guy ever get into the Army?

It didn't make sense that someone who was nearly illiterate like this would be able to enlist.

She re-read the letter again. In spite of the multiple mistakes, if she decoded everything correctly the sentences were actually complete, the grammar correct, and the information included was safe—and refreshingly interesting to boot.

The letter was signed simply *Luke*. She looked at the address on the envelope: Mr. Matthew Hansen, Route 2, Sabetha, Kansas.

She briefly wondered if the writer could be related to Thunder before her ability to reason kicked in.

First, the letter was addressed simply *Hello* so there was no way to know the relationship of the author to the intended recipient. Secondly, he couldn't be the only one here at Camp Hale who had a reason to write to someone in Kansas.

The most compelling argument against it being Thunder, however, was the presence of the Ninety-Ninth Battalion, nicknamed the Viking Battalion, also was training at Camp Hale. That unique group of soldiers was comprised entirely of Norwegian-Americans who spoke the language—and there had to be at least a couple dozen Hansens in that crowd.

And for many of those guys, English was not their native language.

This must be one of them.

Since this was the first time in her six weeks as a censor that she had seen anything like this, it was probably just an overflow letter that had landed in her basket.

Besides, Thunder was bright and witty. His vocabulary was as broad as most of her college friends. And he seemed to know something about every subject they talked about.

Nothing like this poor guy, who was struggling just to be coherent.

Parker stamped the bottom left corner of the letter, signed it, and put it back in the envelope. Then she sealed it and dropped it in the OUT basket.

Chapter Seven

November 1943

The situation at Camp Hale had been shifting in the last few months, ever since the Eighty-Seventh Regiment had been sent away. As an unexpected benefit of being a censor, Parker and the other ladies found out some of what was going on by reading—and then redacting—the camp soldiers' letters.

"So after training with Marines, the Eighty-Seventh was sent to a little Alaskan island called Kiska," she whispered to Emily as they walked arm-in-arm from the mess hall to their barracks after supper. The early winter's night air was crisply chilled and a full moon lit their way. Their boots crunched through a thin icy covering on three inches of snow and their breath formed brief clouds.

"I saw that, too!" Emily looked over her shoulder before she spoke further. "There were supposed to be ten-thousand Japs on that island."

"I wonder how it's turned out…" Parker mused.

Emily leaned closer. "I heard someone say that the reason the

Ninetieth Regiment has been brought here is because the Army thinks our guys will be slaughtered up there."

Parker gasped. She stopped walking and closed her eyes, and her fists clenched at the horrible thought. Of course war meant men would die, but she believed herself protected from that outcome while safely ensconced back here in the mountains of Colorado. This news was literally hitting close to home.

She opened her eyes, now moist with tears. "Am I terribly selfish to be glad that Thunder, David, and Xavier are still here?"

Emily shook her head. "No, ma'am. I feel exactly the same way. I really like those guys."

Parker smiled softly. "You really like *David*."

Emily was probably blushing; it was hard to tell in the dim camp lights. "Is that so wrong?"

"No, not at all." Parker tucked her arm back through Emily's and they resumed their pace. "I assume he likes you back."

"He says he does." Emily's tone didn't match her words.

Though she was certain she knew the answer, Parker still asked, "Then why are you sad?"

Emily snorted and turned a disgusted face to Parker. "You know as well as I do. He's going to war."

Parker had nothing to say to that.

"So what's going on with you and Thunder?" Emily deftly changed the subject.

What indeed.

Parker hadn't mentioned the three badly written letters that she'd read to anyone at first, certain that they were from a Hansen in the Norwegian contingent. Until a letter crossed her desk three weeks after the Ninety-Ninth Battalion deployed in August. A letter which mentioned their leaving and added the writer's wish that his own chance would come soon.

Now she believed the author actually was Thunder and she didn't know what to do about it.

Luke.

His name is Luke.
Parker sighed and forced a smile. "We're just friends."

"I wouldn't be so sure," Emily countered. "You should see how he looks at you when you aren't looking at him."

Parker was not certain how she felt about that. Elated and devastated both pretty much covered it.

"He's a good man, Parker," Emily pressed. "And he's darn good looking to boot."

"I know…"

Now Emily stopped walking. She grabbed Parker's arms and turned her so they were face to face.

"You can't expect *me* to be brave about them going off to fight and not be brave yourself."

Parker hesitated. "It's not just that…"

"Then what is it?"

Parker shook her head. "I can't tell you until I talk to him."

Emily's arms went slack, though she still held on to Parker's. "You're reading his letters, aren't you?"

Parker nodded.

"Is he doing something wrong?"

"No, nothing like that!" Parker couldn't imagine any man with an upstanding character like Thunder's doing such a thing. "In fact, I almost never have to redact anything he writes."

Emily let go of Parker's arms and crossed hers over her chest. "So he has a girl back home, then."

Parker shrugged. "He only writes to what I believe are his parents, as far as I can tell, so I don't think so."

"Then what is it?" Emily demanded.

Parker struggled to find the right words. "His letters are hard to read. That's all. I just want to ask him about it."

"You mean his handwriting?"

"Sure." That worked.

Emily snapped her fingers and Parker saw her expression brighten in the moonlight. "I bet he's left-handed and his teachers always forced him to write with his right hand!"

Parker was stunned. That possibility hadn't occurred to her—and as a former teacher she was deeply embarrassed that it hadn't. "You could be right about that."

"I have a cousin they did that to." Emily shook her head. "Poor guy never got the hang of it and his handwriting still looks like a chicken spilled the ink pot then walked through the puddle onto the page."

That was a pretty accurate description of Thunder's letters. Relief surged through Parker's frame. She smiled at Emily.

"I bet that's exactly what happened." She looped her arm through Emily's and started walking again. "Come on, I'm getting cold and I want to take a shower before the hot water is gone."

*****

Now that the snow had returned to the Rockies, Lucas threw himself into their winter training with renewed effort and unwavering determination.

He climbed the sheer cliff faces at Camp Hale more often than he was asked to and then rappelled down. He skied uphill carrying heavy rucksacks without allowing his pace to slack off. He mastered the steps of setting up bivouacs out in the training areas. Anything he was ordered to do he did to the fullest extent of his ability.

No one pushed him harder than he pushed himself.

Turns out, the men in his platoon were inspired by him to do the same. Probably because he treated them like members of his team. Inspiring his buddies to overcome their environment was just like inspiring his team to win a game.

The difference was that here the stakes no longer involved a fancy trophy, they meant surviving and conquering a vicious and experienced enemy.

Lucas had no respect for those soldiers who tried to get out of their exercises by hiding out in the hospital. That situation got so bad, in fact, that Camp Hale's commander ordered that the core-wracking cough which so many guys developed from breathing the soot-fouled air, dubbed 'Pando Hack' by the soldiers, was not an acceptable excuse for missing field training.

Today when Lieutenant Loose's platoon returned from a thirty-mile cross country ski march, Lucas was both exhausted and exhilarated. "We did well today, guys. I'm proud of us. We're really going to kick some German ass when we get over there."

Martinez wagged his head. "I've got to hand it to you, my friend. I'd never be as strong as I am if you hadn't been kicking *my* ass this whole time."

"Well Xavier, I really *love* kicking your ass." Lucas slapped his friend's back. "You're welcome."

Fraser hefted his skis to his shoulder. "Are we meeting The Lieutenants at the club tonight?"

"Sofia said we are when I talked to her last night." Martinez shouldered his skis. "So let's go."

The six of them had become a tight group—the three soldiers, all now Privates First Class, and the three lieutenants in the renamed and reconfigured Women's Army Corps.

"Never forget that we outrank you," Parker teased.

Lucas leaned across the table and pinned her gaze with his. "So you are saying that your wish is *literally* my command."

The heightened color in her cheeks rewarded his attention.

Damn, she was beautiful.

Lucas guessed her to be about five-foot-five since the top of her head hit the bottom of his chin when they danced. She wore her dark brown hair in a no-nonsense short cut that was unexpectedly attractive. And it made her golden brown eyes look huge.

"It's our turn to buy tonight," Lucas said as they gathered six chairs around a table. "What can I get you?"

"A pitcher of beer for the table is fine with me," Parker replied. "I'm not fussy."

Emily looked at Fraser. "I'd love a glass of white wine. Something sweet if they have it."

Martinez held Sofia's chair. "Irish coffee?"

She smiled at him like he hung the damn moon. "Yes, please."

Conversation flowed easily as the friends talked about the Thanksgiving they were all missing at home the next week, and their plans for a hoped-for Christmas furlough.

"I might be heading to New Jersey," Martinez said casually.

Lucas looked at him, stunned. "Really?"

"He's been invited," Sofia stated clearly. "It would actually be his first white Christmas, since you guys didn't come to Colorado until January."

Lucas exchanged a glance with Parker, who seemed as surprised as he was.

"Sounds like fun," she said with a slightly delayed smile.

Emily shook her head. "My mama would have a conniption if I didn't come home for Christmas."

"So would mine," Fraser admitted, and Lucas wondered if that was his way of getting out of being invited to meet Emily's family as well.

Thank goodness there was no reason for him to expect Parker to extend an invitation. He really needed to spend time with the family he had quietly slipped away from eleven months ago, and to assure them he was doing well. Better than well—he was thriving.

"Have any of you noticed the soldiers from the Eighty-Seventh dribbling back into camp from their deployment?" Fraser asked.

"I have," Sofia said.

"Me, too." Emily faced Fraser. "They left, what, four months ago?"

"Have you heard anything about how it went?" Parker asked.

"Not much," Fraser admitted. "Only that when they got there, the Japs were already gone."

Parker's jaw dropped. "No! Really?"

Emily's eyes rounded. "Then what have they been doing for four months?"

"Waiting for ships to be able to bring them back."

When Lucas first heard that the Army sent the Ninetieth Regiment to Camp Hale as replacements, in anticipation of high casualty rates in the Eighty-Seventh, he was less angry about not being sent. But when he found out that the entire mission was a bust because Navy intelligence somehow missed the evacuation of ten thousand Japanese troops, he was livid.

"Those guys trained for five months at high altitudes," Lucas pointed out. "And then they sat at sea level for four months because the Army thought they'd be wiped out, and so never scheduled ships to retrieve them!"

"And now that they're coming back, the camp is overcrowded," Martinez added.

"That explains the increase in letters coming through the censors." Parker frowned a little. "We've been swamped all of a sudden."

"Speaking of letters…" Emily straightened in her chair. "I got a letter from one of my cousins. He's left-handed but he was forced to write with his right hand in school, so his handwriting is really hard to read."

Lucas noticed Parker's face blanch, then redden. "Emily."

"What?" Emily asked innocently. "I was just wondering if any of us have had a similar experience."

Lucas felt his pulse surge. That question was oddly specific. What was going on?

"Not me. Right-handed from birth," Martinez said.

Fraser nodded. "Yep. Same here."

Emily looked at Lucas. "Are you left-handed?"

Lucas felt like the floor was opening up and he was going to drop into it and disappear. "No."

Emily's brow wrinkled. "No?"

She has seen my writing.

Shit.

Lucas stood. "I, uh. I'll be right back."

He grabbed his coat, spun around, and headed for the door.

*****

"Emily! How could you?" Parker cried. She jumped to her feet and grabbed her coat as well.

"What's going on?" Fraser yelped.

"None of your business!" Parker jammed her arms into her coat sleeves as she ran after Thunder.

When she opened the door of the overheated Servicemen's Center, the frigid wind hit her like a living thing. Parker pulled the collar of her coat closed as she carefully navigated the slick and icy steps.

Thunder had a head start and was he rapidly extending it.

"Thunder!" Parker ran after him as fast as she dared over the frozen snow-dusted pavement. "Thunder, wait!"

She was close enough that she knew he could hear her, especially since the winter wind was coming from behind her and would carry her voice forward. "Thunder! I need to talk to you!"

He kept moving and gave no indication that he heard anything.

"*Luke!*"

That did it.

He slowed to a stop but did not turn around.

Parker caught up to him, panting in the thin mountain air. She planted herself in front of him and looked up. In the dim camp streetlights his handsome face was cut by shadows into grim, harsh planes.

"Can we talk?" Parker asked softly.

He didn't answer. He just stared down his nose at her.

"I'm the one who's read your letters, not Emily," she explained. "But I didn't know they were yours until after the Norwegian guys shipped out."

His brow twitched.

She shrugged. "Hansen *is* a common Norwegian name."

"What do you want?" he growled.

Parker hesitated. "An explanation?"

Even in the faint light Parker could see his jaw muscles flexing. "I was a fool to think no one would find out."

"Find out what?" she pressed. "I don't understand."

His gaze fell away and his shoulders slumped. "I'm not stupid."

Parker took a step back, shocked at his words. "No, you're not stupid! You're a very intelligent man. Why would you even say that?"

His gaze cut back to hers. "I'd explain it if I could. But I can't."

Parker gave him an encouraging look. "Please try, Luke."

"Lucas."

Her brows lifted. "Lucas? Is that your name?"

"Lucas Thor Hansen." He lifted one shoulder. "Luke when I was a boy. Thunder when I was in high school."

"Oh. Okay." Parker bounced a little nod. "So what's the deal, Lucas?"

His jaw worked for a minute before his words came out. "When I look at letters on a page, they don't hold still."

Parker was so startled by his statement that it took her a moment to respond. "They what?"

Now his hands came into play as he demonstrated what he was trying to describe. "They flip around. Sometimes an N will face one way, then it faces another. I don't know which way is right."

Parker could not believe what she was hearing. "Is that true?"

"Why would I lie about this?" he demanded. "And it's not just letters, sometimes it's the whole word."

"Have you had your eyes checked?"

Lucas scoffed and wagged his head. "More times than I can count."

"But you *can* read?" she prodded. "Can't you?"

He heaved a heavy sigh. "Yes… But reading and writing are both difficult for me. I really have to work at it."

Parker didn't know what to say to that, except, "But you're so smart."

"That's why it's so frustrating."

A wave of empathy swamped her. "I can't imagine what that's like."

He kicked the crusty snow piled along the edge of the road. "No one can."

Parker laid her hand on his arm. "I'm so sorry, Lucas."

For a brief moment she thought he might kiss her, but that moment passed.

His tone was resigned. "I knew I couldn't hide it forever."

Parker squeezed his arm. "No one will hear it from me, I promise you that. From now on, give me your letters directly so no one else reads them."

He looked relieved. "Okay. Thanks."

Parker decided right then to be honest about what was on her heart. Even if he didn't feel the same about her, Lucas deserved to know what she thought of him.

"Ever since I met you, I've thought you were one of the smartest, kindest, hardest working men I have ever known. I'm so very glad I know you, Lucas Hansen."

This time, he did kiss her.

Chapter Eight

January 1944

Lucas returned from his Christmas furlough with renewed determination. His visit with his family was good—both of his sisters fussed over him, his dad was deeply impressed with all the things he had learned and accomplished, and his mother was just happy that he was happy.

Because, he realized, he really was.

The thing that surprised him the most was how Parker's discovery of his problem hadn't made his situation at Camp Hale worse—it was actually better. He was set free from the burden now that his secret was shared.

At Parker's urging, he told Martinez and Fraser about his difficulties.

Both of his friends accepted the information as simply that—information. It hadn't changed anything about their friendship, except Lucas noticed that the two men read things out loud more often, like Company notices, or articles in the *Ski-zette*, the camp newspaper.

He really appreciated that, and told them so.

Parker said she talked to Emily and Sofia on his behalf, and after that the subject was never brought up again.

The only thing he hadn't dealt with was the kiss.

Lucas had gained an undeniable affection for Parker, but he didn't feel like now was the right time to start any kind of serious relationship. There was a world war being fought in two hemispheres, after all, and his future was precarious at best.

It didn't help that Martinez and Fraser were both succumbing, either. That meant at some point, he would need to talk to Parker to be sure they understood each other.

Now that everyone was back from furlough, he should probably act on that.

"Hey, there he is!" Fraser wound his way through the bunks in their barracks. "Welcome back, Thunder!"

The men shook hands. "How was your Christmas, Smoky?"

"Cold. Yours?"

"Same. Where's Diego?" Lucas noticed Martinez's bunk was empty.

"He got delayed by a blizzard in Missouri. Should be here tomorrow."

Lucas laughed. "Missouri, eh? So he did go to New Jersey."

Fraser grinned. "Yep."

Lucas dropped his duffel on his bunk and zipped it open. "Anything happening I should know about?"

Fraser's grin dimmed. "Yeah. Since the Kiska screw-up and the departure of the Ninetieth Regiment, it seems the three regiments in the Tenth Light are out of balance again."

Lucas stopped unpacking and faced his friend. "What does that mean?"

Fraser winced. "It means some of us might get moved."

Lucas threw the shirt in his hand onto his bunk. "Shit."

"Yeah."

March 1944

God smiled on Lucas and his buddies once again—he, Fraser, and Martinez stayed put in the Eighty-Sixth Regiment, First Battalion. The men were relieved initially to still be together, and ultimately fall-on-their knees grateful when they heard what challenge they were now facing.

Lieutenant James Loose gathered their platoon for the announcement.

"Army Ground Forces requires that all divisions are tested for battle readiness."

"We're a helluva more ready than we were a year ago," Lucas whispered.

"Damn straight," Fraser whispered back.

"The test is called the Division Series, or D-Series for short," Loose continued. "The Army has a list of criteria for us to meet which includes every aspect of an Infantry Division employed in combat."

Lucas nodded. That made sense.

"All twelve thousand soldiers of the Tenth Light Division will participate this time," Loose continued. "The test will commence on March twenty-fourth and last for three weeks."

Lucas glanced at Fraser and Martinez and smiled.

No problem.
We can do this.

*****

In the midst of a brutal Colorado Rockies blizzard, twelve thousand Camp Hale soldiers set out on skis and snowshoes and took the familiar road up the Tennessee Pass until they reached eleven thousand feet elevation. The temperature was a staggering thirty degrees below zero.

Lucas skied next to Fraser with Martinez right behind them.

Ice and Granite: The Snow Soldiers of Riva Ridge   75

The wind battled against the men, pushing them backwards and shooting stinging snow pellets into their eyes. They skied in silence—there was no point wasting any energy on unnecessary conversation.

The entire Division had been split in half between the red attack force and the blue defense force. The attack force was instructed to conduct reconnaissance patrols to ferret out the defense force. The defense force was instructed to secure positions and remain alert, ready to engage if attacked.

The various companies were given red or blue armbands before the umpires directed them to their designated areas in the surrounding mountains.

A Company wore the red defense armbands.

The umpire initially directed A Company to a location near Tennessee Pass. Lieutenant Loose led the way for his platoon.

Lucas and the others were fresh when they set out, but the skiing, stopping, waiting, and skiing again was exhausting, especially under the extreme storm conditions.

Not only did they need to find their way to their assigned position, but they needed to do so without being seen by the red force.

Exacerbating their discomfort, the body heat generated while on the move created sweat, which in turn chilled when the soldiers stopped and waited in the unrelenting and windy blizzard.

Lucas tried to keep moving as much as he could when the company halted to wait for stragglers and to confirm their compass directions in the gray-clouded snowstorm. Once everyone caught up and the leaders had all consulted the map, they resumed the march.

A Company reached their designated location late in the day as the sky began to darken behind the clouds. They hurried to set up a company command post in the tree line to stay out of sight, then the soldiers were ordered to dig in for the night.

Lucas and Fraser found a protected spot and Martinez and his tent mate claimed the spot next to them. They set up their tents and bolstered them with cut slabs of hardened snow, the trick they had learned from the experienced guys at Homestake.

In spite of the Arctic temperatures, fires were not allowed during the test—the flames were easily observable at night, and smoke could give away positions during the day.

"Remember to change your socks and insoles every night, men," Lieutenant Loose reminded the men as they dug out their K-Rations, pried open the half-frozen tins of food, and spooned the barely palatable sustenance into their mouths. "You're all relying on the health of your feet to survive."

Lucas sat inside his fortified tent and did exactly that. He had no desire to fall victim to frostbite, especially after his experiences during Homestake.

"We'll do better this time than Homestake," Lucas stated optimistically. "We know what we're doing now."

Fraser nodded while he stuffed his dirty socks into his pack. "I hope you're right."

*****

A week later, Lucas seriously doubted his own words.

The soldiers of A Company had encountered obstacles he had not ever considered. When the blizzard passed and the sun returned, the glare on the high snowy ridges was unbearable—and any soldier who didn't guard his green-glassed goggles and wear them religiously risked burning his corneas and going snow-blind.

The intense light reflecting off the snow was more dangerous than some of the men believed, until their vision began to blur and the radiating pain in their eye sockets became unbearable.

Two guys from Lucas's platoon fell victim and were evacuated back to the hospital at Hale.

When Lucas caught Martinez with his goggles on top of his helmet instead of over his eyes he smacked his friend in the back of the head.

"Don't be stupid, Diego! I don't care if they're uncomfortable. We can't afford to lose you."

Sufficiently chastised, Martinez slid the goggles back over his eyes.

The next morning A Company was up before dawn to begin their march up Resolution Road toward Ptarmigan Pass.

But a glitch in radio communications left the men standing around in the frigid predawn air for an hour before they began the ski march that would eventually take them up three thousand vertical feet to fourteen thousand feet in elevation.

In spite of the steep grade, A Company's captain set out at a relentless pace. Lucas pushed himself to keep up, gasping for oxygen in the thinning air.

Keep going.
Be a leader.

The normal pattern was to ski for fifty minutes, then rest for ten. When they took their first break, Lucas shrugged out of his rucksack straps and leaned on his poles, panting and trying to catch his breath in the thinning air. He looked back over his shoulder to see how the rest of the company was doing.

Fraser and Martinez were close behind him and both were panting as hard as he was. The line of resting soldiers grew in length as stragglers caught up.

"Let's go!" The captain bellowed. And he was off.

Lucas could have used another five minutes, but the guys at the back didn't get any rest at all—as soon as they reached the end of the line, the front of the line was on the move again. They never had a chance to drop their ninety-pound packs and recoup.

This was not going to end well.

After five hours of skiing upward around rocks and through trees, Lucas was done in, even though he had kept up and was able to rest the full ten minutes at each break.

Fraser and Martinez were fifty yards behind him and he was pretty certain they got at least eight or nine minutes with each stop. What he could not see was the end of the line farther down the mountain.

When the captain called an end to their current break, word came up the line that some of Lieutenant Loose's men were refusing to move until they had a chance to catch their breath.

As the captain resumed the march, Loose skied back down the line to check on his men. At their next break, Loose headed back up the stopped column, passing Lucas and catching up with the captain.

Loose looked like he was fixing to strangle a grizzly.

Minutes later, Lucas heard aggressive shouting from that direction, but the words were unintelligible and garbled by the wind, trees, and outcropping of granite.

Soon after the shouting stopped, Loose skied back down the resting line until he passed Lucas and stopped by Fraser and Martinez.

Lucas followed him.

The first lieutenant addressed the gathering members of their platoon.

"The captain wants the names of the men who won't march," he groused. "Doesn't care how whipped they are."

Lucas held his breath.

Whatever Loose said or did next would determine whether Lucas could trust the man enough to follow him into battle.

Loose lifted his goggles so now the men were able to see his eyes. "I told the captain that I brought up the men's condition to prove a point, not to get those soldiers court-martialed!"

"What'd he say?" Fraser asked.

Loose shook his head in apparent disbelief. "He threatened to court martial *me* when we get back if I didn't give up those names immediately."

"What did you say?" Lucas pressed.

Loose grinned at him. "I told him to knock himself out."

Lucas let out a spontaneous whoop.

"He also said if this was combat," Loose continued. "He could have me shot."

"What did you say, sir?" Fraser asked.

The lieutenant met Fraser's gaze. "I said if this was combat, then I'd be armed, too."

Lucas laughed.

Yep. I'll follow him anywhere.

Chapter Nine

Due to both the sub-zero weather and the mountainous terrain the Army-issued radios continued to glitch and fail. The extreme cold drained the batteries, and the sub-par radio signals were too weak to penetrate the surrounding mountains.

"If we can't tell Battalion Headquarters where we are, then they can't send us supplies." Loose kicked a chunk of crusted snow and grunted his frustration. Resignedly he told their communications specialist, "Keep trying."

"Yes, sir."

Twelve days into the D-Series test, A Company changed positions again and settled into a huge carved-out rocky bowl below Ptarmigan Peak. The snow in the bowl was eight feet deep and drifted around the edges where the trapped wind had swirled and slowed.

Lieutenant Loose instructed his platoon to set up their defensive position higher up, on a small plateau about a hundred yards or so below the peak.

"Our maps don't show this particular plateau," he told their ten remaining platoon members. "So if any red forces work their

Ice and Granite: The Snow Soldiers of Riva Ridge 81

way up here, we should be able to take them by surprise."

That was the good news, tactically speaking.

The bad news was that because of the failing radios, A Company was effectively cut off from Battalion Headquarters. They couldn't confirm that they had reached their location, so they weren't receiving re-supplies—and they were all running out of food.

The second day at their snowbound post, Lucas dragged Fraser and Martinez with him to talk to their lieutenant. "We'd like to volunteer sir."

Loose looked surprised. "For what, Private?"

"We'd like to scout for food."

Loose frowned. "Do you mean you want to go hunting?"

Lucas shot Fraser a glance. He hadn't thought of that, but he supposed it could be an option. It was obvious from his expression that the mountain-raised Fraser had the same reaction.

"No, sir." Lucas returned his attention to Loose. "We were thinking that maybe we could get supplies from another red force post."

"Or raid a red force post if we find one, sir," Martinez added.

"Huh." Loose flashed a crooked grin. "Permission granted. Just don't get lost. Or caught. That's an order."

"Yes, sir!" the three chorused.

Two hours into their exploration, and skiing over the sharply undulating and tree-covered terrain, Lucas was lagging and beginning to lose hope. "Maybe we should start shooting rabbits."

"We could—if we saw any," Fraser countered.

"Wait..." Martinez froze. "Do you hear that?"

The faint but unmistakable sound of an engine was slowly growing louder.

"To the right!" Martinez pushed off on that direction. Fraser and Lucas skied after him.

A quarter of a mile away they reached a deep ravine—and an

Army Weasel loaded with supplies was climbing right up the center, its tank-like treads carrying the vehicle over the snow and buried rocks.

"Let's take it!" Martinez urged. "If it's headed for red forces, then we have a right to the supplies."

"And if it's headed to blue then we'll capture it," Fraser added. "Guns up!"

The trio skied up the edge of the ravine, then down in front of the Weasel forcing it to stop.

"You are officially captured," Lucas told the driver. "We're A Company, Red Force, and we're stuck up at Ptarmigan Peak with no radio and no food. We're commandeering supplies for our platoon."

The driver put up his hands. "I won't stop you."

The three men unloaded as many cartons of rations that they could manage to drag or carry back to their position.

Lucas banged a fist on the side of the Weasel. "Thanks!"

The driver waved and started up the motor. The sound of another vehicle approaching drew Lucas's attention down the ravine. Another Weasel was rapidly making its vigorous way over the rocks toward them. It pulled to a jouncing stop behind the first one.

"What's going on here?" An irate colonel climbed out and awkwardly stomped on snow shoes toward Lucas and his buddies. "What are you men doing?"

Lucas saluted the officer. "We captured this Weasel, sir."

He scowled. "Why?"

"Because our platoon is in location up at Ptarmigan Peak, but we're out of food."

"You'll just have to wait for your own re-supply." The colonel pointed at the cartons. "Put those cartons back on the truck."

"We aren't getting re-supplied, sir," Lucas countered. "Our radios don't work so Headquarters has no idea that we've reached our assigned location."

The colonel rolled his eyes. "You can't capture a Weasel, Private. That's not how this game is played."

Game?

Men's lives were literally at stake.

Fraser stepped forward. "Sir, with all due respect, our men are cold and hungry, and we aren't able to reach our command."

The colonel glared at him. "I said, put the cartons back on the truck."

"But sir—"

"*Now!*"

While the colonel watched in the fading afternoon light, the three friends begrudgingly loaded the precious supplies back onto the Weasel.

"Fucking asshole's probably one of the observers from Washington. Sleeping in warm barracks, eating hot meals, driving around in Weasels." Lucas could barely keep his rage down to a whisper. "He has *no* idea what kind of hell we're going through."

The Weasel driver blew a soft whistle.

Lucas looked at him and the driver tipped his head to the left.

Lucas looked down the slope and saw the cartons which they were putting back on the Weasel were now resting in the snow on the opposite side. The deep snow had muffled the sound of the driver tossing them out of sight.

Lucas gave him a one-sided smile and nodded his thanks.

When the colonel and the Weasels were gone, the three men laboriously dragged the much-needed supplies through the snow and trees and back to their post under the cover of darkness.

*****

Early on Easter Sunday morning, and sixteen days into the D-Series Test, A Company headed farther up Ptarmigan Peak to

Shrine Pass. The snow was beginning to melt and the resulting wetness made skiing difficult.

Because of the religious holiday the test was halted for twenty-four hours. Even though the Weasels couldn't make it through the soft, sticky snow, the chaplain managed to climb up from Headquarters on snowshoes and held a service late that morning. Several thousand soldiers wearing both red and blue armbands gathered together to celebrate the holy day.

Lucas grew up going to church, but his experiences back home were nothing like this. To be on the top of the world, standing side-by-side with his entire division, and singing *Amazing Grace* in the sweet harmony of thousands of male voices was something he would never forget. Tears streamed down his cheeks, chilling his face, but he didn't bother to wipe them away.

In spite of the cold, the hunger, the exhaustion, and the rough conditions, Lucas had never felt so connected to his brothers-in-arms as he did at that moment.

When the soldiers were dispersing and heading back to their red or blue positions to continue the D-Series test, Shrine Pass was hit by a blizzard of apocalyptic proportions, bringing even higher winds and colder temperatures than those they had experienced up to now.

"Dig in!" Lieutenant Loose commanded. "We're not going any further tonight!"

Lucas, Fraser, and Martinez pulled out their long knives and started cutting slabs of the wind-crusted snow, stacking them in preparation for building a snow cave. Clouds lowered ominously over the top of the mountain cutting their visibility to basically a body's length.

A flash of lightning and the simultaneous crack of head-splitting thunder sent Lucas to the ground. His startled heart tried to beat an exit through his ribs. Curled in a fetal position with his hands clapped over his ears, he wondered if this was how he'd die.

He felt the second flash and resultant roar in his chest, as if the storm was reaching for his heart to stop its protest.

Holy shit!

When there wasn't a third explosion, he opened his eyes.

Fraser and Martinez were on the ground beside him, wide-eyed with fear.

"It's like we're actually inside the thunderhead..." Martinez rasped.

"We are." Fraser rolled onto his back. "At this altitude we are literally inside the storm cloud."

Lucas heard a voice from somewhere in the fog. "Is it over?"

"No way to tell," a disembodied voice answered.

"Come on, guys." Lucas climbed to his feet. "Let's get our snow cave built while we have the chance."

Lieutenant Loose made his way through the swirling snow and the thick icy cloud—still flashing with distant lightning and rumbling with thunder—to tell his men to ignore the restrictions on building a fire. "No one in their right minds would be out in this blizzard looking for us. But if they're stupid enough to try, then being 'captured' by the red forces is preferable to us freezing to death."

Lucas and his buddies didn't need to be told a second time. They got their shovels and dug a wide hole down into the snow, going down five feet before hitting rock. While Fraser lit all three of their camp stoves, Lucas and Martinez used the slabs of hard snow to create a roof over the pit, leaving a small opening to act as a chimney.

Tucked inside their tiny cave, the trio pried open their stolen K-Rations with their bayonets and heated the food over the stoves.

Lucas took a bite of the heated sausages and thought they were the best thing he had ever tasted.

"Our first warm meal in over two weeks, fellas," he said with his mouth full.

"And probably our last until we get back to camp." Fraser hummed his pleasure after putting the first bite in his mouth. "Oh, yeah. That's good."

Lucas looked around the small space. "Once we put the stoves away, there should be room for us to lie on our sides like spoons."

Martinez chuckled. "And word of that never, *ever* is spoken again. Deal?"

"Deal."

The three clunked their tins of food in a toast before polishing off the rest of their generous meal.

*****

By the third week of D-Series, the men of A Company were so tired they didn't bother looking for pine boughs to sleep on and just slept on their overturned skis instead. In fact that was the only time the men ever took their skis off. The snow had gotten so deep that walking around without skis now meant sinking up to their hips in the fresh frozen stuff.

Throughout the test it seemed to Lucas that the evaluators wanted to see just how far they could push the men. Officers would drive by soldiers marching up a mountain and shout from the comfort of their Weasels for the men to pick up the pace.

That disrespect infuriated the exhausted soldiers who were all carrying ninety-pound rucksacks in the below-zero, warmth-sucking, and oxygen-deficient air.

Fucking assholes.

After the umpires finally called the D-Series to a close, and the twelve thousand Tenth Light Division soldiers skied back to Camp Hale, the judges tabulated their scores from all the various trials which the men had successfully completed.

They rated the mountain troops as *satisfactory*.

"Satisfactory?" Lucas jumped up from the chair in front of the A Company office desk and turned in a frustrated circle, his fists clenched in anger. "What the *hell?*"

Lieutenant Loose just shook his head sadly. "I can't even begin to defend the Army right now. I agree with you, this is complete bullshit."

The lieutenant's concurrence with his outburst took some of the steam out of Lucas's engine. "Is that what you called me in here for, sir?"

"No, actually, it's not. Sit down."

He did. Loose slid a paper across the big oak desk.

Lucas's chest clutched at the sight of the form. "What's that?"

"An application for Officer Candidate School."

Lucas blinked. "What?"

Loose smiled. "You showed great leadership skills during the D-Series, Hansen. You always do. I think you should apply."

Hell no.

"I, uh—"

"The course is ninety days long, and you'll be sent to Fort Benning, Georgia to complete it."

Huh uh.

No way.

Lucas was beginning to panic. His pulse surged and thrummed in his ears. There was absolutely no possible way he could be convinced to go back to school, for any reason, on earth, ever.

How do I get out of this?

Loose folded his hands on the desk. "So what do you say?"

Lucas suddenly realized that Loose was still wearing his silver First Lieutenant bar.

Deflect the pass.

"Are you still a First Lieutenant, sir?"

Now Loose blinked. "Um, yes. After a very brief enquiry

Colonel Hampton found no grounds for a court martial, in spite of the captain's threat during the D-Series march."

"Congratulations, sir," Lucas effused. "His reprimand and was not deserved. Not at all."

"Thank you. The board agreed." Loose tapped the application. "Now about OCS—"

The brief shift gave Lucas a moment to craft his response. "I'm sorry sir, but I'm declining."

Lieutenant Loose looked disappointed. "Why?"

"Two reasons, sir. First of all, I don't plan to stay in the Army after the war is over, so the training would be wasted on me." Lucas smiled apologetically. "Send someone with more extensive military ambitions."

Loose slowly pulled the application back across the desktop. "Is there a second of all?"

Lucas nodded. "During the D-Series I talked to some of the ski instructors. They said that not everyone who goes to OCS gets to come back here. To Camp Hale and the Tenth Light."

Loose made a conciliatory gesture. "I suppose that's true."

Good.

Lucas shifted in his seat, ready to deliver his last argument. "Well, sir. I signed up to ski, and that's how I want to serve my country. I don't want to do anything more than that."

Chapter Ten

Parker descended the Headquarters' wooden stairs at the end of the day with Emily chatting by her side. How that gal could be so talkative after a long day of reading others' written conversations was a mystery, but at least her soft accent was always pleasant to listen to—and her southern colloquialisms never failed to amuse.

"Well, I do declare…"

When Emily stopped talking, Parker looked up from the steps and gasped.

Lucas rose from the chair he'd apparently been waiting in. Under weather-tanned cheeks and a clean-shaven jaw, his broad smile lit up the entire building.

Parker was so happy to see him after all these weeks that she wanted to run and jump into his arms. Of course she couldn't—for so many reasons.

Emily hurried forward. "David?"

"He's fine." Lucas's deep calm voice soothed. "But he did go to the hospital to have his toes checked out."

Emily frowned. "Toes?"

Lucas shrugged, unconcerned. "Frost nip. Not as bad as frostbite, but better safe than sorry, right?"

"Yes. Of course." She looked back at Parker. "I'm going to look for him. I'll see you at supper."

And she bolted out Headquarters' front door.

Parker smiled up at Lucas. "I'm so glad to see you."

"Me, too." He glanced at the crowd of departing WACs. "Can I walk you to your barracks?"

"I'd like that." Again she had to resist the urge to act like his sweetie and loop her arm through his or take his hand. She did put on her coat with his help, though, and walked out the door as he held it open. Then she matched his leisurely pace as they crossed the camp in absolutely no hurry whatsoever.

"So? How was it?" she prompted.

Lucas chuckled. "I was always taught that hell was a hot place. But after spending three weeks at the top of these mountains in winter, I think I have solid grounds for another option."

Parker winced. "That bad?"

He nodded. "That bad. Worse, even."

As the pair strolled through the grounds. Lucas told her about the cold, the wind, and the snow. About the marches at high altitudes and up steep inclines. He complained about the inadequate radios and the resultant confusion. He also described the ignorant attitude of the evaluators and their derisive remarks to the soldiers who were actually doing the job.

Parker was appalled. "What a bunch of—of mule headed, arrogant, sons of female dogs!"

That made Lucas laugh. Hard. "Spoken like a true lady."

"Well it's true!" Parker stopped walking, grinning in spite of her anger. "And I do know the real words, but we're in public."

"Yes, Ma'am." Lucas wiped his eyes. "Understood."

Parker's demeanor softened. "I'm really glad you're okay."

"Me, too," Lucas admitted, shaking his head slowly. "I

pushed myself hard—real hard. Wasn't sure how much I could withstand and still go forward."

By now Parker had enjoyed enough conversations with the man to understand how he operated. "You pushed yourself because you are the quarterback and your platoon is your team. They needed someone to follow."

Lucas stared at her like she just figured out how to fly to the moon. "Yes…"

His stunned admiration made her cheeks grow hot, but she could not afford to think about why.

"What's next?" she deflected.

Lucas huffed a laugh. "*Not* Officer Candidate School."

Parker stared up at him. "What?"

"Loose wants me to go to OCS, but I politely declined."

"Why?" she blurted.

He frowned. "Why does he want me to go? Or why did I decline?"

Parker waved a hand in front of her chest. "I know why he'd *want* you to go. You're a born leader!"

Lucas closed the space between them and spoke softly. "And you of all people know very well why I *can't* go back to school."

To be honest, Parker had become so accustomed to reading Lucas's letters that she no longer found them confusing. But that didn't change the fact that his obvious difficulties still existed, and probably always would.

"I'm sorry," she whispered. "You're right. It was stupid of me to ask."

He leaned back and made a face. "You're not stupid, Parker."

"And neither are you," she quickly responded. "And I'm very proud of you for doing such a good job that the Army recognizes your strengths."

"Thanks."

They resumed walking. "When do you start training again?"

"They gave us three days to recoup and repair our

equipment."

"Then what?"

"I don't know. But I'll tell you this." Lucas halted again. "I don't think anything as severe as what we experienced during the D-Series could be experienced anywhere in Austria or Italy."

Parker's eyes widened. "Is that where you're going?"

He flashed a crooked smile. "We certainly aren't training for the south pacific."

"What about Kiska?" she prodded.

"Sea level with hills. And more rain than snow."

He had a point.

"Besides, it's in our name. We're the Tenth Light Division *Alpine*," he continued. "And that's where the German mountain troops are dug in. In the Alps."

Another good point. "Do you know when?"

Lucas expression was sober. "If I had to guess, I don't see us spending another winter in Colorado."

Parker turned and started walking again. They crossed the short distance to her barracks in silence.

Of *course* Lucas and the others were going to be deployed, that was the nature of military life. That was the exact point of them being here. She was just startled by how badly she didn't want him to go.

When they reached the steps to her barracks door, she turned to say thank you. Before she could utter a word, Lucas wrapped her in his arms and kissed her, right out there in the open in front of God and the whole United States Army.

She kissed him back without hesitation.

June 1944

Two months later all twelve thousand soldiers of the Tenth Light Division were gathering their supplies and equipment in preparation for heading to Camp Swift in Texas. The WACs were headed to Camp Carson, to the south but still in Colorado.

Camp Hale was being emptied out.

"The Army runs some sort of maneuvers in Louisiana for every division before they deploy," Fraser grumbled. "Louisiana, for God's sake! Swamps and snakes for the ski troops? What the hell are they thinking?"

Martinez set a fresh pitcher of beer on the table and Sofia began to refill their six glasses. Lucas noticed the ring on her left hand and turned his attention to Martinez.

"Xavier, you have something to tell us?"

"Um, yeah. I suppose we do." He took the pitcher from Sofia and pulled her to stand. "Sofia and I are engaged."

Parker and Emily squealed and jumped up to hug their friend. When they sat back down, Fraser offered a toast. "To old friends and new beginnings."

"Are you waiting until you get back?" Parker asked carefully.

Martinez gazed at Sofia, his expression looking more like a love-sick puppy than Lucas had ever seen on anyone. "No. We're going to the courthouse tomorrow."

Another excited round of female reactions burst out.

Lucas stood. "This calls for champagne."

He made his way to the bar, ordered the sparkling wine, and waited for a bartender to dig it out of the cellar.

"Hansen?"

The tall blond captain standing eye-to-eye with him, and who obviously read his name patch, had a definite accent and an unusual uniform—which also had Hansen embroidered on its chest. "You are Norwegian?"

Lucas shrugged. "Mostly."

He nodded. "You have the looks. *Kan du Norsk?*"

Lucas chuckled. "No, my dad's ancestor came over before the Revolutionary War, from some little town called Arendal."

The captain's brows arched in surprise. "Your family is

Hansen from Arendal?" Then he grinned. "I am a Hansen from Arendal."

"Really?" Lucas glanced at the bartender who had returned with the chilled champagne and was removing the wire which kept the cork in place. "Small world, huh."

"You have maybe been to Norway?"

Lucas chuckled again. "No. I've never been out of Kansas before this."

Nebraska didn't count.

The captain grunted and held out his hand. "Tor Hansen."

Lucas shook it. "Lucas Thor Hansen."

The man's blue eyes twinkled. "If you are a Hansen from Arendal, then we are cousins."

As if to punctuate their improbable meeting the cork shot out of the champagne bottle with a loud *pop*.

Something about the captain made Lucas smile. "I'm very pleased to meet you, sir."

"And I you." He lifted his beer bottle. "Best of luck, cousin."

Lucas accepted the open bottle of wine and tapped it against the man's beer. "And to you. Cousin."

Then he joined his friends once again.

*****

"You have to write to me at Camp Carson," Parker insisted. "As often as you can. Promise me."

Lucas felt the familiar stab of anxiety that rose up every time he was faced with putting words on a page. "I'll try."

Parker squeezed his hands. "Don't *try*—*do* it."

He gave her a stern look from under his brows. "The letters will go through censors."

She shot him a similar look. "So what? You've survived worse."

True.

"Okay," he relented and heaved a resigned sigh. "I'll do my best while we're at Camp Swift."

"And when they send you to Europe. You have to write from there as well." Parker's eyes filled with tears. "Promise!"

Lucas looked down at the woman he'd spent the last year-and-a-half getting to know. The sudden realization of how much she meant to him punched him in the gut so hard he couldn't breathe.

"Say something, Lucas." She wiped her eyes.

"I love you."

The declaration surprised him as much as her. She stared up at him, her lips pinched between her teeth and her eyes wide as hubcaps.

I shouldn't have said that.

"You don't have to—"

"I love you, too," she interrupted and wiped her eyes again. "For months now."

He was stunned. "Is that true?"

"Why would I lie about that?" she countered angrily. "Falling in love with a soldier who's deploying in the middle of the biggest world wide war that's ever happened is the stupidest thing anyone possibly could do."

Lucas pulled her close in the middle of the mess hall, not caring who saw them. With both the WACs and the Army guys being sent away from Camp Hale, all the soldiers who had romantic connections with any of the women here, or in nearby Leadville, had thrown caution to the high mountain winds.

The threat of dying was a powerful motivator.

"What do we do now?" Lucas asked.

"Come out the other end alive, soldier," she blurted. "That's an order."

"That's my plan."

She tightened her arms around his waist. "And after that, come back and marry me."

Lucas tucked his knuckle under her chin and tipped her face upward. "Is that a proposal?"

"It is." She narrowed her eyes. "Are you saying yes?"

Even though Lucas couldn't imagine Parker being happy on a flatland family-owned farm crowded with his parents, sisters, and their husbands, he also couldn't imagine his life without her.

First things first.

They had time to figure out the rest.

"Yes, Parker Williams." Lucas smiled, his chest exploding with joy. "I *will* marry you."

Chapter Eleven

November 1944

Camp Swift in Texas embodied exactly what Lucas previously thought of as hell. Hot, dusty, flat, and infested with snakes, scorpions, mosquitoes, and flies. Lucas could not imagine a more desolate or useless spot on the entire earth.

To compound the soldiers' misery, their maneuvers in Louisiana were cancelled.

"That was the whole damn reason they dragged us away from our training!" Fraser complained as he opened the door to their barracks. Lucas followed him in.

Lucas walked to his cot and sat. Martinez was sitting cross-legged on his cot and threading a needle. His uniforms were stacked and folded in front of him.

"How much longer are we going to be stuck in God forsaken eastern Texas?" Lucas grumbled. "There's a war to get to, damn it."

Fraser watched Martinez pick up a shirt and carefully lay a curved Mountain tab above the barrel-shaped Tenth Light Division patch on his uniform. "We've all lost our altitude acclimation. And there isn't even a pile of dirt for a hundred miles that's high enough to climb ten feet."

"There is one good thing that came out of these five months of banishment." Martinez looked up from his sewing. "The ski troops are officially the Tenth *Mountain* Division now."

"Yeah, you're right," Lucas admitted. "After being called *satisfactory* in the D-Series, I guess recognizing us as an elite division with specialized skills actually does mean something."

"And, we're the very first elite division to be established in the United States Army." Martinez returned his attention to his task. "That's something, too."

Lucas sighed and stretched out on his back. "So when we get to wherever they're sending us, adding a fourth 'weapons' company to each battalion will definitely help…"

Fraser chuckled. "But?"

Lucas met his friend's gaze. "But—they added twenty-six hundred flatland soldiers to our division in the process. These guys can't ski! They've got no high altitude experience! They've never even climbed up the side of a small cliff."

Fraser pulled a deep breath. "I know."

"So?" Lucas prodded. "How is that going to affect us when we're trying to do our jobs?"

"We'll still do what we know how to do," Martinez stated firmly. He looked up and met Lucas's eyes. "Those guys will just have to figure it out along the way."

*****

The entire Tenth Mountain Division was given leave in November, which Lucas and his buddies optimistically figured meant they were finally going to be deployed when they got back. Lucas took the train from Austin to Kansas City and a bus from there to Sabetha.

Lucas was proud to show off the Mountain tab confirmation of his new skills to his family in Kansas, but he was even more proud to show it to Parker. She and the other censors, including Emily and Sofia, were now stationed at Camp Crowder in Missouri. Even though his mom and sisters were upset that he wasn't spending his entire leave on the farm, Lucas had something very important to do before he shipped out, and this was his only chance to get it done.

"This ring is very old." Lucas slid a silver ring onto Parker's finger. It was embellished with Nordic knots on both sides of a rare Baltic amber stone. "It belonged to my great-grandmother, and my great-grandfather had it sent over from Norway."

Parker's eye glittered with tears when Lucas told her the ring's origin. "It's beautiful, Lucas. Thank you."

"It's official now." He smiled down into her golden-brown eyes. "We're engaged."

And then she kissed him very well. Many, many times.

December 1944

Two days before Christmas, Lucas stood on the railing of the *USS Argentina* along with Fraser and Martinez, watching as the ship was tied up to the pier in the Italian port at Naples. The sky was heavy with clouds and the Mediterranean breeze was cold and damp, but the water in the harbor was an incredible shade of turquoise blue.

Lucas had never seen anything like it and wished there was some way for him to send a picture of it to Parker.

"We're in Europe, guys." Martinez looked a bit stunned. "And when we set foot on that dock we're entering a country at war."

This was real.

When the three men walked down the gangplank they were met by a group of uniformed Red Cross gals handing out very welcome hot coffee, fresh donuts, and cigarettes. Lucas didn't smoke but took the free cigarettes anyway, figuring he could trade them later for something he did want.

Fraser and Martinez did the same.

While they stepped to the side to enjoy the unexpected treat one of the guys from Second Battalion caught Lucas's eye. He elbowed Martinez.

"Look at that guy talking to that Red Cross gal handing out the donuts." Lucas grinned. "Either he knows her from somewhere, or he's a real fast worker."

Fraser turned around to see what he was talking about. "She looks familiar." He returned his attention to Lucas. "Hey— wasn't she assisting Captain Jay at Hale with both those ski films?"

Lucas snapped his fingers. "That's it! I bet that's when he met her. I wonder how she ended up over here."

Lucas popped the last sweet bite of donut into his mouth and chased it with the last gulp of the strong black coffee. Seeing the soldier chatting happily with the gal, who smiled back at him like he hung the moon, made him think of Parker. And thinking of Parker made him lonely. As much as he felt like Fraser and Martinez were the brothers he never had—and knew he would take a bullet for either one of them—women were an entirely different deal.

Parker made him feel safe. She knew his secret and loved him anyway. And he loved her back because of it.

"So, what now?" he asked when the lump in his throat cleared.

"Grab our gear when it's brought down and get on a truck," Martinez said. "Fifth Army will take us to our staging area."

*****

It took several hours of standing around and waiting on that windy, wet dock for the Regimental working parties to empty the

Argentina of its contents. Lucas, Fraser, and Martinez were finally able to claim their gear and climb into the back of a truck with a dozen or so other men from A Company. The bumpy ride over cobblestone streets carried them to Bagnoli, about five miles west of the port at Naples.

Lucas watched the unfamiliar city scenery pass by in wide-eyed fascination.

The city of Naples was established six hundred years before Jesus was born. Lucas couldn't fully grasp that reality in his mind. The buildings they drove past by were built two thousand years later—five or six hundred years ago.

Painted stucco covered stone. The solid and sturdy walls were two-feet thick. Roofs were tiled in curved red clay pieces, all handmade. Narrow alleys, only wide enough for a single vehicle, snaked away from the two-lane main road and curved uphill or downhill from there.

If these walls could only talk...

The truck came to a stop in front of an ancient stone-walled warehouse. "Here we are," the driver said. "You're bedding down in there."

When Lucas, Fraser, and Martinez climbed out of the truck Lieutenant Loose walked over to them. "Great—you guys are here. We're only missing two more. Go on in and get settled."

Lucas walked through the tall, heavy wooden doors into the dimly lit building. The cavernous space had plenty of room for the forty guys in his A Company platoon, albeit all of it on the stone floor. Several of the men were heating up rations on their camp stoves.

"At least we're not sleeping out in the open," Fraser said. "The nights are literally freezing."

"I don't care." Lucas turned to his buddies with a wide grin. "We're in *Italy!*"

*****

A Company spent two nights in the warehouse. On a sunny but cold Christmas Day, First Battalion boarded a train headed north to Pisa, accompanied by the ringing of countless church bells.

"Some way to spend Christmas, huh?" In spite of his words, Fraser did not look at all upset about being here.

"I'm with my brothers." Lucas grinned and threw one arm around Fraser's shoulders and the other around Martinez's. "Christmas is about family, right?"

Once in Pisa, the soldiers were transported by truck from the train station to their advance staging area on the hunting grounds of some royal guy Lucas had never heard of. As the trucks trundled past the famous Leaning Tower—Lucas *had* heard of that—he felt a very odd sensation of disbelief.

I really am in Italy.

And that is the famous tower.

Everything he had endured at Camp Hale and beyond was worth this very moment. No one back home in Sabetha, Kansas, just three miles south of Nebraska border, had ever seen this well-known landmark in person.

Now he had.

Lucas knew right then that his life was inexorably changed because he was inexorably changed. No matter what his difficulties were, Lucas had made it here, to this spot, because of his strengths.

Whatever path he took forward after the war would no longer be limited by his handicap, but would be determined by his strengths.

I can't go back to the farm.

That sudden and earth-shaking realization kept him awake for most of that night. He was both terrified and exhilarated by the abrupt but inevitable shift in his future.

He had no idea where he would go, or what he would do, but it was enough for now to just hold on to that idea and grow comfortable with it.

And whatever he did, wherever he went, he would have Parker by his side.

Lucas smiled and closed his eyes.

I will write to her tomorrow.

January 1945

Just two weeks after arriving in Italy, all three battalions of the Eighty-Sixth Regiment took their initial positions on the front line between the American forces and the German enemy.

First Battalion settled in Castelluccio under the command of Lieutenant Colonel Henry Hampton.

"We are charged with holding the territory southwest of Mount Belvedere, here." Colonel Hampton pointed to the designated area on a large map. "This area is one of the most rugged sectors of the front. We'll patrol the territory and beat back any German encroachment we might come across."

Lucas felt a zing of adrenaline at the idea of engaging with the Krauts.

Martinez looked at Lucas. "You ready to kill a man?"

I honestly don't know.

"I guess we have to be." Lucas drew a deep breath. "What do you suppose it's like?"

"I don't know if we can ever be sure that the guy's died," Fraser offered. "I mean, unless you shoot a guy point blank through his heart or head, there's still a chance he could survive."

True.

"But if we want to win this war, we have to shoot to kill." Lucas met Fraser's gaze. "We can't hesitate. We can't let them shoot first."

"We can't think of them as regular men," Martinez added. "These guys we need to stop are working for a madman. He's dangerous, and they're on his side."

Fraser nodded. "Stopping them is stopping him."

Lucas liked that. "So think about it like we're shooting Hitler himself."

"That's the way I'm looking at it."

Martinez rubbed his hands together. "Then I will, too."

*****

The next afternoon Lucas, Fraser, and Martinez took their turn in one of the listening posts which had been dug into the side of a small mountain. The post was camouflaged with three feet of snow and was intentionally hard to see.

"Good thing we had a map," Fraser said to the A Company guys they were relieving. "We'd never have found it otherwise."

"We thought the same thing," one of them said as the three soldiers strapped into their skis. "How's the weather been?"

"Don't be fooled by the sun," Lucas warned. "The wind is brutal."

"Yeah, we can see the top of the snow blowing." The first guy straightened. "You guys ready?"

After the patrol set off on skis, the trio settled in and grabbed binoculars. From the horizontal slit, which faced the open space between Riva and Belvedere, the men had a clear view of one section of the valley.

So far, the area was quiet. Lucas checked the post's log. "The last two patrols watching from here didn't see anything."

Martinez had a pair of binoculars pressed to his eyes. "Too bad. That makes the time drag."

"When we're relieved here and go out to patrol…" Fraser fiddled with the radio. "No matter what the log says, we should expect to shoot and be shot at."

"Permission to approach?"

Lucas looked through a slit in the door. An American soldier on skis stood about ten yards away. He had to be part of the Tenth because no other division skied.

Unfortunately, Fifth Army had forced all the guys to remove their Mountain tabs from their uniforms once they reached the front. They claimed they wanted to "surprise" the Germans with the presence of an American mountain division.

Which was complete bullshit.

Lucas opened the door. "Come ahead."

The soldier skied to the post. "Lieutenant Hollinghurst, Second Battalion," he stated. "Four guys are following behind me."

"What are you up to?" Fraser asked.

"Recon. We're trying to see if there's any way to attack Belvedere from the rear or flank."

The other four members of the patrol skied over to the listening post.

"I'm Lieutenant Traynor," the First Lieutenant said. None of the three privates saluted them—that was forbidden at the front to keep the enemy from identifying and picking off their officers.

"You met Second Lieutenant Hollinghurst," Traynor continued. "Privates Knowlton, Seibert, and Franklin here."

Lucas recognized one of the men immediately. Franklin was the soldier from the dock who was talking to the Red Cross gal.

"Privates Hansen, Fraser, and Martinez," Lucas offered. "First Battalion."

Lieutenant Traynor nodded. "We were searching for possible attack routes behind Belvedere when we spotted your ski patrol from above."

Lucas shot a concerned look at Fraser. "If you could see them so can the Germans."

Traynor nodded. "Exactly."

"Thanks for the heads-up," Fraser said. "We'll let them know."

The reconnaissance patrol rested inside the post, protected

from the wind, for about twenty minutes before they continued on their way.

"We'll have to be careful," Lucas stated after they were gone. "Let's hope those three guys made it back okay."

Chapter Twelve

Lucas, Fraser, and Martinez took their turn at the four-hour patrol before the sun set. The men skied single file with their rifles in hand, taking turns at the lead whenever they stopped to consult their compasses and map.

The day's chilled wind was at their backs as they left the post, meaning it would be in their faces when they returned to Castelluccio. The terrain was rough, full of gullies and rocks, not all of which were visible under the drifting snow.

The men wore their white anoraks for camouflage and spoke very little as they skied parallel to the valley, keeping to the pine tree cover as much as possible to make sure they wouldn't be seen like the last group was.

Lucas was in the lead when he saw ski tracks. He stopped and motioned to the other two.

"They're coming from the opposite direction and heading up," he whispered. "These aren't our guys."

After a brief moment's hesitation, Martinez whispered, "Let's go get 'em."

The trio followed the tracks, which led upward at an angle

through the pines. The men stopped every hundred yards or so and listened for any indication that the Germans they were tracking were close by.

After about fifteen minutes, the answer came in the crack of a rifle.

Lucas fell sideways into the snow and aimed his rifle toward the sound. "Do you see anything?"

His buddies had also taken quick cover in the snow drift.

Fraser's gaze was fixed straight ahead. "Not yet."

"Looks like a ravine ahead. I'd say seventy-five yards. Maybe they're in there," Martinez suggested.

As if in answer, another shot broke the silence. Pine bark from a tree above them showered flakes of black on the white snow in front of them.

"Shit." Lucas unstrapped his skis. "Stay down. We'll crawl up."

Fraser and Martinez removed their skis as well. The three men belly-crawled next to each other through the deep snow toward the ravine. They had not yet returned fire so they hadn't given away their own position.

Three more shots were fired in their direction before Lucas could see the German soldier's head appear over the edge of the ravine. He grabbed Fraser's arm. He pointed two fingers at his eyes then pointed at the ravine.

Fraser nodded, and then turned and motioned to Martinez.

Lucas motioned to stay low.

The three men slithered through the snow, slowly and quietly, until they were ten yards from the edge of the ravine. Then they waited.

Two rifle barrels appeared over the edge. Two helmets followed. Lucas took aim. As soon as he could see a man's eyes, he took the shot.

Both rifles beside him exploded along with his.

Both of the German soldier's heads flew backward and

disappeared.

The trio waited, rifles still aimed at the ravine. When no sounds came, and no additional rifle barrels appeared, they resumed their crawling approach.

At the edge of the ravine Fraser used his fingers to silently count to three, then the men rose up and aimed their rifles over the crusted snow and into the gully.

One German soldier, no older than sixteen, aimed a shaking gun back up at them. His two comrades lay lifeless beside him in splatters of dark red blood—a startling contrast to the pristine white snow.

"*Nicht schießen*," Lucas warned in the basic German they had been taught. "*Kapitulation*."

Don't shoot. Surrender.

The boy lifted his gun and pointed the barrel at Lucas.

Lucas ducked.

Two rifles beside him shot simultaneously.

When he looked over the edge again, the young soldier had no face and a gaping hole was blown through his chest.

*****

The three friends sat in the snow below the edge of the ravine for a quarter of an hour, each man silently considering what just happened.

"I think it's safe to say," Martinez began. "That all of us killed a German today."

Lucas nodded solemnly. "Damn but he was young."

"Just a boy," Fraser agreed. "I wouldn't be surprised if we encounter more of them considering the current stage of the war."

"Hitler's obviously running out of men." Martinez took off his helmet and ran his hands over his hair. "I wish the asshole would surrender rather than send young boys to fight."

"We'll make sure he surrenders, and soon." Lucas was resolute. "That's why we're here."

The other two men nodded.

Martinez replaced his helmet. "What do we do with them?"

"We should probably get their dog tags to prove the kills." Fraser didn't look too happy with the prospect. Even so he added, "I'll go get them."

He scrambled over the edge of the ravine and slid down the side. Lucas tossed down a rope so Fraser could pull himself back up the slippery snow-covered slope.

Martinez reached for the bloody dog tags and stared at the names. "Now what?"

Lucas shrugged. "Leave them. We sure can't haul them back with us."

Martinez crossed himself. "*Pater, Filius, et Spiritus Sanctus.*"

Fraser chuckled. "I didn't know you were religious."

"I wasn't an hour ago," he replied. "But I'm rethinking that right about now."

Lucas climbed to his feet. "Let's get our skis and head back. It'll be dark soon."

*****

When they returned to Castelluccio the three men went straight to First Battalion's intelligence tent to give their report.

"Lieutenant Ward's busy," his corporal said as he accepted the dog tags. "So each of you needs to write out your report and turn them in by the end of the night."

"You want three separate reports?" Lucas asked, startled by the order. "Or do we write it together?"

"Separate." The corporal peered at him. "So he knows exactly what happened, and if every man followed orders."

Lucas shifted a nervous gaze to Fraser, but Fraser wasn't

looking at him.

"Yes, Corporal. We'll have them ready for you by ten-o'clock," Fraser promised the aide.

After the men left the building, Fraser spoke softly to Lucas. "Dictate your report to me and I'll write it out."

Lucas appreciated the offer but, "Then two reports will be in the same handwriting."

"I'll print yours, and write mine in cursive."

God bless David Fraser.

Lucas heaved a sigh of relief. "Thank you."

Fraser slapped him on the back. "That's what brothers do."

*****

Before the first of February all three regiments of the Tenth Mountain Division were settled in along the front line. And every single soldier in the Division was livid about having to remove the Tenth Mountain patch and curved tabs which they'd fought so long and hard to earn.

"This is bullshit," Lucas said again every time anyone brought the subject up. "Fifth Army wanted to keep us a secret, but obviously *that* didn't work."

Another barrage of harassing announcements was currently being broadcast across the valley between the line of Tenth soldiers and the entrenched German army.

"Welcome to Italy, boys," the accented and disembodied voice taunted. "We hope your journey from Camp Hale was a pleasant one."

"It's a long way from Colorado to Mount Belvedere."

"Don't worry about our mountains. We have them secured. Sit back and enjoy the willing Italian women."

"Our Fuhrer sends his regards to your little ski troops."

"You can always go back to Camp Hale and train more."

Fucking Krauts.

With the arrival of the Eighty-Fifth and Eighty-Seventh, the Eighty-sixth was sent behind the lines to the town of Lucca for two days of rest and recuperation. Lucas took the opportunity to write to Parker, but he never told her about the German soldiers they killed.

When the Eighty-Sixth returned to the front, Lieutenant Colonel Hampton assembled his First Battalion in a church in Castelluccio. Once again a large map was posted in front of the soldiers, this time on the altar.

"The Germans are dug in high up on Mount Belvedere. From that vantage point they can see everything below them and use their artillery to control the highway, effectively cutting off Allied supply lines."

Hampton used a stick to point to the location, then he moved the point to the opposite side of the valley. "The Germans are also entrenched high on the sloping side of Riva Ridge over here, facing and protecting their position on Mount Belvedere across the valley."

"Riva Ridge is the key," Lucas whispered.

"How do you know?" Martinez whispered back.

"It's the play that makes the most sense."

"Oh."

"In order to take and hold Belvedere," Hampton continued. "American forces must first take control of the Ridge…"

"Show off," Martinez whispered.

Lucas smiled. "Knock out the defense and the offense falls."

"…but unfortunately three uphill attempts by Fifth Army to defeat the Germans on Riva Ridge have failed. Miserably."

Lucas would have expected Colonel Hampton to be perturbed by that, but their battalion commander looked almost giddy.

"This brings me to the point of this briefing."

"Guys." Lucas straightened on the bench. "Something big is happening."

Hampton continued, speaking slowly and clearly. "After all of their reconnaissance expeditions, Fifth Army has arrived at the conclusion that a *single battalion of soldiers* could attack and hold Riva Ridge…"

He paused while his gaze moved over the crowded sanctuary and a smile spread his cheeks. "But *only* if they make use of the Tenth Mountain's training, and have our men climb up the back side and attack the Germans from above and behind."

Lucas swiveled to look at Fraser and Martinez. He hoped he was right about what Hampton would say next, but he didn't want to jinx it. His pulse surged so loud in his ears that he was afraid he'd miss the colonel's next words.

"So, because we are positioned closest to Riva, we are that single battalion. The First Battalion of the Eighty-Sixth Regiment is going to eliminate the Germans from their stronghold on the front of Riva Ridge!"

Lucas leapt to his feet and whooped his excitement as the church full of soldiers did the same. He smiled so broadly at Fraser and Martinez that his cheeks hurt.

"This is it! Exactly what we trained for!"

*****

Experienced scouts from First Battalion evaluated the steep incline of Riva Ridge's back side found several possible climbing paths, all which should be negotiable by soldiers carrying heavy rucksacks loaded with weapons and ammunition. The best part of the plan was for the men to climb the ridge at night.

"The Krauts won't expect that play," Lucas murmured in the briefing. "We're going to take them by surprise."

Martinez grinned at him.

"Because of the size of our task, I've asked for an additional infantry company to bolster our numbers," Colonel Hampton told the men. "And since Second Battalion is located closest to us, they'll be sending F Company to join us in the mission."

Lucas's first reaction was that the request was akin to asking another team to help him win the state title—and it made him angry.

"You're looking at this all wrong," Fraser told him later when he expressed that idea. "We're on the same team."

"Yeah—it's more like calling the best junior varsity players up to varsity," Martinez said. "Just bolstering your numbers, because the opposing team is ferocious."

"And undefeated after three tries," Fraser added.

That analogy made sense to Lucas. "Well I hope we'll get to renew our climbing skills at least. The last time we practiced rock climbing was before we went to Texas—almost eight months ago. I have to admit I'm a little rusty."

In answer to his hopes, First Battalion marched out to a marble quarry the next day to do precisely that.

Back at Camp Hale their climbing instruction took place in the summer when the weather was pleasant and there was no snow. Now they were climbing in February in finger-numbing temperatures. The hard marble wall radiated cold, bolstering the chilling effect of the constant damp and frigid wind.

The lead climbers went up first, pounding pitons into the solid marble which proved much harder than the composited granite of the Rockies. As they scrambled upward they clipped carabineers to the eyes of the pitons and threaded a heavy rope through the carabineers—ropes that the men below would use to climb the vertical wall.

There were only two pitches at the quarry so the soldiers all had to wait their turn to climb. When Lucas started climbing he was relieved that his muscle memory kicked in. But while his body remembered what to do, the stamina required to complete the task was long gone, stolen by months of flatland inactivity.

Lucas's arms and legs burned. His hands cramped. His breath

Ice and Granite: The Snow Soldiers of Riva Ridge 115

came in gulps. At least they weren't at high altitudes here, so the air held plenty of oxygen.

When he reached the top his legs felt like rubber bands and he sat down hard.

And I don't even have my rucksack on yet.

Though the training for most of the men was the same as back at Camp Hale, the flatlanders which were added to the division at Camp Swift were starting from scratch. The new guys had to be shown everything from tying into the rope harnesses, to how to loop and hold the ropes.

At the moment, Lucas was glad for the respite that their slower pace on the two pitches provided.

Martinez, unfortunately, fell back into his fear of heights and needed some coaxing when he climbed the marble wall the first time. By the time he reached the top he was dripping sweat in spite of the cold.

"I. Hate. Heights!" he growled as Lucas gave him a hand up at the top. "At least when we climb at night I won't be able to see the ground."

Second Battalion's F Company arrived on their second day of training to join the climbs. Lucas was pleased to see the same guys they'd met at the listening post a couple weeks earlier.

He, Fraser, and Martinez went over to say hello while they waited for their next turn, and watched while the three men climbed. Franklin, Seibert, and Knowlton clearly knew what they were doing, but were felled by the same malady that they all suffered from.

"Swift Syndrome," Fraser quipped. "Caused by spending too damn many months on a landscape that's as flat and brown as a pancake."

When he shared that gem with the F Company guys they all laughed and agreed. Lucas blew a sigh of relief.

They already feel like my brothers-in-arms.

After they climbed for a couple days unhindered, the soldiers started carrying their heavy packs, weapons, and supplies up to the top to become accustomed to the task ahead. It was like starting all over again, and every muscle in Lucas's body ached when he stretched out on his cot at night.

Before the end of the week they switched their training from day to night.

The soldiers did not have lights on their helmets so they had to rely on the moon and stars to find their way. And in this, the second week of February in nineteen-forty-five, there was no moon.

Just after sunset the men marched to the quarry through the snow, and Lucas's eyes gradually adjusted to the dark.

"When we climb Riva, we should have some moonlight," he said to Fraser and Martinez.

"Assuming we aren't waiting another month, of course," Martinez countered. "Fifth Army isn't giving us any clues as to the timing of their plan."

"True," Lucas admitted.

Night climbing in the dark while wearing a ninety-pound rucksack with a rifle hanging off one side was not a simple task. The steep, icy cliffs would have confounded any flatland infantry division, but the Tenth Mountain Division was no flatland outfit. And the Eighty-Sixth Regiment's First Battalion understood the job ahead of them very well.

"Practice climbing as silently as possible," Lieutenant Loose urged them. "We'll be relying on the element of surprise. The Germans think the ridgeline is impossible for any large number of troops to scale, especially at night, so they won't be expecting us. But if we give away our presence, they'll pick us off like sitting ducks."

As the soldiers practiced for the next several nights they grew quieter and quieter. Grunts were held in. Boots were placed more carefully against the marble. Socks were used to muffle the sound of the pitons being hammered into the rock wall. Pitons near the top were wrapped in torn fabric to prevent the metal rings from clanking.

Lucas stood at the top of the wall and listened to the men climbing up below him. If he was standing fifty yards back, he would not have heard a thing. The highest German position on the slope of the ridge was at least two hundred yards downhill. Maybe three.

We're ready.

Chapter Thirteen

February 18, 1945

The attack on Riva Ridge, and the coordinated attack on Mount Belvedere the following day, was dubbed Operation Encore—because this was the *fourth* attempt by Fifth Army to dislodge the Germans from those dug-in and heavily defended positions.

During the night before the climb, eight hundred soldiers from the Eighty-Sixth's First Battalion plus Second Battalion's F Company were carried by truck twenty-five miles from Castelluccio to the town of Vidiciatico. From there the five companies involved each hiked along snow-bordered roads in the dark and settled into one of five villages at the base of Riva Ridge's eastern wall. Once they arrived in the villages they were instructed to search out farmhouses, barns, sheds, or any other form of shelter in which to hide from the Germans' detection during the following day.

The next night after sunset they would climb the backside of Riva and hold the ridge once it was captured.

It sounded so simple.

But Lucas was under no illusion that it would be. He and his best buddies Fraser and Martinez—*call them Smoky and Diego, now*—found a shed attached to a farmhouse. Diego knocked on the farmhouse door just before dawn and asked in simple Spanish if they could hide there for the next eighteen hours, hoping the words were close enough to Italian to get his point across.

The flannel-clad man who answered the door flashed a gap-toothed smile and cried, "*Si si! Ti porterò un po 'di formaggio, pane e vino!*"

Smoky and Lucas looked at Diego. "What did he say?"

"I think he's bringing cheese, bread, and wine."

Lucas had no problem with that.

Sure beats cold K-Rations.

As the sun rose, ringed by a hazy ice-crystal rainbow, and with the wine-accompanied breakfast placating their bellies, the three men tucked into their warm sleeping bags and tried to get some sleep. After training at night for the past week they were somewhat adjusted to sleeping during the day, but knowing what was coming that night kept Lucas's thoughts reeling.

Tonight he was going into battle for the first time. Not just exchanging shots with a German patrol, but facing heavy artillery, machine guns, and multiple battalions of the enemy.

If he wasn't scared, he'd be worried.

Fear heightened the senses. Made men cautious. Careful in their decisions. Lucas knew he would fight to the best of his ability, but he could not allow himself to become reckless.

I have a fiancée to get home to.

As always, thinking about Parker soothed his mood. He'd packed her letters in his rucksack so he would have them with him at all times. It was the closest thing to having her there.

Parker continued to be faithful in her writing, sending her letters to the Red Cross office in Lucca so they could be forwarded to the Battalion wherever in Italy they were at the moment. And Lucas kept to his word, writing her back every single time.

He'd lost his fear that she might not be able to make sense of what he had written, because she responded to every bit of news or description that he included.

When they first received their assignment to climb Riva Ridge and began their training at the quarry, Lucas wrote to Parker and told her that he was immeasurably proud to be there—and immeasurably petrified, as well.

I'm not afraid of dying, he wrote, *but of disappointing you.*

She wrote back immediately: *Nothing you could ever do will make me disappointed in you. You are honestly the bravest man I have ever met and I love you with all my heart.*

Lucas only knew he'd slept that day because he awoke from a dream. Martinez still snored softly, but Fraser was awake and cleaning his gun in the dull afternoon light seeping through the boards that formed the walls of their hidey-hole.

When he saw Lucas's eyes were open, he flashed a grim smile.

Lucas sat up, keeping his sleeping bag wrapped around him in the unheated space. "Did you get any sleep?"

"A little." Fraser tipped his head toward the outer wall. "Clouds have rolled in. There'll be no moon tonight."

"Well, we'd only have a quarter moon anyway." Lucas stretched to release his cramped muscles. "Good thing we spent the last week climbing without any light. We know we can do it."

Fraser gave him another tight-lipped smile and continued to clean his gun.

*****

All the First Battalion soldiers were ordered to stow their tents, sleeping bags, and other non-essential supplies in their duffel bags and leave them behind in the villages that they'd hidden in.

Lieutenant Loose assured the men in his platoon that, "Captain Niedner will assign a guard here, and we'll come back for them when we've completed the mission."

Unfortunately their skis were considered non-essential.

"Only the bear paws, I'm afraid. They'll fit in your rucksacks and won't get in your way while you climb," Lieutenant Loose explained. "Wear your whites, obviously. When you're done packing everything else in your duffel, pick up your ammunition. We march at seven-thirty sharp."

Each soldier climbing Riva Ridge was issued ninety-six rounds of ammunition, two grenades, and either an extra machine gun belt or mortar rounds to carry up the ridge. Lucas shifted the heavy load trying to settle it on his back and shoulders, but the ammunition was bulky and unwieldy and seemed to have a mind of its own.

"If we hadn't trained with our packed rucksacks we'd never make it up the ridge loaded down like this," he grumbled.

Diego looked at Lucas like he was facing certain death. "I don't know if I can do this… It throws me off balance."

Lucas clapped his hand on his friend's shoulder. "Once you're tied in, you can't fall. Remember?"

Diego nodded slightly. "But at the top—"

"At the top, I'll pull you up. I promise." Lucas crossed his heart.

Diego crossed himself as well with a shaking hand. "*Pater, Filius, et Spiritus Sanctus.*"

"It's seven thirty," Lieutenant Loose announced. "Time to go."

A Company was scheduled to climb the ridge first, so they were leading the line of eight hundred First Battalion soldiers to the base of Riva Ridge's back side.

Loose's platoon walked to the end of the village's main road and met up with the rest of the A Company platoons. Captain

Niedner checked to make sure everyone in the company was accounted for.

"This is it men. From now on, we march and climb in absolute silence. You've all been told that our lives depend on completing this mission without alerting the Germans of our presence." He paused and drew a deep breath. "You have each other's lives in your hands. Keep your brothers safe."

Without another word, he turned and led the silent march toward Riva Ridge. Lucas followed Smoky, and Diego followed Lucas.

The night was cold and damp, not freezing yet but headed in that direction. The wind in the valley had died with the sunset, so that was a blessing. On the opposite slope of the Ridge ahead of them the German Army's klieg lights fired up and began their nightly ritual, sweeping back and forth across the sky in search of an air attack. Tonight they were powerless in that endeavor and only succeeded in tracing repeating figure eights across the bottoms of the low-hanging clouds which accumulated that afternoon.

The soldiers walked in a single file column through snow that wasn't deep enough to require their bear paws. As they marched toward Riva Ridge, the four other companies also making the climb fell in behind them, until their line stretched back half a mile or more.

The line halted when they reached the Dardagna wash, twenty-yards wide and swollen with snow that melted during the daytime. Captain Niedner found the rudimentary path of decent-sized rocks piled in a line across the waist-deep wash and he crossed first. Balancing precariously with their heavily-weighted packs, the men of A Company carefully followed, picking their way across the swirling ice-cold stream.

Halfway across, a rock tipped and Lucas bobbled, windmilling his arms to keep his balance.

Do. Not. Fall.

He righted himself, paused to steady himself, and with his pulse thrumming loudly in his ears, kept going. He heaved a relieved sigh when he reached the opposite side of the wash. Getting soaked to the waist with icy water in freezing weather was no way to start a mission.

Three hours and twelve miles into their silent march, A Company arrived at the bottom of the trail leading up the steep lower slope on the backside of Riva Ridge. This trail would take the companies to the base of the vertical face, where the eight hundred Tenth Mountain soldiers would start their unprecedented climbs.

Captain Niedner briefly halted the column so that the company's lead climbers could gather up the coils of rope and bags of pitons which recon teams had left for them. Lucas grabbed the chance to take a drink of water from his canteen. Others took advantage of the stop to relieve themselves on the side of the trail.

Lucas chuckled silently.

Water in, water out.

Niedner signaled to move again and his forty soldiers began the hike up the trail. The men walked deliberately and slowly, careful where they stepped in the dark. The path climbed upward through ice-rimed rock and increasingly snow-dusted brush. In some parts the ledge they traversed was only wide enough to set one boot directly in front of the other.

Above them, and much closer than before, the swirling German searchlights reflected off the low clouds and washed the soldiers with a pale ambient glow—brighter and more helpful than the quarter moon which was currently hidden in the heavily overcast conditions.

Good thing the Krauts don't know they're lighting the way for their enemy's attack.

The irony was delicious.

*****

Lucas was breathing hard now. He heard Diego panting behind him. Hiking uphill in the dark, on a steeply angled and snow covered trail, under the life-or-death requirement of silence, the soldiers had no chance to hurry their steps and gain any sort of forward momentum to make the climb easier.

After two hours of non-stop movement, the soldiers reached the base of the nearly vertical backside of Riva Ridge. Captain Niedner signaled a break to let the men catch their breath and the signal passed down the line to the companies who were following them.

The weather had chilled steadily through the early night and Lucas knew the temperature had dropped below freezing by now. Even so, he sat on a boulder and opened the front of his jacket. Sweat from the extended exertion dripped into his eyes and ran down his backbone. He swiped his arm across his forehead before opening his canteen and taking a long, deep drink of the cold water.

A thousand feet below their position Lucas could still hear the tumbling water in the Dardagna wash. Above him, the search lights continued their silent, eerie dance. Sitting on a snow-covered rock in the peaceful silence it was hard to believe that eight hundred American mountain soldiers were approaching imminent battle with a vicious and experienced enemy.

A metallic clang ripped a jagged hole through that peaceful silence.

Lucas froze, wide-eyed with fear, as whatever it was that made that jarring sound continued down the trail below them, clanking and banging the entire way until it splashed into the wash.

What the hell?

No one around him moved.

Lucas held his breath, hoping his pounding heart wasn't

audible to anyone but him.
Did the Germans hear that?
Surely they did.
They must *have.*
Minutes ticked past, each one lasting an hour. Soldiers all around him silently checked their weapons, expecting a German sentry above them to shout a warning any minute now.

Lucas looked at Diego.

Diego shrugged.

Then he looked at Smoky who was watching the sky.

Nothing.

Lieutenant Loose was slowly making his way up the column. "Some idiot machine gunner dropped his helmet," he whispered angrily as he passed by. "Make sure yours is secure."

Lucas tightened his helmet strap, his hand shaking with rage. How could anyone on this critical mission behave so carelessly and endanger all eight hundred members of their First Battalion in the process?

If he was on my team he'd be benched for life.

After another quarter hour of silence from the Germans on the ridge above, A Company slowly resumed their hike, with the rest of the Battalion following behind them.

The nearly vertical face of Riva Ridge had been divided into four sectors and A Company was assigned to climb at Pizzo di Campiano. And another quarter hour after the dropped-helmet scare, Captain Niedner split A Company off from the other companies and hiked north toward their assigned climb.

Once there, the company's soldiers sat in the snow and waited while their three lead climbers went to work, each one creating a path up the granite wall. As they had practiced at the marble quarry, they used socks to muffle the blows of their hammers as the pitons penetrated the composite rock more easily than the solid marble.

The process of creating three climbing paths to the top of the two-thousand-foot rock face took an hour. While A Company waited, other groups who were assigned to climb at the same spot hiked up and joined the waiting men of A Company.

The German klieg lights still moved in their hypnotic patterns overhead. It was odd to sit with the other soldiers in silence and Lucas wondered if the other men were as nervous as he was.

*****

A low fog rolled in after midnight which would help hide the soldiers from German detection. When the pattern of tugs on the rope signaled that it was safe to start sending men up, Lucas was one of the first to step forward.

Diego stepped up next to him. Lucas looked at him, surprised at the man's apparent eagerness.

Diego, however, looked terrified. He pointed a stiff finger at Lucas, then himself, and then clasped his hands together. Lucas nodded his understanding.

We are doing this together.

Lucas waited for Diego to settle into his rope harness before they took their first step together, climbing side-by-side. Then the second. And the third.

With each step, Diego seemed to relax in minute increments. He kept his eyes on Lucas and his hands on the ropes. When they had climbed about a hundred feet, Lucas motioned to Diego, *don't look down.*

Diego's eyes rounded in fear and he mouthed, *HELL no!*

On the way up, however, Lucas did take the opportunity to look down—and around. What he saw was astounding.

Eight hundred Tenth Mountain soldiers were climbing up out of the low fog in absolute silence. Spaced at eight foot intervals on the various routes, each of the parallel guide ropes wobbled with their concerted efforts. The reflection off the clouds above

Ice and Granite: The Snow Soldiers of Riva Ridge

was their only source of light. Even so, each man moved soundlessly with skill and determination.

They all had trained so long and so hard for this, and at last they were accomplishing a mission that only an elite division was capable of completing. All the missteps of Homestake and the brutality of the D-Series were paying off.

We are making history.
Right here, right now.
And I'm part of it.

Lucas had never been so proud. This climb trumped any state championship—hell, even a national championship—because what he was doing this night *mattered*.

He resumed climbing, feeling a shift inside his head and his heart. He wasn't a quarterback anymore.

He was a member of one of the first elite Army divisions created, embarking on a mission which only he and his brothers were capable of implementing.

And with God's help, they'd blow the hell out of the Germans who had no idea they were coming.

Chapter Fourteen

February 19, 1945

It took Lucas and Diego well over an hour to reach the top of Riva Ridge. Lucas's muscles strained and cramped with the effort, but there was no other choice except to keep going up. The base of the vertical face of the ridge was several hundred feet down now, and the path blocked by other soldiers climbing below him.

The constant wind blowing across the top of the ridge showered him and the other climbers with snowy ice crystals that got in his eyes, but he didn't have a free hand to wipe them with. He looked sideways at Diego. His buddy was about five feet ahead of him and climbing steadily in spite of his dread of heights.

When Diego reached the top, he nervously looked toward Lucas. Remembering his promise, Lucas pushed himself harder up the last few feet until he could climb over the edge onto the top of the ridge. He swiveled on his belly and held out his hand to Diego.

Diego let go of the rope with one hand and grasped it. Lucas rolled away from the edge, pulling Diego with him, until the man plopped face down in the snow next to him.

"Thanks," he whispered.

Lucas patted his shoulder.

Smoky climbed up behind Diego. The three friends reached the top at three o'clock that morning. They joined Lieutenant Loose and waited silently for the rest of their platoon among the dozens of soldiers climbing at the same spot.

Loose kept squinting at his watch in the dark. "We're supposed to be in position at Pizzo di Campiano and ready to attack by five," he whispered to the dozen assembled men. "If the rest of the platoon doesn't get up here soon, we'll have to go on without them."

"Just us?" Lucas whispered back, startled by the thought.

"Intel says we're attacking an observation post," Loose explained. "Should be lightly defended."

That was some consolation, though Lucas was actually disappointed. After all their intense training, and the adrenaline rush of climbing the ridge, he'd hoped for a bit more action than that.

The drifting snow on top of the ridge was four to five feet deep. Lucas and the eleven other men in Loose's platoon strapped into their bear paws in preparation for hiking through the snow to their assigned position at Pizzo di Campiano. After another hour, Loose made the call.

"It's almost five now. We're out of time." He shouldered his pack and the men did the same. "We can't wait for the other guys. They'll have to catch up with us."

A thin, pale line along the horizon to the east hinted at the coming sunrise as the dozen men of their A Company platoon struggled to cross a portion of the slope that was covered with egg-sized gravel under a disguising blanket of snow, rendering the bear paws useless. The only way to cross a scree slope like that was to take them off and scramble as fast as possible.

They removed their snow shoes and clambered across the rocks, which kept rolling downhill under their boots. And of course, the tumbling rocks eliminated any chance of remaining silent.

Within five minutes of beginning their crossing the first German grenade landed about a hundred yards below them on the slope of the ridge. Lucas flinched, alarmed by the sudden blast.

Shit!

Lucas watched Loose at the front of the line. The lieutenant kept his head down and his feet moving. So every man in the squad did the same.

The grenades kept coming and, even though they were landing below the soldiers' current position, their continual explosions rumbled in Lucas's chest and set his heart to pounding harder than the exertion and relatively low altitude could account for.

When the men regained snow-covered ground they marched silently and rapidly forward on bear paws again. Thankfully the German grenade assault stopped when the damned rocks no longer betrayed their position.

The squad reached Pizzo di Campiano half an hour later than scheduled. Lucas nudged Smoky and pointed across the valley. Mount Belvedere was directly in front of them.

"No wonder they wanted someone to take out the observation post here," he whispered.

Smoky nodded. "This has got to be the closest spot to Belvedere on the whole ridge."

Loose told the radioman to inform Lieutenant Colonel Hampton and Captain Niedner that a third of their platoon had arrived at their assigned position—and was attacked by German grenades along the way.

Then Loose ordered, "Form a perimeter and dig in. The

bastards know we're here now."

While there were wooded areas further down the slope, on top of the ridge only a few small saplings managed to survive between the rocky ground and the heavy snows. The twelve soldiers spaced themselves every seven or eight feet and dug foxholes in the snow, shoveling down until they hit rock.

Wearing their white anoraks and crouching in holes deep enough to cover them, the men were in a good situation to engage with their enemy below. Smoky was to Lucas's right, and Diego was the next man over. They settled in and waited.

Until the Germans fired, the platoon didn't know exactly where the enemy was. The soldiers were not going to waste their limited supply of ammunition by shooting randomly, but the wait was excruciating.

Lucas watched the sky lighten. The cloud cover was slowly evaporating, hinting that the coming morning might be clear.

The downhill sound of a German officer giving commands broke the silence. Lucas didn't understand what was being said, but when he heard the unmistakable *whoosh* of a mortar round sliding down the inside of a metal tube, he was able to put the pieces together fast.

That was no observation post below.

"Did you hear that?" he asked Smoky, incredulous that he had. "They're loading a launcher!"

Smoky looked as astonished as Lucas felt. "I did!"

Thoomp.

The Germans shot the round and Lucas watched the launched explosive sail over his head and land uphill behind the squad.

They're too close.

Now what?

Lieutenant Loose stood so the top half of his body was visible above his foxhole. "Observation post my ass! Before they wake up and realize that they need to move down-slope, we're going down to get 'em!"

Hell, yeah!

Lucas stood as well. From his new vantage point he could see what was coming behind Loose. He pointed urgently, but didn't say anything.

Loose turned around.

In the growing daylight, Platoon Sergeant Boyd trudged toward them with the rest of their platoon in tow—thirty more men if they all made it up the difficult climb.

Loose didn't ask where the soldiers had been, he just ordered the men to dig in as well. Then he pointed at Lucas.

"Thunder, Smoky, Diego," he called quietly, adding two more names. "You men come with me."

Lucas practically leapt from his foxhole.

Armed with grenades and rifles, the five soldiers followed Loose in a crouched and careful descent through the drifted snow toward the sounds of the launched mortars. When they could finally see the German bunker, the six men stretched out on the snow, side by side.

Loose held a grenade in front of his face and met each man's eyes. "On three," he whispered.

Lucas took off a glove and dug one of his two grenades from his pack. He gripped it in his gloved right hand and hooked a bare finger through the ring on the pin.

Once they were all readied, Loose whispered, "One, two, three—"

Six grenades flew through the chilled morning air and hit their targets, exploding simultaneously with an ear-ringing intensity.

Lucas shouldered his rifle as shouts in angry, startled German pierced the air. He took aim at the backs of the departing Kraut soldiers and squeezed off six shots.

Two men fell.

Beside him the other five men were shooting as well, so Lucas couldn't be certain his bullets had been the only ones to reach their targets, but that didn't matter. All that mattered was that the bastards were dead.

Loose jumped to his feet. "Let's go!"

Lucas didn't need to be asked twice.

The six men ran in leaping, bear-pawed steps through the snow toward the armed dugout while its former occupants escaped in a similar fashion down the mountainside.

Loose grinned when he saw the abandoned artillery they had just captured. "Great start men. Let's keep going!"

The men followed the tracks of the German gunners, slowing their pace when they saw another bunker sprouting a dark mortar tube out of the white slope ahead of them. Once again, they approached cautiously until the half-dozen soldiers were lined up on their bellies in the snow.

On the lieutenant's count of three, Lucas pulled the pin on his second and last grenade and threw it with deadly accuracy. Another shattering burst of grenade explosions rewarded the men.

This time, however, the Germans shot back.

Lucas's elbows dug into the snow as he aimed his rifle at anything in the bunker that moved. Shot after shot reverberated against his shoulder, setting his right ear to ringing. He knew at least one German went down because *he* was the one who put a hole right between that Kraut's eyes.

When the German counterattack stopped, Loose waited a few minutes then motioned for the men to advance. Lucas counted twelve bodies when they reached the bunker, eight the victims of the grenades.

"See if they have anything valuable on them," Loose ordered.

Lucas and the others carefully went through the pockets of the dead soldiers looking for maps or orders—anything military. Smoky, however, collected their watches.

He shrugged when he caught Lucas's inquisitive glance. "Souvenirs.

Loose retrieved his radio from his pack and called back to their platoon's position above them. "Able eighty-six one? Do you copy?"

"Go ahead."

"Send down two carrying parties." He smiled at the group. "We have some ordnance to dispose of."

The men from the platoon arrived swiftly, led by Sergeant Boyd. The stunned looks on their faces attested to the incredible feat that Loose and his five guys had just accomplished.

"I don't believe it." Boyd shook his head and his gaze moved over the six men grinning back at him. "A *rifle* squad just routed *two* artillery posts, and captured *two* eighty-two millimeter mortars?"

"And about five hundred rounds of mortar ammo, give or take," Loose replied with a chuckle and a modest shrug.

Lucas shot a proud look at Smoky and Diego, both of whom looked like they were about to burst.

We're off to a great start.

After lugging the mortar out of the dugout, the soldiers set fire to the German bunker. They hurriedly retreated to a safe distance before the flames hit the ammunition. Once it did, the stockpile exploded, the concussion and heat hitting Lucas hard even at their protected spot. The resulting fireworks rivaled the most elaborate Fourth of July celebration Lucas could possibly imagine.

When the display ended, thick black smoke from the exploded ammo drifted straight up on the windless morning—a testimony to the Germans below that their position had been thoroughly destroyed.

Loose and his six-man advance squad led the way back up to the first bunker to retrieve the second mortar and then set that abandoned ammunition on fire as well. Once that equally explosive, concussive, and snow-melting fire died down, Lucas and the others helped the carrying party heft both of the heavy eighty-two millimeter mortars through the deep snow back up the slope to their platoon's dug-in position.

There Loose ordered the men to bury the weapons as deeply as they could. "I expect by the time the spring thaw melts the snow up here, and these tubes are poking out of the ground, the Germans will be long gone."

Lucas shared another triumphant and determined look with Smoky and Diego.

"That's what we expect too, sir," he stated. "And we aim to make sure it happens."

*****

The enemy might have lost two artillery posts, but Lucas was under no illusion that the setback was going to stop the Germans from trying to reclaim their stronghold at the closest spot on Riva Ridge which faced Mount Belvedere. After resting and eating a breakfast of cold K-rations, Loose ordered his platoon to reload, rearm, and start patrolling the ridge at Pizzo di Campiano.

Lucas, Smoky, Diego, and a guy named Payette joined Lieutenant Loose on a patrol into the evergreen woods below them. Above the woods, a ridge of gigantic granite boulders stuck out of the snow.

I bet those could hide a lot of Germans, too.

As if Payette heard Lucas's thoughts he suddenly left the group, climbed up the hundred yards or so, and disappeared behind one of the boulders. Meanwhile Lucas, Smoky, and Diego followed Loose into the trees. Lucas pulled his green-glassed goggles up to his forehead so he could see in the shadowy woods.

Chug—chug—chug—chug—chug!

The sound of a Tommy gun echoed above them. "That's Payette," Lucas shouted. "He's in the boulders!"

Movement under one of the sweeping evergreens about ten

yards to Lucas's right caught his attention. He turned his head and saw a machine gun barrel poke out, aimed straight at him.

Shit!

Lucas felt like he was whirling in slow motion as he shouldered his rifle, certain without a doubt he'd be riddled with holes before he could get a single shot off.

Smoky must have seen the movement too, because he got a shot off before Lucas did. Smoky hit the gunner and Lucas got the loader. Both men screamed and writhed on the ground before Diego fired off two shots, hitting each German soldier squarely between the eyes.

Smoky slapped Diego's back in thanks.

But Lucas was shaking so hard that he could see his rifle barrel trembling.

Why didn't he fire at me?

He had me dead to rights.

Payette bolted into the woods. "It was gonna be an ambush! When I shot at them, they ran!" He stopped and looked at the dead machine gunners. "Hey—good job, guys!"

"Take all of their weapons and drop them in that hole up top with the rest of what we captured," Loose ordered. "Then check their pockets. We'll leave the bodies here."

Lucas forced his unsteady legs to carry him toward the cold machine gun that should have ended his life. He grabbed the thing like it was a snake he'd spooked in the fields back home, gripping it hard enough to choke the life from it.

*****

Six hours after the platoon was reunited at sunrise, and soon after Payette spooked the Germans and truncated their ambush attempt, the Krauts counterattacked. The fight for the prime position at Pizzo di Campiano escalated rapidly.

Tucked inside their snowy foxholes, the forty white-camouflaged soldiers of Lieutenant Loose's A Company platoon literally threw everything they had at their German aggressors, including two badly aimed German grenades which Lucas threw back at the enemy before either one exploded in his lap.

As the gradually graying day eased into another overcast evening, snow began to fall. The flakes were large and wet, and dampened the soldiers' white anoraks. The previous night's wind had died away so the flakes fell straight down as if they were rain.

Lucas shivered. Even though the temperatures were nowhere near as cold as the Rockies, the air up there was dry. This air was not. The wet chill seemed to seep right through his snow gear.

The German attacks fell into a pattern which continued through the night: fight, recoup, and fight again. Lucas lost count, but he was pretty certain they had been attacked at least four times and from two different directions so far.

The amazing thing was, as far as Lucas could tell, his platoon could count far more German casualties than American ones. And though some were injured, none of his guys had died.

Sure, he'd been grazed by a bullet and had to keep wiping away blood that trickled down his forehead and into his left eye, but that was nothing more than an annoyance. Sure, it was a terrifying annoyance, truth be told. But he'd survived the very close call with the German bullet.

And he hadn't let it slow him down at all.

The snow stopped falling sometime during the night after dropping only a couple inches. As soon as the following morning's gradual light was bright enough to see by, someone knocked on Lucas's helmet. "Come with me."

Lucas wiped his eye again and looked up at Diego, who was lying on his belly in the snow behind Lucas. "Where?"

His friend's expression shifted to alarm. "You're bleeding."

"Just a scratch," Lucas deflected. "Might be deep enough to leave a scar to show off, though."

"If you say so." Diego scowled and pointed to Lucas's left. "The shots from the German trench over there have slowed down. Let's go finish 'em off."

Lucas eased himself out of the foxhole with his rifle gripped in his gloved hand, and belly crawled through the snow behind Diego until they reached the evergreen area.

Diego pointed to a trench at the edge of the trees. "Right there—do you see them?"

"Yep." Lucas felt for his grenades. He didn't have any.

Damn.

"How many grenades you got?" he asked Diego.

Diego held up a grenade. "Just one. I figured it's enough fire power to get most of them, then we'll finish 'em off with our rifles."

"In that case…" Lucas held out his hand. "Let me throw the grenade. You might hit a tree."

And I can hit a wide receiver's hands at fifty yards.

Diego handed the grenade to Lucas. He pulled out the pin, stood, and threw the grenade in a perfect arc which hit its target dead on. It exploded inside the Germans' trench.

No one climbed out to run.

Diego and Lucas approached low and carefully, rifles at ready.

One man out of six was still alive. Diego shot him in the back of the head and then turned to Lucas. "You see the size of these backpacks in here? These guys came up here to stay."

Lucas opened one of the packs. What he found there closely matched the contents of the duffel he'd left behind in the farmhouse shed.

He looked up at Diego. "If I had to guess, I'd say these guys are mountain troopers."

"The guys we engaged with this morning didn't have packs," Diego observed. "And their patches were different."

Lucas nodded. "I think we've been fighting two different

units since yesterday."

Diego looked gobsmacked in the pinkening light. "You could be right. *Damn.*"

"That explains why the attacks are coming so close together." As incredible as it seemed, Lucas was certain he was right.

"Do you think they know they're both attacking us?"

Lucas shrugged. "I don't know how they could miss all the noise."

"Right." Diego climbed out of the trench and offered Lucas a hand up. "Let's go report this to Loose."

Chapter Fifteen

February 20, 1945

When the sun had risen high in the sky, thirty-six hours after they started up the trail to climb Riva Ridge, Loose and his men were still in position. Exhausted, hungry, freezing cold, out of grenades, and dangerously low on ammunition, they still held their ground against the constant attacks from both enemy units.

All of the Germans they had closely engaged with up to now had either fled or were killed. The one exception was an SS lieutenant that Payette and Smoky took prisoner in the wee hours of last night.

Lucas came up to take a turn guarding the big man who was badly wounded. Blood stained most of the front of his uniform.

"Shot in the gut," Smoky said as Lucas relieved him. "If the bullet nicked his colon, he'll be dead in a couple days."

The lieutenant growled something at Lucas in angry, guttural German.

"So he's not interested in mercy, huh?" Lucas gave Smoky a wry grin. "Doesn't want medical treatment either?"

"Nah, he's an arrogant son-of-a-bitch." Smoky punched Lucas's shoulder. "Maybe he'll be nicer to you. You've got those Aryan looks, after all."

Lucas cut his gaze back to the prisoner. "Trust me. We are *not* going to be friends."

"Loose is checking with the regimental command post to see what they want us to do with him." Smoky stretched and yawned. "But we can't afford to lose any guys to escort him down."

That's quite the understatement.

"Might they want to question him?"

Smoky shrugged. "We'll see."

Half-an-hour later during a lull between the constant attacks, Loose and Payette made their way up to where Lucas sat guarding the prisoner.

"I called the Regimental Command." Loose rubbed his forehead and sighed wearily. "They aren't interested in questioning the guy."

Lucas considered the German lieutenant. There was fresh blood on his jacket. His face was pale and the sheen of sweat made his brow glisten in the gray light. Even so, the man still regarded his captors with undisguised disgust and vitriol.

"I'll take him down, sir," Payette volunteered.

Loose peered at the private. "You will?"

"Yes, sir." Payette's expression was grim yet resolute. "I'll take care of the lieutenant."

From the way Payette said *take care of*, Lucas had a pretty good idea of what was about to happen.

"I'll go too, sir." Lucas shot Payette an approving look. "To make sure everything goes as it should."

Loose waved a hand at the men. "Go on then. Come back as soon as you can." Then he turned away and headed back down toward their perimeter of foxholes.

Lucas grabbed one of the German's arms and Payette

grabbed the other. They hauled the big man to his feet.

"Let's go." Payette grinned without mirth. "And don't give us any trouble."

The prisoner spat at him.

Payette yanked him forward and Lucas followed.

The trio walked toward the edge of the slope to where the ridge dropped off. There was no path to follow and the downward angle was impossibly steep.

Payette pointed. "Go. *Gehen Sie.*"

The lieutenant glanced over the edge, then glared defiantly at Payette. "*Nein.*"

Payette stepped a few paces behind the German, lifted his pistol, and shot the Kraut in the back of the head.

The man tumbled forward and his lifeless body rolled down the side of the mountain leaving a stark and bloody trail on the pristine white snow. Lucas and Payette watched until the corpse came to rest against a tree trunk about a hundred-and-fifty yards below them.

Lucas looked at Payette. He felt no remorse and that bothered him some—but this was war and that man was clearly their enemy. Besides, Payette's actions were actually merciful, since the man was dying a bad death anyway.

"He should not have disobeyed orders," Payette said softly.

"No," Lucas agreed. "He should not."

*****

Their second full day spent holding and defending Pizzo di Campiano felt like it lasted a month. Lucas had never been so tired or hungry in his life. It was hard enough to stay awake when the weak winter sun was out, but as it slid lower in the southwestern sky, Lucas felt like it was pulling his eyelids down with it.

If he didn't get so cold when he sat still, he would've been tempted to curl up in his foxhole—even without the sleeping bag he'd left behind—and give in to his overwhelming exhaustion.

To his great credit, Lieutenant Loose proved to be an exceptional leader. Not only did he not question why Lucas and Payette returned so quickly from escorting the German prisoner, he nodded and smiled knowingly when they did.

Now he was making his way from foxhole to foxhole, encouraging his platoon to stay strong. Besides Lucas's superficial head wound, a couple of other guys had been hit—but none seriously enough to warrant evacuation. They just patched each other up and kept fighting.

God's watching out for us.

Loose squatted next to Lucas, who was sitting on the snow-crusted edge of his foxhole. "How you doing, soldier?"

"Never been better, sir." Lucas grinned at the lieutenant and removed his green-glassed goggles now that the sun was almost gone. "In fact, I'm thinking about vacationing here next year."

Loose chuckled and wagged his head. "Maybe I'll join you."

Lucas's gaze shifted. "Someone's coming, sir."

Loose followed Lucas's gaze. "Shit."

Then he shouted at the approaching group, "Hey! Get your heads down, you stupid asses! Unless you want to lose 'em!"

The soldiers immediately dropped to the snow and continued to advance in a crawl.

"Shit," Loose whispered again when the men were closer. "That's Lieutenant Colonel Hampton."

Lucas laughed silently. "You just called our First Battalion Commander a stupid ass."

Loose looked stricken. "Yes. I'm aware of that."

Hampton crawled up to Loose and patted his knee. "How you boys doing?"

"Honestly? We haven't slept for forty-eight hours and we ran out of food yesterday." Loose paused then wisely added, "Sir."

"Ammunition?"

"Gone, except for bullets."

Hampton nodded. "You've done well. And, your relief party is on the way. They should be here before midnight. You boys can go down when they get here."

Relief flooded Lucas's frame so strongly that it almost made him collapse into tears.

"Thank you, sir." Loose's voice sounded thick, like he might cry as well.

Colonel Hampton's gaze moved along the perimeter of foxholes. "What's the situation here?"

"We've engaged with the enemy every couple hours since we arrived. In fact—" Loose looked at Lucas before he continued; the lieutenant appeared to have regained his composure. "Hansen here was one of the two men who discovered we've actually been fighting against two different units."

Hampton regarded Lucas. "Is that so?"

"Yes, sir." Hansen pointed in Diego's direction. "Martinez and I captured a bunker, and judging by what was in their packs they were German mountain troopers."

Hampton nodded. "We knew they were up here."

"But the Germans we encountered previously did not carry packs," Lucas explained. "And they had different patches on their uniforms."

"We believe they were regular infantry sent up to support the mountain troops," Loose interjected.

Hampton's gaze intensified. "What you're telling me, Lieutenant, is that your *platoon* has successfully held off two German units for forty-eight hours?"

"Yes, sir."

"How many men have you lost?" Hampton pressed.

Loose looked surprised by the question. "None, sir."

Now Hampton looked surprised. "None?"

Loose shrugged. "A few of the men have sustained injuries, but we're all still fighting."

"And we captured two eighty-two millimeter mortars, a few machine guns, and a shit-load of rifles and pistols," Lucas added, bragging on Loose's behalf.

Loose shot him an appreciative glance. "Not to mention a thousand rounds or so of German ammunition blown up."

"You should've seen it!" Lucas grinned. "It was like the Fourth of July up here, sir."

Hampton huffed a chuckle. "Thank you, Lieutenant. Your men's exceptional bravery won't go unnoticed, I assure you."

February 21, 1945

While Loose's weary platoon waited in the frigid darkness for their replacements, they watched the battle raging on the slopes of Mount Belvedere.

German support from Riva Ridge had been eliminated by First Battalion's successful nighttime climb and surprise attack, so the rest of the Tenth Mountain Division was currently blasting the German stronghold on the other side of the valley as planned.

Artillery blasts flared and then lit up the targets they hit with eerie orange glows.

Machine gun fire flashed in staccato bursts of white light from both sides of the battle

Loose's platoon was close enough to hear the explosions as well as see them, though the distance across the valley between their position and the battle delayed the powerful booms.

"Which side is winning?" Lucas asked Smoky.

"Can't tell from here." Smoky pointed in the dark. "But if our guys are the ones going uphill, they seem to be making headway."

"Fourth time's the charm," Lucas murmured. "At least we're quiet up here at the moment."

The replacement unit arrived at half-past midnight. After a

briefing by Lieutenant Loose, their platoon was finally given the go-ahead to withdraw around one o'clock in the morning.

The only way down was essentially the same way they came up, minus the ropes. Loose led his men around and down the steeply sloping side of the ridge—the same slope where Payette shot the German lieutenant.

It was slow going through the snow and in the dark. Several men slipped and were caught by their platoon mates who also slipped.

Lucas wondered if they'd encounter the officer's corpse but it was hard to see in the dark. Still he couldn't keep himself from looking for it until he thought he saw it.

Whether it was really there or he was hallucinating from his lack of sleep was impossible to tell. Either way, he shuddered involuntarily.

When they reached the trail at the base of the vertical wall Loose called a halt so the already spent men could take a brief rest. Lucas pulled his canteen from inside his coat and took a long drink of body-heat-melted snow—their only source of water up top—and tried to erase the image of the frozen German corpse, real or imagined, from his head.

After a quarter hour Loose roused the men and they began their cautious descent down the narrow and rocky trail.

"There's no rush, men!" Loose reminded them. "No one's chasing us. Just get down safely. That's an order."

The snow on the rocky path had been trampled by the boots of eight hundred soldiers on the way up, and two days of sun had cleared the remaining layer away. Lucas was glad they didn't have to be silent on their descent, as they had been on the way up, but ironically the soldiers were far too tired to attempt any conversation.

The platoon rested again before they crossed the Dardagna wash.

"Where are we headed from here, Lieutenant?" Diego asked.

"The Battalion Command Post in Vidiciatico," Loose replied. *That's twenty-five miles from here.*

Lucas groaned and lay back against his pack.

"Will they send any trucks?" Diego's pleadingly hopeful tone was unmistakable.

Loose sighed heavily. "I don't know. We'll just keep going and rest when we need to."

*****

Nine hours after their replacements arrived on top of Riva Ridge, Lucas and his foot-weary platoon mates stumbled into First Battalion's Command Post. Along the way to Vidiciatico they retrieved their duffels from the village which they overnighted in, and begged for food from the farmers. All of them had a little to eat and it was enough to keep them going.

Barely.

Once inside the relative safety of the command post, Lucas sat down on the ground, too spent to go any further. Thirty-nine men in the line mimicked that action as they entered the gates.

"Tell Colonel Hampton the platoon from Pizzo di Campiano is here," Loose told the sentries. "And then direct us to the mess tent."

Lucas managed to stay awake long enough to finish a bowl of oatmeal and a scoop of scrambled eggs. Then he followed Loose to their billet—a half-bombed-out barn.

Lucas was far too tired to care where he slept. He unrolled his recently retrieved sleeping bag in a stall, pulled off his boots for the first time in three days, and crawled inside.

The last lucid thought he remembered having was to wonder once again why he wasn't shot in the evergreen grove when he should have been.

Chapter Sixteen

As the First Battalion soldiers were pulled off of Riva Ridge following their triumphant assault on the German stronghold, Loose's platoon was joined by the rest of A Company in Vidiciatico. The Eighty-Sixth Mountain Regiment as a whole—soldiers who trained at Camp Hale—had just succeeded in one of the most difficult maneuvers in military memory.

Because that's what we were prepared to do.

Lucas picked up two letters at the command post, one from his parents and one from Parker. He read Parker's first.

> MY DEAREST LUCAS,
>
> I HOPE YOU ARE DOING WELL. EMILY, SOFIA, AND I ARE STILL AT CAMP CROWDER AND WE ARE STILL WORKING IN THE CENSOR'S OFFICE, THOUGH THERE ARE VERY FEW SOLDIERS HERE SO THERE IS NOT MUCH WORK TO DO.

> SOUTHERN MISSOURI IS VERY DIFFERENT FROM COLORADO AND I CAN'T SAY THAT I LIKE IT HERE. HOPEFULLY YOU BOYS WILL PUT A STOP TO THIS WAR SOON, AND THEN WE CAN ALL GO HOME!
>
> I DO HAVE NEWS, MY LOVE: I MET YOUR FAMILY.

Lucas read that line twice to make sure he saw what he thought he saw. Convinced he understood the words correctly, he read on.

> BECAUSE CAMP CROWDER IS LESS THAN 300 MILES FROM SABETHA, WHEN WE WERE GIVEN A 3 DAY PASS EMILY AND I BORROWED A CAR AND MADE THE TRIP.

Lucas drew a deep breath. He had told his parents about Parker, but he hadn't bothered to mention that he intended to marry her when the war was over.

> YOUR MOTHER IS A DEAR. YOUR FATHER IS KIND. AND I LOVE YOUR SISTERS ALREADY.
>
> I DID NOT TELL THEM THAT I PROPOSED MARRIAGE AND YOU ACCEPTED. THAT IS UP TO YOU. BUT I DID TELL THEM I AM IN LOVE WITH THEIR SON, SO THEY MIGHT HAVE FIGURED IT OUT WHEN THEY SAW THE RING YOU GAVE ME.

Lucas let the letter fall to his lap.
Parker drove for hours just to meet my family.
Now he felt guilty that he had not asked to meet hers before leaving Colorado. But then, she didn't offer it either. If there was a reason for that, he'd worry about it later.

Lucas looked at the neat writing, all in capital letters so they were easier for him to decipher, and realized that this amazing woman was the absolute love of his life.

I need to let her know that.

A pang of loneliness pressed into his heart. When he finished carefully reading and rereading Parker's letter, he opened his parents' missive before answering hers.

> *Dear Lucas,*
> *We just had the most amazing visitor…*

*****

Lucas tried to put his experiences into words for Parker, but it was just too hard for him to do. He ended up asking Fraser to write some of the letter for him.

"Say that nothing in Italy is as severe as the training we had at Camp Hale," Lucas dictated. "The top of the highest ridge at Riva is just six thousand feet—Camp Hale was ninety-five hundred."

Fraser nodded as he wrote. "And Mount Belvedere is only fifty-four hundred at the top."

Lucas pointed at the paper. "Write that too," he said. "And say I promise to tell her everything when I get back."

"Okay." Fraser finished writing and handed the letter to Lucas to sign. "You're a lucky man, you know that?"

"I do." Lucas tucked the single-page letter into an envelope. "Want to walk to the post office with me?"

On the way across the post, Lucas and Fraser passed F

Company from Second Battalion—the guys who trained with them at the marble quarry and then climbed the ridge with First Battalion. The F Company guys were leading a rag-tag group of two dozen German prisoners.

Lucas nodded a relieved greeting to Jack Franklin.

He made it.

Franklin flashed a crooked grin and nodded back.

"Is it just me?" Fraser posited. "Or do those guys look relieved to be captured?"

Lucas caught the eye of one soldier—fifteen if he was a day—and the boy flashed a tentative smile. Lucas did not smile back.

"The Tenth is pushing the Germans pretty damn hard and they're getting desperate," he said. "It's better to surrender than die."

Fraser looked over his shoulder at the group making their way to the POW enclosure. "We have hundreds of Krauts here now—hell, maybe a thousand—who have to be guarded, housed, and fed. Not at all what I expected when we deployed, I have to say."

Lucas hadn't thought much about prisoners of war either, before coming to fight. He knew there was a POW sector at Camp Hale, but he never went to look at it.

"I just hope *we* get fed first," he muttered.

February 25, 1945
Camp Crowder, Missouri

Parker listened to Emily cheerfully relay the information from David's most recent letter while she tried not to think about the handsome captain who was undoubtedly waiting for them in the censors' office.

Captain Thomas Boone became their commanding officer when the Camp Hale WACs returned from their Christmas furlough and were transferred from Colorado to Missouri. The trim man was well-spoken, quick to smile, always the first one in the office every morning and the last one to leave. Apparently, he had no faults.

Unless his obvious attraction to Parker could be considered a fault, of course.

She opened the front door of the masonry building, stomped snow from her boots on the covered entryway, and let Emily go in first to briefly deflect the attention she expected would soon be focused in her direction.

"Good morning, Lieutenants." Captain Boone's smooth baritone slid over Parker like silk stockings. "I'm glad last night's snowstorm hasn't deterred your path."

"We all spent a year and a half in the Colorado Rockies," Parker reminded him. She found his comment irritating for some reason so she added, "A six-inch snowfall is nothing."

Captain Boone helped Parker remove her coat before she could do it on her own. He hung it on one of the empty hooks that lined the hallway leading to the censors' workroom. Emily pointedly cleared her throat and Captain Boone jumped to help her with her coat as well.

"It looks like another light day," the captain said while he hung up Emily's coat. "I think we'll be out of here early again."

Parker regarded her superior officer. "Do you ever wish you were deployed somewhere, instead of being stuck here with us?"

A shadow crossed Boone's brow. He ran his fingers through thick dark hair that was solidly graying at the temples.

"After Pearl Harbor I signed up to serve my country in any capacity," he stated. "And I knew when I enlisted at thirty-seven that my age might limit my usefulness."

"But still," Emily pressed. "Did you hope for more?"

Captain Boone sighed and his expression dimmed.

"War is glorified by those who can't go. But I'm not under any illusion that the actual experience meets that optimistic description."

Parker's heart clutched at his sobering words. She hadn't heard from Lucas in several weeks, even though she kept writing faithfully. She prayed every night before she went to sleep that he was alive and unharmed.

And again every morning when she woke up.

A few officers at Camp Crowder who had experience in the First World War assured her that he would get her letters as soon as his unit was bivouacked near a command post, but while the soldiers were on the move during a campaign there was no safe way to deliver mail.

And no reason to risk soldiers' lives by doing so.

Parker turned away and walked into the workroom and straight to her desk. The WACs assigned to the censors' office were half in number from what they were at Camp Hale so the room was much smaller.

Several of the gals were already at work when Parker took her seat and they exchanged brief smiles of greeting before turning back to the letters in their baskets.

Parker picked up the top letter in her basket. When she looked at the neat handwriting, her vision blurred with tears.

Where are you Lucas?

Parker's decision to visit the Hansen family unannounced was gutsy, but she never doubted it was the right thing to do. If she and Lucas were to be married when this mess was finished, she needed to know whether or not she would fit in with his parents and sisters.

She had seen evidence in her own parents' lives of the damage that could be caused when a daughter-in-law was pitted against her husband's mother. She had no desire to live out her life in that same fraught situation.

Thankfully she was met by the Hansen family with surprised

but very welcoming arms. And when she spoke openly about their son's training at Camp Hale, including information which she had personally redacted from his letters, Lucas's father and mother thanked her repeatedly.

Lucas's sisters, Mary and Suzanne, both chuckled at Parker's lack of farm knowledge. Her lesson in milking a cow left the three women in hysterics, but the retelling at supper that night was even funnier.

By the time Parker left Sabetha, Kansas her fears were eliminated and she dearly looked forward to finally having sisters of her own.

"Where are you?"

Parker looked up into Captain Boone's warm brown eyes, framed by the sort of wrinkles that came from smiling. She could smell his aftershave—a mix of cloves and cedar. The scent was clean and soothing.

"Just wondering when this war will be over," she lied. "And wondering if the guys who are training here will actually get a chance to fight."

Captain Boone pulled over a chair. He straddled it and rested his arms on the back of the seat. "Which war do you think will end first?"

Parker blinked. She had not considered that the fighting might end on one front, but continue on the other. "I have no idea. What do you think?"

The captain's gaze held hers. "My money's on Europe. The Pacific Theater is too big to get a handle on just yet, in my opinion."

Your mouth to God's ears.

Parker's gaze fell away—staring into Boone's eyes was too intimate. "I hope you're right."

Boone touched Parker's elbow. "I do hope your guy makes it back. I mean that."

Parker only nodded. She didn't raise her eyes.

"Please know this…"

When he stopped, Parker lifted her eyes to his.

"I am here, Lieutenant," he said softly. "You will always be able to count on me, no matter what."

"Thank you," she whispered.

Chapter Seventeen

March 2, 1945
Northern Italy

After a week of rest, First Battalion was assigned to take the town of Sassomolare, fourteen miles northeast of their battalion command post at Vidiciatico. Though nighttime temperatures still dropped well below freezing, during the day the sun raised temperatures just enough to melt the accumulated snow.

As a result, the unpaved roads through the hills were turning into mud.

"So much for our skis," Lucas peered out the back of a truck as A Company jounced painstakingly along the mucky early morning path toward their objective. "We might not even need the bear paws anymore."

Diego sighed. "I'm going to miss skiing."

Smoky laughed. "You can always take up skiing when we get home, you know."

Diego made a face. "In California?"

One of the other guys in the truck leaned forward. "There's a ski resort called Sugar Bowl up by Donner Pass. I've skied there a few times and it's worth the trip."

"Huh. Didn't know that. Thanks." Diego looked pensive as he considered that information.

The trucks came to a stop by Mount Forte and the soldiers climbed out. The late afternoon was gray with a sporadic and chilly breeze and hazy clouds.

At least it's too warm to snow on us.

Loose gathered his platoon. "Dig in for the night, men. Try and stay warm."

That was ironic advice, since the soldiers were armed with only a single Army blanket each. Just like on Riva Ridge they were forced to leave their sleeping bags and tents behind.

The equipment which was so meticulously tested in Colorado now remained packed away in their duffels back at their battalion's command post.

Lucas sat on the edge of the shallow foxhole that he and Diego dug out and the men used their bayonets to pry open their K-rations. The food was cold, of course. Fires would give the Germans a clear target to shoot at.

At this point Lucas had learned to just chew and swallow, and not think about the flavor or texture of his meal. The point was sustenance, and no more. Fuel for his energy. Just calories and protein to keep his strength up.

"I wonder if we'll be able to take some of these home with us." Lucas held up the tin can. "They'd make an interesting souvenir."

"My mother would have a heart attack if she knew what we were eating out here." Diego chuckled. "She'd sit me right down and feed me a big bowl of menudo with fresh tortillas and watch me finish it all. Meanwhile she'd keep up a steady stream of indignant Spanish about how her poor little boy was being treated."

Lucas was intrigued. "Menudo?"

"Soup made with cow's stomach and hominy." Diego shrugged. "It tastes better than it sounds."

Lucas did not make the face he wanted to. "On the farm we call it tripe." And he hated it.

Once they finished eating there was nothing to do but check their weapons and go to sleep, even if they weren't ready. Lucas laid down and settled his back against Diego's, and pulled their two shared wool blankets over his shoulder.

"So I guess testing all that equipment was just for fun since we aren't actually using it," Lucas grumbled.

Diego grunted his agreement. "Look at the bright side. It's not thirty below zero here, either."

True.

The next morning the Battalion was up before dawn. Loose ordered the men to reverse their jackets from the all-white snow camouflage side to the regular Army olive drab side.

"We'll be on the ground for the next few days. You don't want to be a target."

The order infuriated Smoky. "Loose has a good point," he grumbled, "but now we look like every other flatland soldier."

Lucas understood exactly what Smoky was angry about. Without their Tenth Mountain tabs, and now stripped of their white anoraks, the highly trained and elite snow soldiers would be impossible to differentiate from the guys who signed up late and only went through basic flatland training before being deployed.

After enduring so much hardship to get to where they were, it was understandable that the men in the Tenth Mountain Division wanted their efforts and skills to be acknowledged.

After all, a man's uniform told the world where he belonged and what he could do.

*****

As soon as A Company had their gear packed and their weapons ready they set off walking down the winding, beaten up road toward Sassomolare. The morning was quiet and still as the sky gradually lightened on their right.

If it wasn't for the countless mine holes, and half-destroyed houses and barns along the way, Lucas would not be able to prove there even was a war going on at the moment. Birds sang in the surrounding trees as the day brightened and a rooster crowed somewhere. It sounded like home.

That illusion didn't last.

As the sun peeped over the hills to their right the first blast of Army artillery fired off from half a mile behind them. Lucas flinched at the sudden ear-ringing booms, but didn't turn around to look back. His objective was up ahead.

The launched ordnance sailed over the heads of A Company with telltale whistles and landed a half a mile in front of them. Dirt and rocks fountained upward fifteen feet in a solid line across the A Company soldiers' intended path.

Loose halted the line until the debris fell back to earth, and the smoke cleared enough for the soldiers to see what was in front of them, before he motioned the men forward again. Lucas heard the engines behind them rev up as the big guns moved forward as well.

Machine gun fire exploded from the side of a hill just beyond the blast line. Lucas and the others leapt for cover behind nearby rocks or tucked into ditches and immediately launched their counterattack.

Lucas squatted behind the remnant of a stone fence and aimed his rifle at the flashes emanating from a German machine gun. He held his breath, and took the shot. The gun recoiled against his shoulder as rifle shots banged all around him in a deadly stuttering cadence. He moved his aim to another target and shot again before aiming back at his first target.

He watched for a moment, but no machine gun fire retaliated.

I got him.

In the deafening cacophony of machine gun and rifle fire Lucas didn't hear the mortar rounds dropping in their tubes, so once again he wasn't prepared for the enormous and now much closer blast from behind.

He reacted instinctively, dropping his head and pulling in his limbs. His heart pounded with the shock.

Damn.

Lucas unfolded from the defensive position and peered through the smoke and debris from the blast. As visibility returned he caught a satisfying glimpse of fleeing German soldiers.

*****

For two hours A Company moved forward with the artillery's support in a manner that Lucas could only think of as an inchworm. The big guns fired half a mile ahead of the company. The soldiers advanced. The artillery moved up behind them, and then fired again.

And in between the men on the ground attacked the Germans with fierce fire and grenades. Lucas was damned good at throwing those little bombs with pinpoint accuracy.

When they halted and waited for the next round of mortars to be launched, Lucas took a long drink from his canteen then passed it to Smoky.

Smoky took a smaller drink and handed it back. "You're bleeding."

Lucas nodded and flexed his left arm. "I got grazed again. But this one's probably not bad enough for a decent scar."

"They got my pants here." Smoky pointed to a tear where his drab green trousers ballooned above his boots. "But missed me."

Diego squatted next to Smoky behind the boulder the two men were leaning against.

Lucas offered him his canteen but Diego shook his head. "I got water, thanks."

Diego adjusted his helmet and Lucas saw a deep groove where a bullet had scraped a horizontal dent along the side. "That was a close one."

"Yeah." Diego's hand reached up and slid his fingers along the gash. "Thought they got me for a minute there."

The whoosh of mortars sliding into multiple tubes made Lucas cover his ears. Smoky and Diego did the same before the chest-thumping launch sent the ordnance over their heads once more.

"Let's go." Lucas climbed to his feet.

A burst of machine gun fire dropped him to the ground.

"Are you hit?" Smoky shouted.

Lucas ran his hands down his body. "No." He lifted his rifle barrel. "Where are they?"

Diego peered over the rock that the three men were sheltered behind. "They're pinned between us and the artillery target ahead."

Immediately the A Company guys returned heavy fire aimed at the pinned German machine gunners. Rifles barked nonstop and grenades punctuated their impact. The result was deafening.

The three friends crouched side by side and steadied their rifles on top of the boulder.

Remember BRASS.

Breath, relax, aim, slack, squeeze.

After taking down at least four Krauts, Lucas pulled back to reload. He was careful not to touch the hot barrel of his rifle as he refilled the weapon, but his fingers trembled with the surge of adrenaline and the exhilaration of the battle.

The dug-in German unit continued to answer A Company's attack. Battalion artillery was useless at this point because the enemies were positioned too close together—and A Company might get hit if they tried.

Some of their comrades were hit. Shouts for medics brought forward the guys with stretchers and red crosses on their helmets. Lucas, Smoky, and Diego left the shelter of the boulder and inched forward, staying low and taking shots whenever they could.

Half an hour or so after the first shots were fired, the German guns fell silent. Lucas listened for the groans of injured men from the enemy's position but heard nothing.

Lieutenant Loose waited about ten minutes before motioning their platoon forward.

Crouching and moving slowly, the men spread out and approached the enemy's position. Lucas stepped over multiple dead bodies and collected German machine guns along the way. Off to his left, someone fired a shot.

"Got him!" the American shouted.

Two shots to his right were also followed with, "Got 'em!"

By the time the platoon reached the line where the artillery fire hit, there were no living Germans left.

Loose spoke into his radio. "We're secure up to the line. Fire when ready."

*****

Five hours after First Battalion began their early morning push they had secured the hills south of Mount Terminale—their first objective. Every German soldier on the southwest side of that small mountain had been captured or killed.

The battle-weary men took a break, ate, and waited for Third Battalion of the Eighty-Fifth to move up and hold their secured spot. Meanwhile Colonel Hampton briefed them on their next task.

"We're going to move around to the eastern base of Mount Terminale to where Eighty-Sixth's Second Battalion is launching their attack on Campo del Sol," he said. "We're going to give them support, and once we take Campo, First Battalion will move on and take Sassomolare."

Lucas closed his eyes and tried to picture the map they'd been shown yesterday afternoon. He could draw a diagonal line from where they were now northeast to Terminale, then Campo del Sol, Sassomolare, and on to Mount Grande d'Aiano, their ultimate objective.

Sassomolare was probably eight or nine miles from where they sat now. The eastern base of Mount Terminale should be three.

And Campo del Sol was right between the two.

Eighty-Sixth's First Battalion caught up with their Second Battalion in the early afternoon as they were moving toward Campo del Sol.

The inchworm's at it again.

In the same way First Battalion had reached their objective, Second was advancing toward theirs. Artillery fire, march forward and eliminate the enemy, more artillery fire, more marching forward.

First Battalion stayed behind Second, assuring that no German soldier was missed. That meant Lucas and his platoon were stepping over dead German soldiers every few yards. Medics were already in place, treating and evacuating injured Americans. Injured Germans would have to wait—and if they bled to death first, no one cared.

The occasional pistol shot around him proved that for many American soldiers, letting their injured enemy live even that long was not an option.

Lucas approached a small outbuilding on the farm they were currently traipsing through, his rifle ready. He motioned Diego to join him and pointed at the little stone structure.

"You go left, I'll go right," he whispered.

Diego nodded.

Lucas heard a sound through the window opening, but

couldn't tell if it was a human or an animal. Either way, the barrel of his rifle preceded his entry.

A rustle of boots and rocks answered.

Lucas and Diego stepped through the doorless opening and looked down their barrels at the stone hut's lone occupant.

The German soldier was trying to hold up his Luger but didn't appear to have the strength. His face was a grayish white and the sheen of sweat shone in the dim interior. His uniform was soaked with blood.

Lucas took the mercy shot.

Diego collected the man's weapons. And his watch.

Chapter Eighteen

March 4, 1945

The capture of Campo del Sol was accomplished late that same afternoon. And well before sunset yesterday, both Second and First Battalions had established their bivouacs in Campo del Sol. The soldiers settled in for the night to lick their battle wounds and regroup. Many of their guys had sustained injuries, but like Lucas's most of them weren't serious and didn't require the men to be pulled off the line.

We might look bloody and battered, but we're standing strong.

"Plans are to take both the town of Sassomolare and the high ground beyond at Mount Grande d'Aiano tomorrow," Loose told his platoon once their bivouac was set up. "We'll get our specific assignment in the morning. In the meantime, eat and get some rest."

This morning Lucas and Smoky climbed out of yet another cold, damp foxhole. Lucas started shivering as soon as he straightened. Though the day before had been relatively mild, a chilly wind decided to blow just before dawn and now it sent frigid tendrils through every gap in Lucas's uniform.

Ice rimed the edges of their hidey hole and covered the ground with incongruently sparkling beauty in the sunrise. Once again Lucas had the odd sensation that the horrors of war—guns blazing, artillery launching, bombs exploding, and men dying—were just a nightmare, and the peace of this frosty early morning in the mountains of northern Italy was reality.

A look at the men coming to life around him quickly restored their true reality. None of them had showered for three weeks and all had sprouted beards. Shaving outdoors with cold water wasn't a viable option, but beards did keep their faces warmer. Superficial wounds had left blood stains on grubby uniforms. Helmets were scratched and dented.

Yet etched on the face of every single member of the First Battalion of the Tenth Mountain Division was a grim and undimmed determination to finish the job they'd been given.

Lucas was more proud than he knew how to express that he was a member of this very special group of men. It occurred to him then that for the rest of their lives, they would all share a bond that no one else could.

*****

The first artillery launch of the day was just before eight that morning. Colonel Tomlinson had ordered First Battalion to take the lead this time, with Second Battalion to follow.

As usual Colonel Hampton would march in front of First Battalion. Lucas adjusted his helmet, checked for his grenades and ammo, and then gripped his rifle at the ready as the platoon began their march toward the town that lay almost six miles to the east.

"The hills surrounding Sassomolare aren't secured, so be prepared for German artillery and mortars," Captain Niedner warned A Company before confirming that, "Our first objective is to secure the town, our second is take Mount Grande d'Aiano."

Surprisingly, there wasn't much engagement with the Germans as First Battalion made its usual inchworm-like approach toward Sassomolare. Lucas figured all the Krauts had retreated to the relative safety of the town's solid buildings rather than risk being blown up or shot out in the open.

Two-and-a-half hours after they started moving, First Battalion entered the mess of a town that was called Sassomolare. Every street was pockmarked with the kind of holes that landmines leave, and most of the stone-and-stucco buildings were missing chunks from their outer walls or had gaping holes in their red-tiled roofs.

First Battalion was immediately fired upon.

Lucas and Smoky dove through a doorway and rolled away from any windows. Lucas grabbed his pistol and pointed it at the empty room. Smoky climbed to his feet and unholstered his pistol as well.

The men made a quick sweep of the abandoned two-story home before establishing themselves in an upstairs window. From their vantage point, Lucas and Smoky were able to fire on the German soldiers who were fighting hard to hold on to the town.

Lucas heard an unfamiliar sound and looked in the direction that he and the others had approached the town from. He laughed out loud when he saw an Army tank rolling down the street.

Captain Niedner was standing on the tank like some medieval knight on his battle steed and shouting directions through the turret. "The house across the square with the red door!"

Lucas watched in amazement as the tank's blunt-ended and lance-like gun swiveled in that direction and fired, hitting its target dead on.

Boom!

"Now two doors to the right!"

Boom!

The routed Germans scattered, so Lucas and Smoky began picking them off like they were playing a game at a carnival. Obviously not every shot they took was fatal, but then they weren't the only ones firing.

Three hours after marching out of Campo del Sol, Colonel Tomlinson declared Sassomolare secure.

First Battalion regrouped and Colonel Hampton assigned A Company to establish their battalion's command post.

When Captain Niedner found a structure that seemed less damaged than the others around it, he claimed it for First Battalion. Colonel Hampton gave it a brief once-over from the outside and approved the choice.

"Let's hurry and get set up in there." He turned to the headquarters' sergeant. "Let me see the map."

With the command post decided on, Loose's platoon moved down the street, carefully checking inside every shop and house for inhabitants, German or Italian. Lucas and Diego exited an empty butcher shop when Lucas heard the unmistakable *thoomp* of a mortar shell being launched.

"Shit!" Lucas grabbed Diego's arm and yanked him back inside the building.

The pair froze, waiting for the shell to land.

The bomb exploded right next to the building they'd just claimed for their command post. The Germans were obviously watching them from the temporary safety of the slopes of Mount Grande d'Aiano. And they'd targeted the battalion's commanding officer.

Hampton was down.

Medics ran to the bleeding Lieutenant Colonel lying in the street. Lucas heard one radioing for an evacuation team. He didn't want to get in the way, but he wanted to know how badly Hampton was hurt.

He and Diego approached slowly, on the alert for another telltale *thoomp*.

The medics lifted Hampton onto a stretcher and carried him to a jeep. The man was conscious, but Lucas could see blood from his shoulder to his wrist. He watched the jeep drive off, sorry to lose such a good leader

God be with him.

*****

For the next several hours the sweep of buildings in Sassomolare continued. Lucas, Smoky, and Diego worked as a team with two of them entering the front door and the third watching the back. Whenever they found hiding pockets of German soldiers, Lucas made a quick assessment and decided which one was likely the most timid. Then he'd pull that man aside.

He'd straighten to make a clear point of his physical size and ask, "*Wo sind die anderen?*" Where are the others?

After blustering and acting brave, the defeated soldiers eventually caved and ratted out their comrades. The trio turned over their prisoners to their command post before proceeding to the next disclosed location. When they found it, they confronted the cowering enclave that was invariably hiding there and repeated the process.

By two o'clock that afternoon, the town of Sassomolare was cleared. It was time to move on to their next objective.

The terrain on Mount Grande d'Aiano was mostly pine forest, and though the altitude wasn't impressive, there were still huge patches of hard, crusty snow in the shadowed dips and ravines.

Not enough for bearpaws or white anoraks.

Lucas swallowed his disappointment and lined up with A Company. C Company took the lead and advanced up the slope of Mount Grande d'Aiano under heavy German attack. Machine guns, grenades, and bazookas rained down their firepower as C Company returned fire and doggedly made their way up the slope.

A Company followed C Company and was subjected to the same sort of assault, albeit from fewer sources. Captain Niedner's men also responded with full fire power, taking out any enemy soldiers which had escaped the initial attack by C Company.

Lucas realized with a shock that he had become used to the idea of killing German soldiers. Diego's comment that to kill a soldier was akin to killing Hitler had resonated with him. He no longer thought of the enemy as human.

Does that make me inhuman as well?

Lucas pulled a deep breath and resolved to think about that later. After the war. After he got home. When life returned to normal again.

While the continuous German attacks on the advancing companies were fierce, they also exposed individual pockets of Krauts which were scattered across the slope—undetectable mountain soldiers who were skillfully camouflaged and concealed.

Once they exposed their own positions by opening fire on the Americans, however, the A Company soldiers fired back. Their counterattack was supported by Army heavy artillery from below which targeted the exposed soldiers' locations and fired on them, blasting the Germans out of existence.

While the soldiers fought on the slopes, Army aircraft flew low above them and strafed the opposite slope of Mount Grande, thereby eliminating the Krauts' only escape route.

It only took an hour and a half for First Battalion to rout, kill, or capture the German soldiers who were entrenched on Mount Grande and thereby secure the objective. First Battalion now held the south sector of Mount Grande d'Aiano, and Third Battalion held the north. Second Battalion had moved into Sassomolare while the First made their advance on Mount Grande.

After two hellish days spent battling their brutal opposition, the Tenth Mountain Division's Eighty-Sixth Regiment was firmly established right where it was supposed to be.

And at midnight that night, Colonel Tomlinson sent word to all three entrenched battalions that Major Harold Green, Executive Officer of Second Battalion, would replace the injured Lieutenant Colonel Hampton as the new Commander of First Battalion.

March 5, 1945

The Germans were defeated, but that didn't mean they were gone. Seven rounds of enemy mortar fire landed near First Battalion's Command Post during breakfast alone. A Company could hear the explosions from their overnight post on the south side of Mount Grande.

None of the guys in Loose's platoon had gotten much sleep during the night. Besides the rough conditions on the side of the steep mountain and the below-freezing temperatures, Lucas and his buddies bedded down on the damp cover of pine needles with only a single blanket per man to keep warm.

And A Company was still responsible for keeping their part of the line impenetrable, which meant that every three hours a new platoon was sent out on patrol to look for any Germans still hiding in the forest.

When the soldiers on patrol routed any Krauts out of cover there was always an exchange of fire, the sounds of which could clearly be heard from A Company's position. Awakened several times last night by the shots, the soldiers from the resting platoons leapt from their foxholes and rushed to the aid of the embattled patrol.

Loose's platoon started their assigned patrol at three o'clock in the smoke-hazed afternoon. Twenty-four hours after securing Mount Grande, Lucas expected that all the Germans holding the mountain had been captured or killed, and he was too tired to care if they weren't. Loose called a break at three-thirty and the men plopped on the ground where they were.

Lucas yawned, stretched, and rubbed his eyes. When he opened them again, he didn't trust what he saw.

He elbowed Diego. "Did you see that?"

Diego looked as done in as Lucas felt. "See what?"

Lucas pointed down the slope. "Down there—"

Smoky scooted toward him. "Did you see them too?"

More movement, definitely human and definitely more than one, jolted Lucas from his lethargy. He scrambled to his feet and ran to Loose. "Tell Captain Niedner we're under attack. Look."

Lucas pointed. A detachment of German soldiers was working its way up First Battalion's flank.

Loose's eyes rounded. "Everybody up. Back to company position. NOW."

Armed with automatic weapons, the German detachment below fired round after round up at A Company as they continued their advance. And once again, the forty men of First Platoon, A Company found themselves single-handedly repelling the uphill attack of a heavily fortified German unit with only their rifles and grenades.

The A Company men spread out in a line which took advantage of their uphill position. Lucas decided to make use of his arm and his eye and began tossing perfectly placed grenades down at their attackers.

Their radio man contacted their new commander, Major Green, requesting support. C Company appeared an hour into the battle, thankfully carrying their own supply of grenades and bullets.

The Germans were clearly intending to fight to the death and

Ice and Granite: The Snow Soldiers of Riva Ridge 173

Lucas understood their desperation. When the game looks hopeless, a quarterback calls any plays he thinks will work.

The Krauts had to know by now that they were losing the war, so they had nothing else to lose but their lives.

By the battle's end, four straggling hours after it began, Lucas's arm burned from throwing grenades and his shoulder was bruised from the recoil of his rifle. But the remaining Germans finally withdrew down the mountainside, straight into the waiting arms of Second Battalion in the town below.

Chapter Nineteen

March 16, 1945

Operation Encore was a rousing success.

On March sixth at Mount della Spe, three miles east of Mount Grande d'Aiano, and where the Tenth Mountain Division as a whole was gathered, Fifth Army declared Mount Belvedere and Riva Ridge secured.

Not a single man had been lost during the Tenth's climb of Riva Ridge. And during the subsequent mountain battles on the Ridge, only twenty-one soldiers had died, and just fifty-two were wounded seriously enough to be transported off the battle line.

One week later, on March thirteenth, General Mark Clark of Fifth Army responded to their unprecedented and impressive victory by ordering the Tenth Mountain Division to stand down until all of the Fifth Army divisions were aligned laterally across northern Italy—even though the Germans had already established a new defensive line where their canons, artillery, and heavy mortars could reach the established American positions.

Lucas stared at Captain Niedner, not believing what he'd just heard. "Could you repeat that, sir?"

"We are ordered to stand down, Thunder." Niedner didn't look any more pleased than Lucas was.

Who in their right mind stops a drive when it has this much momentum?

Apparently Fifth Army does.

"The good news is that, while we're waiting, Major General Hays is giving each Tenth battalion four days of furlough in a rear area." Niedner flashed a resigned half-smile. "And First Battalion of the Eighty-Sixth is once again going first."

So at ten o'clock tonight, after their other duties were finished, a bunch of canvas-topped trucks rolled into Mount della Spe to take the First Battalion guys south and west to the Tenth Mountain Division's rear command post at Camp Tizzoro, located just outside the pretty little mountain village of Montecatini.

The winding fifty-mile drive took three hours, navigating through the mountainous back roads of northwestern Italy. The worn-out A Company arrived at the command post around one o'clock in the morning. Division Command had set up cots in a school house, so each of the hundred-and-forty soldiers gratefully claimed one and stretched out to grab some uninterrupted sleep.

This was the first night in a month that Lucas wasn't sleeping on the ground or in a foxhole. Even though the cot was—as they always were—three inches shorter than he was, Lucas had no complaints. The thin mattress, pillow, and sheets were luxurious by comparison. Besides that, he could finally mail some letters. There might even be a letter or two from Parker waiting for him here at the command post.

He missed her so much.

His last wakeful thoughts were what he wanted to tell her when he wrote to her tomorrow.

*****

The next morning after breakfast, Lucas prepared himself for the next bit of luxury that this unexpected furlough offered: his first shower in a month. Fifth Army Engineers had set up portable showers inside a long tent on the main street of the town, and the soldiers took turns going in by company.

When they entered one end of the tent, the men stripped off their filthy, and no doubt stinking uniforms, and dropped them into huge canvas bins. Next they were each handed a towel and directed toward an area behind a hanging tarp. That area was lined with two dozen nozzles spraying hot water toward a central drain.

The tingle of the hot water spray made Lucas's skin pucker with pleasure. He tipped his head back and let the water run against his face, through his beard, over his chest, and down his legs. Then he turned around and let the spray flush his short but tangled hair and heat his stiff shoulders and back.

Lucas held the bar of soap in his hand but didn't move to wash himself yet, and wondered how long he could just stand there in the hot shower before some grunt shooed him out.

Someone cleared his throat and Lucas opened eyes he didn't realized he'd closed. He caught the grunting corporal's eye and the man tilted his head as if to say, *get on with it*.

Lucas nodded and set about lathering up every square inch of his body until he thought he must look like the soap version of a snowman. He noticed by the feel of his ribs that he'd lost weight, thought that wasn't really surprising. He didn't believe his K-Rations were designed for more than survival—and some days he'd run out of those.

Lucas rinsed his hair and body thoroughly, satisfied only when his skin squeaked under his palm. Then he reluctantly grabbed his towel and began to dry off.

Padding barefoot out of the shower area with the damp towel draped around his hips, Lucas moved past the next tarp to a long

Ice and Granite: The Snow Soldiers of Riva Ridge

table set up on both sides with razors and mirrors. When he stepped to take his turn to shave and looked in the mirror, he was shocked at his appearance.

His face was thinner than he'd ever seen it before and his skin was weathered and tanned by the elements. But his eyes, rimmed with lighter skin which had been protected by his green-glassed goggles, appeared to be a brighter blue by contrast.

Lucas lathered his face—again—this time with a shaving brush, and then put a new two-sided blade in a communal razor.

He'd grown a beard twice before, when he lived rough during Homestake and the D-Series, so shaving this much hair from his face was not a completely new experience. He kept checking the mirror for stray reddish-blond hairs until he was satisfied that he hadn't missed a spot.

The final stop was an attached tent with more long tables, these stacked with clean uniforms. Lucas made his way along the piles getting a complete set of clean clothes, down to plenty of extra socks and boxers.

Now that he was rested, fed, clean, and dressed, he felt like he could conquer the world.

Smoky and Diego were waiting for him at a table outside a small café across the street and they waved him over. When he sat down Diego handed him a little glass of a reddish liquid.

"What's this?" Lucas asked as he accepted the drink.

"Cherry brandy."

Lucas cocked an eye at him. "Did you try it?"

Smoky leaned closer and spoke softly. "We had to. It's a thank-you gift from the proprietor. Because we're chasing the Krauts out, and all."

Ah.

Lucas lifted the glass to toast his friends. "Skoll!"

The three clinked glasses and Lucas tossed back the brandy. He had to restrain himself from spitting it back in the glass. His eyes watered and he clamped his jaw shut.

When he could speak again, he rasped, "That's *god-awful* stuff."

Smoky and Diego grinned at him.

"Yeah, we know," Diego said gleefully.

Smoky took the empty glass from his hand. "Come on. Let's go over to the command post and check for mail."

*****

The trio waited in a long line of First Battalion soldiers—some clean, some still waiting for their turn in the showers—who were also eager for their first mail call in two weeks. Diego got his mail first, then Smoky, and finally Lucas. The trio left the command post tent and looked for another little café where they might be able to order a beer.

"Don't give me that look," Lucas chided Smoky. "It's almost lunchtime."

The men found an establishment very eager to please, and again chose a table outside. The weather wasn't exactly warm—Lucas guessed in the fifties and breezy—but after living mostly outside since arriving in Italy nearly three months ago he'd begun to feel claustrophobic in small spaces.

Obviously Smoky and Diego felt the same way because both of them chose the outdoor table without consulting each other.

Lucas opened the letter from his parents first. In addition to general farm business and small-town gossip was the unsurprising announcement that on Valentine's Day his youngest sister Suzanne had accepted the Ag major's proposal. The wedding was set for June. Lucas sighed.

I doubt I'll be back by then.

He folded the letter and stuck it in his pocket, then turned his attention to the three letters from Parker. While he was reading the first one, Diego jumped to his feet.

Lucas and Smoky looked up at him. Diego's jaw hung slack

and his eyes rounded with apparent shock under a lowered brow.

"What's wrong?" Smoky asked.

Diego lifted wide eyes from the paper and looked at Smoky, then Lucas, then Smoky again. "It's—I—"

Lucas frowned. "What happened, Xavier?"

"It's Sofia…" his voice trailed off.

Lucas's heartbeat stuttered. "What about Sofia?"

"She's—I mean I'm—we're…" Diego held up the letter and pointed to it as if that would somehow make things clear.

"Spit it out, man!" Smoky urged.

Light dawned in Lucas's brain. "A baby?"

Diego nodded spastically. "I'm going to be a father."

Lucas and Smoky jumped up. Smoky pounded Diego on the back while a grinning Lucas shook his hand.

"That's great news, Xavier."

Smoky was beaming, too. "Congratulations!"

Diego sank back into his chair, still looking stunned. "Thanks, guys."

Lucas lifted his beer and knocked it against Diego's. "We need to celebrate."

*****

After spending four days on furlough in Montecatini where Lucas slept on cots, ate and drank in restaurants, and even went to the movies, living in foxholes in the dirt again and eating lousy food from mess kits made his furlough seem like just a dream.

The Red Cross had done a bang-up job with the servicemen's clubs in Montecatini, and the town had plenty of pretty Italian girls willing to keep the soldiers company. An Italian hotspot called Club Trianon even boasted a swing orchestra and a burlesque show, both of which were popular with the guys.

But the highlight for Lucas was the surprise visit by General

Duff, who showed up in Montecatini and presented Lieutenant James Loose with a Silver Star for his actions on top of Riva Ridge. Not only that, he also presented all thirty-nine members of his A Company platoon with Bronze Stars.

"During Operation Encore you men were isolated and outnumbered," General Duff declared. "But you held your position at Pizzo di Campiano against a formidable enemy for forty-eight hours. You deserve these stars. Wear them proudly."

Lucas did.

The Germans were unimpressed, however, and continued to launch round after round of harassing mortar fire in and around the Mount Della Spe command post, usually at supper time.

"I can't wait to get back into action," Lucas grumbled while he cleaned his rifle. "If I'm going to be miserable like this, then I want to be able to take my frustration out on the Germans."

"Same here," Smoky held up the rifle he was cleaning and sighted down the barrel of the gun. "Plus I need a few more 'Krauts killed' notches on my stock so I can impress the girls when I get back home."

Diego silently cleaned his rifle without looking up.

April 1945

To Lucas's relief, First Battalion was finally on the move again, this time heading eleven miles south in a single-day's march from Mount Della Spe to a bivouac position in the vicinity of Riola. Over the next two days they were joined there by the Second and Third Battalions. The Eighty-Sixth Regiment was whole again.

By April tenth, the Tenth Mountain Division's three regiments formed the American front line, stretching along Italy's Highway Sixty-four, the principal route from the south into the city of Bologna.

"Something big is in the works," Lucas opined at supper in the mess tent. "You see all the stuff being trucked in?"

"About damned time," Smoky grumbled and stabbed his corned beef on toast with his fork. "I came here to fight, not sit around and wait."

"I think you're right." Diego made parallel lines in his gravy with his fork. "We're pretty bulked up here."

Diego didn't just mean the countless truckloads of supplies and ammunition that had been rolling into the command post for the last week. Most of the men in the Eighty-Sixth had been asked to turn in their rifles, and were issued new Thompson submachine guns in their place—Tommy guns for short. The submachine guns had an effective range of one-hundred-and-fifty meters.

Lieutenant Loose took his platoon out to practice with their new weaponry and Lucas was impressed with both the range and the speed of the compact gun.

This sure beats the heck out of a rifle.

An announcement summoned A Company that afternoon. All hundred-and-twenty men lined up in formation while Captain Niedner stood in front of them.

"We're about to embark on Operation Craftsman," he began. "This is a concentrated offensive which will make full use of the strengths of both Fifth and Eighth Armies."

"Told you it was big," Lucas whispered to Diego.

Diego shot him a nervous glance.

"The final objective of this 'big push' is the complete destruction of the German Army in Italy, and the subsequent liberation of Italy." Captain Niedner grinned broadly. "And because of our successes in the Italian theater, the Tenth Mountain Division has been tapped to spearhead the enemy's pursuit through the Po Valley."

Lucas's pulse surged. The tough guys who trained at Camp Hale, originally unwanted and generally underappreciated by the

US Army were now the point of their spear.

They've finally figured out what we can do.

Lieutenant Loose asked the question that was on Lucas's mind, and probably everyone else's. "When does it start?"

"The day after tomorrow." Niedner grinned. "Now go get ready to fight. Dismissed."

*****

Lucas collected his mail that afternoon, making certain he would have time to answer Parker and his parents before this big push started. As usual, he read his family's letters first, saving Parker's for last.

When he read her words, he had to stop and reread them to make certain he wasn't mixing things up. He finally searched out Smoky and asked him to read the letter aloud.

"Are you sure?" Smoky asked. "I mean, is it personal stuff?"

"Yes," Lucas admitted. "But it's important enough that I want to make sure I'm reading it right."

"Okay." Smoky glanced around to make sure no one was in earshot, and then he began.

> MY DEAREST LUCAS,
>
> I HOPE YOU ARE DOING WELL. I CAN'T TELL YOU HOW MUCH I MISS YOU, AND HOW MUCH I LOVE YOU, AND HOW MUCH I THINK ABOUT YOU.
>
> I HOPE YOU MISS ME, LOVE ME, AND THINK ABOUT ME AS WELL. DO YOU? IT'S SO HARD DURING THE LONG WEEKS WHEN I DON'T HEAR FROM YOU. I CAN'T HELP WONDERING IF YOU ARE STILL

UNHARMED, AND IF YOU ARE STILL MINE.

I KNOW IT'S NOT YOUR FAULT. I UNDERSTAND THAT YOU ARE AT WAR, FIGHTING GERMANS AND LIVING ROUGH. SO PLEASE DON'T THINK THAT I AM SCOLDING YOU!

BUT YOU HAD BETTER COME HOME TO ME, LUCAS THOR HANSEN. BECAUSE I JUST TOLD A VERY NICE CAPTAIN THAT, AS MUCH AS I APPRECIATED HIS OFFER, MY HEART IS SOLDLY CLAIMED BY A PRIVATE WHO WAS BORN IN A THUNDERSTORM.

Smoky lowered the letter and looked at Lucas. "So she was approached by a captain with romantic intent and she flatly turned him down."

"But she doubts me?" Lucas pressed. "Is that what she's saying?"

"I don't think so." Smoky looked back at the hand-printed pages. "She misses you, and she worries about you."

Lucas nodded. He understood that.

He reached for the letter. "I am going to write her the mushiest love letter that has ever been written by a lonely soldier in the entire history of war. She will not have a single reason to doubt me ever again."

Smoky chuckled appreciatively. "I believe that is a sound tactic, Private. A *very* sound tactic."

*****

As prepared as Fifth and Eighth Armies were to begin the

push, the weather failed to cooperate. Mild and sunny for the last week or so, the morning of April twelfth presented the collected American Armies with darkly overcast skies and heavy ground fog, thus eliminating any possibility of Air Corps bombers being able to provide air support for the planned advance.

Hoping for an improvement in the conditions, the soldiers and flyboys waited at the ready for a change in the conditions. Late in the afternoon, however, the air attack was postponed until the next morning.

"Even if the weather does clear there aren't enough hours of daylight left to accomplish our objectives," Lucas grumbled when the men were told to stand down.

Smoky nodded his agreement. "This was a wasted day."

"An exhausting day," Diego added. "The anticipation of battle kept us all on edge the whole time."

April thirteenth wasn't better. In fact, it was worse.

Lucas huddled inside the partially destroyed house where his platoon was sheltered and watched a steady downpour drench the pockmarked landscape. Adding to the general miasma of the day was the unsettling news that President Franklin Roosevelt had died suddenly of a cerebral hemorrhage at his home in Warm Springs, Georgia.

Lucas remembered when the man was first elected in November of nineteen thirty-two. Lucas was seventeen and still too young to vote, but when he was twenty-one he did vote for Roosevelt when he ran for reelection in nineteen-thirty-six. By nineteen forty-two, however, Lucas was disillusioned by the man's apparent lack of leadership where this war was concerned.

Looking back now, and knowing what they did about the utter madman who was terrorizing and destroying Europe, Lucas wondered if the president might have made different choices about getting America involved sooner, and not wait until Pearl Harbor was bombed by the Japanese and his hand was forced by Hitler's subsequent declaration of war on the United States.

In any case, God rest his soul.

Thankfully on the morning of April fourteenth the fog finally lifted. Lucas and the others prepped and waited for a sign or a signal that something was going to happen at last.

At eight-thirty the anticipated roar and welcomed sight of the Air Corps' B-24 bombers flying overhead set Loose's platoon to cheering. Waves of Thunderbolt fighter bombers followed, setting Lucas's blood on fire.

Come on boys, get us into the fight.

For the next forty minutes Lucas heard the constant explosions of what had to be thousands upon thousands of rounds of artillery hammering the German positions ahead. Great geysers of flame and heavy black smoke rose up to two-hundred feet in the air, and even from their position over half a mile back Lucas could feel the concussions from the repeated bomb blasts.

Give the bastards hell.

Chapter Twenty

The next day, April fifteenth, dawned sunny and breezy. The Eighty-Sixth was finally directed to advance in the direction of Tolé, fourteen miles northeast of Riolo.

Their twenty-four-hour holdup before they moved was apparently caused by Regimental Commander Colonel Tomlinson insisting that their entire assembly area, plus the four miles of road from Cereglio to Tolé, be swept for mines before the attack.

Sweeping started yesterday and continued all night before the area was declared clear. In spite of Lucas and his buddies practically jumping out of their skins, anxious to enter the fray, most of them had to admit they were glad to know that they wouldn't have to worry about landmines as they advanced.

"We can concentrate on what's ahead of us, not what's below us." Diego looked decidedly relieved. "One less thing trying to kill us."

Lucas glanced at his friend, concerned. Ever since Diego received word that Sofia was expecting, his enthusiasm for fighting had dimmed. Lucas couldn't fault the man—if Parker was carrying his child he'd probably be more cautious too.

But too much caution could make a man hesitate, and hesitation in battle was often fatal.

Lucas shifted his gaze to Smoky.

Smoky's expression was somber. His eyes met Lucas and he gave a little nod.

Lucas understood that Smoky understood. It was up to the two of them to make sure that Xavier Martinez's wife did not become a widow and that his child would not grow up without a father.

Nearly three hours into their march, the Eighty-Sixth was approaching Tolé half-a-mile behind Colonel Tomlinson's forward reconnaissance squad when massive machine gun fire shattered the air in front of them.

Captain Niedner immediately ordered First Battalion to advance at double time. As they jogged forward Lucas saw two officers running back toward the Eighty-Sixth with a bleeding and stumbling Colonel Tomlinson carried between them. When they passed each other, the colonel looked bad. Really bad.

First Battalion halted when they saw the rest of Tomlinson's recon squad hunkered down under heavy fire a hundred yards ahead of them. Companies A and C moved to the right, B and D to the left.

Then they rained hell down on the Germans.

With their Tommy guns blazing and grenades launching so quickly there wasn't time to catch a breath in between, First Battalion completely obliterated the recon squad's attackers.

And when Lucas and the others walked forward through the smoking debris and destroyed bodies, collecting weapons and looking for survivors, he felt no remorse when none were found.

Serves the bastards right.

As soon as the smoke cleared and order was reestablished, the executive officer of the Eighty-Sixth Regiment, Lieutenant Colonel Robert Cook, took over as Regimental Commander in place of the severely injured and evacuated Colonel Tomlinson.

Then he led the triumphant Eighty-Sixth Regiment into Tolé.

April 16, 1945

Though the town of Tolé was secure, the mountainous hills to the south of the town were not. Long into the night German artillery high in the mountains rained down mercilessly on Tolé. And before morning, First Battalion had a plan.

"Just like Riva," Major Green told his men. "We'll circle around and climb up behind them. When the sun comes up, we'll attack."

Lucas grinned and nudged Smoky.

Smoky grinned and nudged him back, whispering, "Hell, yeah."

The mountain wasn't nearly as steep as the ridges at Riva, but the climb still wasn't easy. The moon that chilly night was no more than a sliver in the sky and offered the soldiers no help. It took the one-hundred-and-twenty-five men of First Battalion two hours to complete the circuitous route around the base of the mountain and hike up the back side.

And just as they had before, they approached the enemy in silence. Judging by the lack of fire in their direction, their presence was not detected.

Lucas, Diego, and Smoky hunkered down in the forest behind a huge felled pine tree. From their vantage point they could see flashes through the trees about a hundred yards in front of them, as the German artillery continued to fire on the town of Tolé below.

The constant noise from their blasts disguised the sound of First Battalion's approach and helped the soldiers settle in closer to the enemy's position than they expected they'd be able to. Then the men waited for the sun to lighten the sky enough to see their targets.

Impatient for the signal to fire, Lucas aimed his new Tommy gun downhill toward the dug in German unit. Birds began to chirp and sing in the forest as the clear morning sky slowly lightened, an incongruent accompaniment for the slaughter which Lucas expected was about to take place.

When Major Green finally gave the signal, a hundred-and-twenty-five weapons fired through the trees at the unsuspecting Germans. The Krauts scrambled to turn their mortars around to shoot uphill, but Lucas knew that even if they were able to do so, the ordnance would fly impotently over their heads.

Under the continued assault of First Battalion, the Germans fell just like the sitting ducks that they were. And fifteen minutes after they took the first shot, no Germans were shooting back.

The Tenth soldiers approached the bunkers slowly, watching and listening for movement or sound from the enemy. Shots echoed through the morning as German soldiers hiding in the area were killed.

This time, they didn't even bother with collecting the weapons. The Germans were clearly retreating, evident by the fact that the Americans only encountered them in defensive positions and never on the advance.

Our job is to completely eliminate the Germans from Italy. And that's what we're doing.

*****

Even though First Battalion had been up all night sneaking up on the German artillery guys, that didn't stop Major Green from marching them out of Tolé right after breakfast. Their objective was the village of Marzabotto, eight miles east of Tolé, and through the town of Bortolani.

"None of this area is secured," Major Green warned. "So clearing the hills of Germans is more important than reaching

Marzabotto today."

The terrain around Bortolani was flat, fallow farmland with hills at a distance. The men in that village told the soldiers that the Germans had been there, but that they moved on. Even so, the soldiers searched the shops, homes, barns and outbuildings in case the townspeople might be lying to them under German threats of retaliation.

Finding nothing, the battalion continued their march along the paved road which led from the flat farmland into a sunny and narrow valley. Walking openly through the valley between the mountains—some of which were still topped with snow—would put them at risk of attack. But without those possible attacks on the Americans, the soldiers couldn't know where German squads were hiding.

Major Green stopped their advance before they entered the valley and broke the battalion up by company. "A, B and C Companies move up the slopes and continue forward through the trees. Use the forest for cover, and follow the road."

The company captains nodded their response.

"Flush 'em out, men. Radio if you need help," Green continued. "D Company and I'll see you all in Marzabotto."

Captain Niedner led A Company up the slope to the right of the road that snaked through the bottom of the valley. Because they had all day to cover a mere eight miles, the men spread out in a line perpendicular to the valley and advanced through the trees slowly and silently, sweeping the area for any signs of German occupation.

Lucas walked slowly through the woods, the floor of the forest dappled in bright, moving discs as the sun shone through the breeze-fluttered leaves. He passed the ashes and blackened logs of long dead fires, caught the whiff of shallowly buried human shit, and resisted the urge to kick the discarded ration tins with German labels.

But as yet there were no actual German soldiers to be found.

When the sun was straight overhead Niedner signaled for the company to halt. Lucas sat on a tree stump and took a drink from his canteen while deciding whether or not to open a tin of his own rations. Smoky was uphill from him about five yards or so and he walked down to where Lucas was.

"What do you think?" he asked quietly. "Are there any Krauts left?"

"Yeah. Gotta be." Lucas looked up the slope. "I just hope we aren't passing them and getting ourselves pinned between units."

Smoky's gaze followed Lucas's. "It's awfully quiet. I mean, obviously they were here at one point. But I'd expect them to fire on us if they're hiding somewhere up there."

Maybe.

After half an hour Niedner gave the order to continue and A Company resumed their slow advance. When they reached the edge of the downward slope at the far side of the mountain they were traversing, they took another break. Down below, the hazy valley widened out and was populated by a cluster of typical stone walled and red tiled buildings in its center. Lucas estimated the vale only stretched maybe a mile or so before narrowing again between the next rise of mountains.

Niedner spent several minutes looking through binoculars before addressing the gathered men. When he did, he looked strangely pleased.

"The Krauts are down there." He turned to his radio man. "Alert the rest of the battalion."

Lucas asked for the binoculars and took a look for himself.

"What do you see?" Smoky asked.

"I see several men in uniform patrolling the street," Lucas reported. "There are gunners in the windows. None of them are on alert, I don't think. They look pretty relaxed."

He handed the binoculars to Smoky. "What do you think?"

Smoky peered through the implement. "I think there are mortars in the barns at both ends of the street."

Diego stepped closer. "Can I look?"

Smoky handed him the binoculars and he pressed them to his eyes. "You're right, Thunder. They look pretty relaxed right now."

Diego handed off the binoculars to another guy. "If we can sneak up on them, we can take 'em."

"And that's what we need to figure out." Niedner turned to the radio guy again. "Find out where Major Green and D Company's artillery are."

*****

In the middle of an otherwise peaceful and sunny afternoon, First Battalion's big guns came rolling down the road toward the tiny village which turned out to be called Montasico. D Company's artillery took the opening shot to draw out German firepower before the A Company soldiers approached on foot.

Their attack was not in any way stealthy as the rumbling and roaring artillery rolled quickly toward the German stronghold, stopping, firing, and rolling again.

Lucas and the rest of A Company trotted behind the earth-shaking guns vigilantly watching for individual shooters or flying hand grenades. For some reason, the Germans seemed to be holding back. The gunners in the windows up ahead weren't firing yet. And even though the men patrolling the streets had scattered, they weren't fighting back either.

The German mortars did come to life at last, but their first volleys landed behind the soldiers' position. The D Company guys aimed their mortars at the German ones and shot off with ear-splitting accuracy. The mortar on the far side of the town center exploded.

German machine gun fire suddenly opened up from the left. Lucas spun around and aimed at the open window. At the first hint of movement he fired.

That exchange seemed to awaken the other Germans.

A Company soldiers dove for cover as Germans shot from random positions and with an odd variety of weapons: machine guns, rifles, and Lugers.

From his position tucked in a deep-set doorway, Lucas heard the unmistakable clicks of empty guns from across the road.

They're running out of ammunition.

One platoon of A Company held back and captured the mortar that first shot at them, and Lucas watched the soldiers fire into the barn before lowering their weapons. They led five prisoners out of the structure and made them lie face down in the street before tying their hands.

At the other end of the street one lone German soldier, blood streaming down his face, staggered away from the exploded mortar with his hands in the air. He made it about ten yards before collapsing face down on the cobbled pavement.

Lucas took aim and fired several shots into an open doorway. No one exited that building, but three men ran out of the building next to it. One ran left in Lucas's direction, two ran to the right. Lucas shot the man heading his way. Someone else took care of the other two.

Every time Lucas thought the battle was over, some stubborn German shot off his weapon. And each time they did the American response was brutal.

It dawned in Lucas's thoughts that those soldiers were drawing fire on purpose. Rather than surrender, in their minds it was better to be killed fighting the enemy—that made the dead man a hero. Not that it would make much of a difference in the battered and defeated country that Germany was quickly becoming.

Clearly not all of the Germans had the same viewpoint, however. By the time the random shots finally stopped an hour later, thirty-one remaining and disorganized Krauts were disarmed, gathered together, and restrained.

One guy from another platoon spoke German and he grilled the prisoners about the locations of any nearby units. After an intense conversation, in which he finally pulled out his pistol and pointed it at the head of one prisoner, some of the remaining prisoners were still openly defiant.

"*Ja? Ist das was du willst?*" Is this what you want?

Without turning away from the faces of the angry Krauts the American shot the German POW through the head.

Ringing echoes of the shot reverberated against the surrounding mountains as the soldier's body crumpled to the cobbles. His blood ran between the stones in bright red rivulets.

A German with captain's insignia stepped forward. Lucas didn't know what he was saying, but if he was asked to judge, the man was speaking the truth.

The American addressed Captain Niedner. "He says they're headed toward La Palazzina, but he doesn't know how fast they're moving."

"Do you believe him?" Niedner pressed.

"I do," Lucas offered. "The fear in his eyes is real."

Niedner nodded. "Let's go then. But don't a single one of you let your guard down for a second."

With the thirty remaining prisoners in tow, A Company resumed their slow, sweeping march through the mountains bordering the road toward Marzabotto. While they found more evidence of German occupation, every site they came across had already been abandoned.

Lucas was glad that it appeared—so far—that the captain whose expression he believed was telling the truth.

A Company arrived in Marzabotto at eight-thirty that evening, exhausted both by their painstaking routes through the mountainous terrain, and from not having slept for thirty-six hours. Once the prisoners were handed over to a local jail to be held until all of First Battalion arrived, the three platoons of A Company split off from each other in search of shelter.

Lucas laid down on a pew in the unheated Catholic church, too tired to eat. His body ached with exertion and he was drained by the repeated surges of adrenaline that the last day-and-a-half's fighting had sent through his frame.

At least the pew was longer than he was tall. His last coherent thought was that he should shelter in churches from now on.

Chapter Twenty-One

April 17, 1945

There seemed to be more men in First Battalion—about five hundred—than lived in all of Marzabotto. The influx swelled the village and stretched their resources beyond what the locals could provide. But not a single one of the locals complained.

Instead, the Italians continually expressed their gratitude that the Americans were pushing out those *dannati tedeschi schifosi*—hideous damned Germans. And the Tenth soldiers were happy to not be sleeping in foxholes and to have the occasional indoor toilet at their disposal. Showers and shaving, however, would have to wait until the campaign was completed.

Food was sparse and the soldiers were careful with their personal rations, but those like Lucas who didn't smoke shared their cigarettes with the townspeople. Some soldiers even broke up their chocolate bars and gave pieces to the children who dared to approach them.

This cloudy morning, relatively rested and with a little something in their bellies, A Company marched out of

Marzabotto. They were assigned to clear and secure the mountains on the east side of the Reno River on their six-mile sweep northeast toward La Palazzina.

The Germans had blown up the only bridge across the Reno River as they stormed out of Marzabotto, so the A Company soldiers searched up and down the riverbank for a way to cross the river on foot. They found a likely spot east from the center of the village at about two hundred yards.

The water in the river was as freezing cold as the nights had been and was comprised of recently melted mountain snow and chilly spring rain. Lucas held his Tommy gun and his rucksack over his head as he waded up to his thighs through the swift downstream current and fervently wished that the sun hadn't decided to hide on this particular day.

Once on the eastern bank, the soldiers removed their olive drab pants and helped each other wring them out before putting them back on. As uncomfortable as that was, it was preferable to changing and stuffing wet clothes into their packs, making everything they owned damp.

The day's activity should warm them well enough even though the sun was hiding, and they'd all change into dry clothes later once they achieved their objective. Besides, this northern Italy weather was nothing compared to the frigid Colorado winters to which they'd become accustomed.

However the soldiers did change into dry socks before moving on. Maintaining healthy feet was critical to their ability to keep fighting. Trench foot was nothing to take lightly, so wet feet were avoided first and foremost.

"My guess is that the Krauts made a beeline for La Palazzina," Captain Niedner stated when every man in A Company was ready to march. "But we can't afford to be sloppy along the way."

Then he pointed to the hills on their right. "Same drill as yesterday. Stretch bottom to top and look for anything speaking

German."

Lieutenant Loose led his platoon toward the hills. "We'll go high up this time."

Lucas, Smoky, and Diego took the highest point. Lucas liked the feeling that no one could descend on him from higher ground, especially after personally experiencing on Riva Ridge the advantages that a small squad had when they held that position.

The men walked at a steady pace, their gazes moving back and forth in search of evidence of occupation. There was far less debris up this high than they'd found yesterday at the lower altitude. All Lucas and his buddies found today were one old fire with cigarette butts in the ashes, which truthfully could have belonged to hunters, and shell casings which they couldn't positively identify.

After a mile or so, the hill tapered back down toward the river. Rising in front of them, another two hundred yards to the north, was an imposing ridge with multiple visible ravines leading to the top.

A Company took a break, camouflaging in a grove of trees helpfully sprouting thousands of new pale-green leaves, while Captain Niedner consulted his map. "There are five ravine approaches to the ridge and a flattened top big enough for artillery. Let's radio for reinforcements."

*****

Within an hour, B and C Companies joined them. The company captains each claimed one of the five ravines to climb.

"Once the area up top is secured, we'll sweep down the remaining two ravines into the town of Panico and clear them along the way." Niedner pointed at the map. "We'll regroup right here up top, and all descend at the same time."

"Do we know if there are any German posts up there?" one of the captains asked.

Niedner shook his head. "No, I haven't received intelligence either way. But I think it's best for us to assume that they're up there."

The captain nodded. "Okay. Let's go get 'em."

The three companies of soldiers followed a dirt road from their hiding place to the ridge, using the mature trees lining the path on either side as cover. The men sprinted the last and open fifty yards to the bottom of the heavily wooded slope of the ridge.

No one fired at them.

Niedner had chosen the widest ravine—which was also the farthest east of Panico—for A Company. The combined companies stood at the opening of that ravine now. B and C Companies turned left and moved west along the bottom of the ridge toward the next two ravines.

The sides of the forested gorge were steep; Lucas estimated a forty-five degree angle. But they had to climb up the ravine that way. If they climbed up the center they'd be sitting ducks for their enemy who was quite probably defending the ridge from above.

Niedner looked resolved. "Half of you go up each side. Do your best."

The company split up with two platoons climbing the left side and one platoon climbing the right. In spite of the forest cover they would probably be able to keep an eye on each other—and if either side drew fire they could easily shoot across the gorge with the range of their Tommy guns.

The day remained gray and cloudy, but in spite of his still damp trousers Lucas was sweating. Keeping his footing on the steep slope was hard enough without struggling to be undetectable in the process.

Again the men stretched along the slope from top to bottom and moved in a line, but this time Lucas, Diego, and Smoky were in the middle. Huge outcroppings of granite, exposed by the ancient waters that created the ravines countless centuries earlier, slowed their process. Each one had to be approached with caution, as if it harbored an enemy ready to attack.

After half an hour, both groups of soldiers were nearing the top of the mountain on either side of the narrowing ravine. So far none of the men on Lucas's side had seen anything indicating Germans were present, and there had not been shots fired on either side of the gorge.

Maybe they're not up here after all.

As soon as the thought formed in his head, somewhere above him and to his left Lucas heard the swish of a mortar round sliding into a tube.

He aimed upward to his left and shot his gun into the trees above them in case he might hit someone, but mainly to warn the men on the other side of the gorge.

The *thoomp* of the launch made Lucas dive for protection under the closest granite outcropping. He counted the seconds until the expected explosion—which landed twenty five yards below him and in the center of the ravine.

Small mortars, probably sixty millimeters.

Lucas figured the round was shot from about two hundred yards away, so there had to be scouts at the top warning the artillery guys that the Americans were approaching. Lucas signaled to Smoky and Diego, and the three friends scrambled straight up toward the top edge of the ridge, following the A Company guys who were scouting the slope above them.

The first guys to see over the edge pulled back and launched grenades in a flurry of blasting aggression. Lucas stopped a little below them and threw all four of his in rapid succession, listening for their corresponding explosions.

Diego handed his grenades to Lucas. "Your aim is better than mine."

Lucas grinned and pitched Diego's four grenades with what he hoped was deadly accuracy.

Another mortar round launched, its bomb still landing in the center of the ravine but now ten yards closer to the top. The impact was terrifyingly loud and Lucas felt pressure from the blast all along his frame.

"We have to move in!" he shouted at Diego. "We have to get too close for them to use their artillery!"

As half of the A Company soldiers climbed over the upper edge of the gorge, Lucas saw the other half of their company running in their direction, scrambling down the shallow top of the narrowed ravine and then back up to join them.

Other than the mortar fire, Lucas didn't think anyone was shooting back, but now that they were on top of the ridge Lucas heard gunfire at the same distance where he believed that the mortars were set.

After Captain Niedner arrived with the second half of the company he motioned the men forward, leading the way through the flat-bottomed forest on top of the ridge and toward the sounds of battle.

*****

Lucas pressed his back against the thick trunk of a tree, wiped rain from his eyes, and reloaded his Tommy gun. In the cool late morning temperatures the low clouds couldn't hold their moisture and they were currently dumping it on top of the ridge.

At least it was raining on the Germans as well. Acting like they were impervious from their high ground position, and ready to fire on unsuspecting Americans moving through the Reno River valley below, the Krauts clearly weren't prepared for an attack from the rear—as usual.

The German artillery squad tried to pull their big guns backward to a range where they could fire at the Tenth soldiers streaming over the edges of three ravines, but the top of the ridge wasn't big enough and they continually overshot their target. So instead, they blasted a constant barrage of machine gun fire at the three quarters of First Battalion who had dared to climb up and surprise them.

That seems to be a theme for the Tenth.

Even though the battle was lopsided in the American's favor, the win wasn't easy. Lucas's thigh was gouged with a bullet and Smoky was grazed in the arm. Diego stayed on the ground, peering out from beneath his gashed helmet and firing with deadly accuracy.

Lucas swung out from behind the tree and with deafening effect emptied his Tommy gun's magazine at the helmets tucked under the sixty-millimeter mortar. When he finished, no one moved.

*****

Before noon the guys from A Company flushed five German snipers out of the soggy and mist-filled woods. Once their artillery squad was wiped out the remaining Krauts dropped their rifles and surrendered, standing still and holding their hands high in the drizzling rain. Smoky and another guy searched them for additional weapons while Lucas and Diego aimed their Tommy guns at the clearly nervous POWs.

With the prisoners restrained and in tow, A Company and B Company descended the closest of the last two ravines after being assured in English by their prisoners that no one was waiting in the village below. C Company continued over the ridge top to climb down the shortest and northernmost ravine.

Walking into the cluster of buildings optimistically labeled *Benvenuto a Panico*—Welcome to Panico—was eerie. The town apparently consisted of one main road, several shot-up buildings, and no current inhabitants.

"Take a break someplace dry and patch yourselves up," Captain Niedner told his guys. "B and C are returning to their objectives."

The soldiers broke out their first aid kits and dressed each other's wounds. Thankfully none of them was hurt badly enough to be taken off the line.

"Even if I was hurt worse, I'd still stay," Lucas said with determination. "It's going to take a hell of a lot more than a flesh wound for me to quit, I'll tell you that."

He ground his teeth when he poured the stinging antiseptic over the deep gouge in his thigh left by the bullet.

This one's definitely going to leave a scar.

He sprinkled sulfur powder on the wound, and then securely taped a couple gauze pads over it. Satisfied with the job, he helped Smoky dress the hard to reach gash in his arm.

When Lucas was done, he put the supplies back in the first aid kit. "I'm up to one Purple Heart and two Oak Clusters so far. I hope my dad's impressed."

Smoky snorted. "As long as they're not pinned to your corpse, I'm sure he'll be thrilled."

Lucas laughed. "Good point."

Since joining the Army and becoming fast friends with Smoky and Diego, Lucas had found his rest-of-his-life's team. The three men had been through hell together in their training, and now they were in the hell that their training had prepared them for.

And here in Italy the success which the Tenth Mountain Division was continually experiencing in their relentless push against the German army was showing the world that, tabs on their uniforms and white anoraks be damned, they were still elite soldiers. They had finely honed skills and indomitable fortitude, and they were a driving force to be reckoned with.

After the men put themselves back together, A Company marched around the bottom of the ridge they'd just cleared and headed a mile to the next mount. Thankfully the rain stopped, though the skies were still heavy and the ground was soaked and sodden.

Doing the same as they'd done before, A Company spread out in a line and climbed up the south side of the small wooded mountain and down the opposite side.

There were no signs of German occupation anywhere, but when they descended the north slope they were once again on the shore of the Reno River.

"Our orders are to clear this side of the river," Niedner stated. So let's follow it until we can cross into La Palazzina."

"How far is that?" Lucas asked.

"Less than two miles."

Lucas shouldered his pack. "Sounds good to me."

*****

While First Battalion's A, B, and C Companies had been scouring the surrounding hills for Germans, they could see D Company—their weapons guys—traveling right down the center of the river valley with their big guns and First Armored Division's tanks. By the time Niedner's group approached their objective in La Palazzina, the battle for that town was already raging.

Lucas heard mortars launching, tanks firing, and grenades exploding, all against the constant backdrop of automatic weapons firing on both sides. He was eager to join in the fight.

With the rest of their battalion's arrival, the battle for La Palazzina didn't last long. By late afternoon it was over, and A Company now had a total of sixty-three prisoners to turn over before First Battalion pushed into the high ground and A, B, and C Companies each established a presence on one of the three mounts surrounding the town.

Captain Niedner met with Major Green and then reported back to his guys while they changed into dry clothes and dug in for the night.

Ice and Granite: The Snow Soldiers of Riva Ridge

"The Eighty-Sixth has captured nearly four hundred prisoners," he said proudly. "What's even more important than the number, is that most of them are from the Three-Sixty-First Regiment of the Ninetieth Panzer Division." Niedner crossed his arms over his chest and looked extremely pleased. "That marks another German regiment which had been crushed by our advance."

"Hell, yeah!"

"Fuck the Krauts!"

Lucas laughed. "We'll be home by the Fourth of July."

Diego sighed and looked wistful. "Then I'd be there when the baby's born."

Smoky smiled at his friend. "We'll do our best to make that happen, brother."

Lucas patted Diego's back. "That's a promise."

Chapter Twenty-Two

April 18, 1945

The Eighty-Sixth Regimental Command Post was moving forward to Case Costa, sixty-seven miles to the north-northeast of La Palazzina.

Rather than send First Battalion forward into the German stronghold city of Bologna, General Hays ordered them to move seven miles to the west, around a ridge of mountains and through very rugged terrain, to seize the village of San Chierlo.

"Rugged terrain is what we do." Smoky observed as the battalion moved by company out of La Palazzina. "At least we have some semblance of a road to follow."

"A muddy road, after yesterday's rain." Lucas's boots were caking with mud that he tried to scrape off in nearby tufts of grass. If the surrounding terrain was more hospitable he'd walk beside the road instead of on it, but the scraped road dropped off sharply into rock-and-moss slopes which were impossible to traverse.

"Maybe we'll get to climb through the forest soon," Diego offered. "There's bound to be less mud there."

Lucas considered the steep and wooded hills around them. "I doubt there are any Krauts hiding up there. This road is barely wide enough for one automobile. It's not worth maintaining an observation post for."

Smoky chuckled. "Lucky for us they weren't expecting a battalion of mountain troops to come slogging through."

After three hours of hiking uphill, filing along the edge of ridges, and traipsing through the shade of countless trees on that damp-chilled morning, A Company gathered on top of the final mount and stared down at the San Chierlo valley.

Two or three square miles of peaceful farmland spread out on the flat ground below them. The scudding clouds overhead spotted the fields with slow-moving shadows.

Lucas was confused. "What are we supposed to attack?"

Captain Niedner shrugged. "Taking San Chierlo was our objective. So we'll go down there and set up a battalion bivouac."

"Food," Smoky said suddenly. "There's food down there in those barns."

Lucas smacked his forehead—as a farmer himself, he of all people should have thought of that first. "And it takes food to feed an army."

"It sure does." Niedner huffed a laugh. "This way we can deny our enemy while we feed ourselves."

The mood in A Company was significantly brighter now on this almost-sunny day than on the unrelentingly wet day before. Knowing that they weren't likely to encounter any Germans *and* might have a chance to eat fresh food instead of tinned had raised their combined spirits.

The soldiers climbed down the slope of the wooded mount and picked their way over low stone fences, and across fallow grain fields and sprouting grasses, until they passed a large stone church. Beyond that was a barely two-hundred-foot long cobbled street lined with six ancient two-story stone and red-roofed buildings.

"Welcome to downtown San Chierlo, men!" Diego quipped with a smirk on his face as they approached. "Don't get lost."

There were several Italians chattering in the center of the cluster of buildings. They turned as one to consider the approaching soldiers.

One well-dressed man stepped forward, his face etched with concern. *"Benvenuto all'esercito Americano."* Welcome American Army.

"Grazie," Captain Niedner replied, smiling before he used one of the sentences from their training manual. *"Ci venderai cibo?"*

Will you sell us food?

The man's expression eased. *"Sì."*

"E vino?" Niedner added.

Now the other man grinned broadly. *"Sì! Certo!"*

Captain Niedner shook the man's hand. *"Grazie!"*

Lucas could see First Battalion's B Company already setting up in the woods beyond the tiny village center. When he looked behind him he saw C Company emerging from the woods at the bottom of the mount in the same place that A Company had.

Captain Niedner turned to his men. "I'll let Battalion Command know we're all here and get our next orders. You men settle in. You can buy food and wine from this gentleman afterwards."

April 19, 1945

Having accomplished the mission of securing the peaceful little valley at San Chierlo, First Battalion had now cycled to the Eighty-Sixth Regiment's rear position, with Second and Third

Battalions at the front. This brief lull gave the Tenth's Quartermaster the opportunity to gift First Battalion with transportation.

Because the Germans were under constant and unrelenting air attack by Army Air Corps, they had no way to refuel their vehicles. The Tenth, on the other hand, had plenty of fuel trucks. So they simply claimed abandoned German trucks and jeeps, filled up their gas tanks, and used them to transport the Tenth's soldiers.

The Quartermaster was in charge of redistributing these rolling assets according to need. And it would seem that First Battalion had the need.

"We're heading into the main objective next, men. The Po Valley," Captain Niedner told the assembled A Company soldiers who huddled together for a morning briefing. "And here is why we'll need them."

The captain held up a map of Italy, fragile from its constant folding and unfolding, and swept his hand across the northern region.

"The Po Valley runs east-west here. It's four-hundred miles long and runs from the western Alps, here, to the Adriatic Sea, here. Eighteen thousand square miles in all."

Lucas let out a low whistle.

No wonder Operation Craftsman was such a big deal. The Po River Valley encompassed the majority of northern Italy.

"Here is San Chierlo." Niedner pointed to a spot on the map on the southern edge of the valley and then swung his arm away from the map and around to the northeast. "And the Po Valley is just five miles as the crow flies over those hills."

*****

In the middle of that afternoon Major Harold Green pulled all the companies of First Battalion together. The soldiers crowded into the church in San Chierlo—the largest building in that valley—until they were packed on the pews like sardines and standing two or three deep against the outer walls.

"Eighty-Sixth Regimental Orders for the next phase of the operation have arrived," he announced. "First Battalion will head northwest from here this evening and descend into the Po Valley tomorrow. At that point we'll be positioned just outside of Bologna on the city's western edge."

Lucas had a strong mental picture of Niedner's map and understood exactly what Green was talking about. After approaching from the south, First Battalion was currently circling through the mountains southwest of Bologna, both to clear them of any Germans, and assure that the combined Armies attacked from different sides of the heavily occupied city.

"Our specific task is to destroy a section of Highway Nine, completely severing the German supply route to Bologna," Green continued. "We plan to blow up the road at Martignone. Any questions?"

No one spoke up, so Major Green continued. "We march at six o'clock. Eat supper before we move. Dismissed."

He didn't have to tell Lucas twice.

Even though the eight hundred soldiers of First Battalion far outnumbered the occupants of the valley, the Italians were happy to sell the men anything they had left in their bins and larders.

"Spring's here," Lucas explained. "They'll have fresh vegetables soon, and a whole new crop of grain to store."

"Because the Germans will be long gone by then," Diego said as he worked the cork from a wine bottle. "We're seeing to that."

Smoky broke a loaf of bread and inhaled the scent, smiling like it was the first time he'd eaten in days. "I don't care if the Krauts took all their butter and cheese. This bread is heaven all by itself."

Diego poured the young red wine into their tin cups. "And

God bless them for hiding their wine."

Lucas took a drink. It was actually pretty good. He looked at the ancient buildings clustered in the little town's center. Life here was so different than Kansas that he couldn't grasp what it must be like.

"I can't imagine growing up in a house that's four or five hundred years old…"

Smoky snorted. "That's because nothing *in* America is four or five hundred years old."

"Not true." Diego wagged one finger. "Indians built pueblos and monks built missions."

Lucas frowned. "In the sixteen hundreds?"

"Yep."

Lucas was intrigued. "Are they still standing?"

Diego poured him more wine. "The missions are."

Smoky held out his cup. "I'd like to see that someday."

"Then come visit me. I'll show you." Diego filled Smoky's cup. "Both of you."

"Is Sofia in San Diego?" Lucas asked.

"No, she's in New Jersey with her family. We'll move to San Diego once I'm home." Diego tossed the empty wine bottle aside. "We'll both have the GI Bill to help out, so we should be set."

Lucas chuckled. "Would you believe our house was made from a Sears and Roebuck's kit? My dad built it himself after he came back from the First World War."

Smoky's jaw dropped. "Are you serious?"

"Yep. He got half of my grandpa's land and built it so he could marry my mom."

Diego stared at him. "He ordered a kit for a *house?* From a catalog?"

Lucas laughed at his friend's shocked reaction. "And we still use the windmill he built to pump water for the house."

"So you have indoor plumbing," Diego clarified.

"Well…" Lucas dragged out his response for effect. "The pot was in an outhouse at first, until my mom got pregnant and pitched a fit about having to traipse out there in a blizzard."

"Are you sure you aren't actually a hillbilly hick from deep in the Appalachians?" Smoky joked, his expression bright with amusement.

Lucas laughed again and good-naturedly punched his arm. "Shut up and open the other wine bottle."

*****

At six o'clock sharp First Battalion headed out, cheered on by their cluster of hosts. They walked north, climbing up and out of the valley on a narrow winding road from San Chierlo until the road t-boned into Highway Twenty-six.

From there they headed west and eventually back down, until they stopped at the swiftly flowing Samoggia River.

The two-lane road paralleling the river was already crowded with rumbling American Army vehicles. Soldiers from the Second and Third Battalions of the Eighty-Sixth Regiment, all on foot, headed northeast.

White dust from the riverbank filled the dimming evening air so thickly that it was difficult for Lucas to see. Some guys had already tied handkerchiefs around their noses and mouths to keep out the dust, so Lucas did the same.

The reassembled Eighty-Sixth Regiment guys were in good spirits, laughing and joking with each other as they marched. The long columns moved steadily forward until the convoy was called to a halt at nine o'clock near the town of Stiore, eleven miles from San Chierlo.

"Settle in for the night, men," Major Green told First Battalion. "We're at it again in the morning.

April 20, 1945

First Battalion was given their much-anticipated vehicles before moving out of Stiore. They received four transport trucks—enough to carry two companies—and four jeeps.

Lucas volunteered to drive one of the trucks. Smoky and Diego climbed in the front with him and a bunch of other guys from A Company filled the back.

After resuming their advance on that clear morning, the soldiers stopped at the top of the last ridge of the Apennine mountain range. The enormous Po Valley was laid out below them, visible through an unnerving haze of artillery smoke. Mile after mile of fertile fields stretched as far as they could see.

"Going into the Po Valley reminds me of coming down from Hale into Denver," Smoky said softly.

Diego snorted. "Yeah. Except the Rockies are *way* higher than these hills they call mountains."

By noon First Battalion had advanced thirteen miles in just five hours, completing their descent into the valley. After a break where they switched out drivers and riders, the soldiers advanced on the town of Crespellano, prepared for tough German opposition.

There was none.

Even though the town sported common signs of attack—red roofs with holes or missing tiles, chunks of plastered walls gouged out of centuries-old homes, roads pocked with mine blasts—the enemy had already moved on.

"Do you think they're guarding the highway instead?" Lucas asked his buddies.

"I would be," Smoky replied. "It's their only supply line into Bologna."

"And any army without a supply line is in deep shit." Diego checked his Tommy gun, which was still fully loaded since the soldiers hadn't seen any action in the last two days. He looked up at Lucas and winked. "Let's make sure the Germans are covered with it."

From Crespellano, First Battalion headed east to Via del Martignone, then turned north and followed that road until they reached Highway Nine. Still advancing without opposition, the soldiers took their time setting explosives along a quarter mile of the paved highway in order to completely disable it.

They also concentrated a massive ordnance on the little bridge where the highway crossed a long canal. Not only would that eliminate the ability for trucks to continue by simply driving over land, it would also disrupt the supply of water to the entire area.

By three o'clock that afternoon First Battalion retreated to a safe distance while their weapons guys detonated the bombs. Lucas watched in awe as the four hundred yards of highway erupted into a long, booming, ear-splitting and chest-thumping dirt fountain.

He put his handkerchief over his face again as the wind blew dirt and smoke toward the waiting soldiers, covering them in soil and soot. Lucas blew gritty snot on the ground and wiped his face with the handkerchief, unconcerned with the filth.

By now he knew from experience that combat was a grimy, showerless business, and that all of the soldiers were in the same condition. None of them knew when they would be able to wash or shave again. That was just part of the job for an Army at war.

The soldiers stood when the mess settled and walked forward to assess their efforts. Smoky laughed and did a little jig. Diego pumped his arm in the air.

Lucas just stood still with his fists on his hips, enormously satisfied. For four hundred yards stretching from side-to-side in front of them, only a wide jagged scar of fresh earth remained. All traces of Highway Nine were completely obliterated.

Chapter Twenty-Three

After the successful completion of their operation, Major Green marched his satisfied but exhausted battalion west a couple miles to their assigned bivouac area outside the town of Calcara. Along the way, it became obvious to Lucas by their lack of opposition that the German army was quickly retreating from the now-secured area.

As the American soldiers walked toward Calcara, German soldiers actually approached them, hands in the air, and eager to surrender. Unable to speak English, the capitulating soldiers just handed over all of their weapons and equipment without being asked, then fell into step alongside the Americans.

"What the hell?" Lucas blurted.

Major Green stopped their march when the German infantry numbers swelled to equal First Battalion's. "Do any of you speak English?"

"*Ja.* Yes." A soldier wearing artillery patches approached the major. "I do."

"Can you tell us what's going on here?"

The man looked confused. "We are surrendering."

"I *know* that," Green snorted. "But why?"

"Most of us were artillery," the German said slowly. "But when you Yanks broke into the valley our officers were caught by surprise. They told us *we* were the infantry now."

Lucas stared at Smoky and Diego. "They're running scared."

The pair nodded their silent agreement.

"But you Yanks came so fast," the German continued. "That all the officers just got in their trucks and drove away."

"They abandoned you—the foot soldiers," Green clarified.

The man appeared embarrassed by the statement. "*Ja.*"

Major Green looked over the ragged German soldiers who, in Lucas's opinion, resembled a frightened and defeated Boy Scout troop more than a fierce army. "Tell your men to drop every weapon they have right now."

He did.

A few knives were tossed on the ground, but the soldiers had already handed over their guns.

Major Green pointed south. "Now walk that way, keeping west of Bologna, until you meet up with Fifth Army. They'll know what to do with you. Do you understand?"

The German nodded. "*Ja.*"

"Good. And tell your men that I put you in charge."

The German looked relieved. "*Ja. Danke.*"

April 21, 1945

After a night of rest the Eighty-Six Regiment was on the move again. Regimental orders came down for them to advance on foot northeast beyond Modena and seize the bridge over the Panaro River at Bomporto, a brutal distance of thirty miles.

Second Battalion was given all the regimental vehicles and took the lead. The First and Third Battalion soldiers were on foot and forced to move at a rapid and exhausting pace to keep up.

The sun smiled down on the column making the foot soldiers sweat, though a welcome and accommodating breeze helped cool them off.

Today would be a beautiful day under different circumstances.

Lucas considered the Army-controlled vehicles that passed by him as well as those abandoned ones that the soldiers marched passed along the road. Together they presented an odd assortment of German personnel trucks, motorcycles, Volkswagens, buses, and kitchen trucks.

"I wish some of those guys would give us a ride," he grumbled. "My feet are killing me."

Nine hours into their march and well after dark, Regimental Command radioed Major Green and he halted First Battalion. "Regimental Command Post has moved to Bomporto. Army engineers discovered that the Germans had rigged the bridge to explode when we crossed it."

Lucas said a silent prayer of thanks that the engineers discovered the trap and no one was hurt.

"The engineers removed the dynamite charges and now we control the bridge." Green pointed to the lights of a small town about half a mile away. "That's Ravarino. We're stopping there for the night."

Lucas, Smoky, Diego, and four other guys took shelter in a barn outside of the town. Once he could finally sit still, Lucas pulled off his boots and his bloodied socks.

Smoky frowned. "That doesn't look good."

Lucas didn't think it did either.

He examined his sore feet and thankfully found only one raw spot on each heel. "It's a lot of blood, but only two blisters."

Smoky was already pawing through his pack. "Still, any wound can fester when we're living rough like this. Do you have any sulfur powder?"

"In my duffel." Lucas mentally kicked himself for leaving

the antiseptic powder behind. "But who the hell knows where *that* is now. Haven't seen it since we left Riolo a week ago."

He poured the remaining drinking water from his canteen over his dusty kerchief and cleaned as much blood from his heels as he could.

"Here." Smoky held out a tin. "Use mine."

"Thanks." Lucas sprinkled the powder on his big, broken and bloody blisters then handed the tin back to Smoky.

"Do you have tape?" Smoky asked.

"I think so." Lucas rummaged in the bottom of his pack and pulled out a small roll of white adhesive tape. "Yeah."

Lucas used his knife to cut patches of fabric from the hem of his kerchief and pressed them against the blisters. Smoky helped him cut strips of the fabric-backed tape and he secured the fabric and powder against the wounds.

"That should hold it." Lucas pulled out a clean pair of socks—his last one—and put them on. He'd leave his boots off until morning.

Then he stretched out on a hay bale, using his pack as a pillow, and slipped into an exhausted slumber.

April 22, 1945

Eighty-Sixth Regimental Command was moving again—this time northwest from Bomporto to San Pietro. First Battalion left Ravarino at dawn and hurried to catch up. They crossed the salvaged bridge at Bomporto and reached the command post two hours after setting off.

Lucas's heels ached, but when they took a break in San Pietro he took off his boots and thankfully saw no blood on his socks.

Diego sat down next to him and handed him a cup of hot black coffee. "How're you doing?"

Ice and Granite: The Snow Soldiers of Riva Ridge

"I'll live." Lucas accepted the coffee. "Thanks."

"Do you miss Parker?" he asked out of nowhere.

Diego's question twisted the dull knife of loneliness that never moved from Lucas's chest and it caused him fresh pain.

"Yeah. I do." Lucas set the coffee down and pulled one boot on so he wouldn't have to look Diego in the eye. "I bet you miss Sofia something fierce."

"You have no idea." The man sounded miserable.

"We're gonna get home before the baby comes. I'm sure of it." Lucas finished tying that boot and grabbed the other one. "Look how fast we're moving. The Krauts are on the run."

Diego nodded and stared into his canteen's coffee cup. "It's just hard. That's all."

Lucas tied his second boot without saying anything. There really wasn't anything he could say, and he was never the sort to talk just for the sake of talking.

Captain Niedner gathered A Company to give them their next objective. "First Battalion is tasked with securing the city of Concordia Sulla Secchia, seventeen miles north of here."

Lucas groaned. "Any chance of a ride, Captain?"

Niedner smiled a little. "Actually, yes. We'll be part of a convoy so you men can hitch rides anywhere you can find them."

Thank the Lord for small mercies.

"There is one word of warning, though." Niedner's smile vanished as suddenly as it had appeared. "We've been advancing so quickly that some of the German units have been abandoned by their commanding officers and left behind, like those guys who surrendered yesterday."

"So we'll do the same thing when we encounter them?" Lucas asked. "Take their weapons and aim them back toward Fifth Army?"

"Yes. Unless they shoot at us." Niedner's expression was grim. "In that case, we obliterate them."

*****

The convoy rumbled north out of San Pietro an hour later under the cover of white and gray clouds which couldn't decide whether to rain or disperse, so they did a little of both.

Lucas and his two buddies snagged a seat on the rear bumper of a confiscated German personnel carrier and held on as if their life, not just their sore feet, depended on remaining in place—though with so many vehicles and foot soldiers traveling northeast along the two-lane road the convoy wasn't moving very quickly. Falling off would have been more annoying than dangerous.

Lucas had no complaints about the pace. As long as he was able to ride instead of walk, he and his feet were happy.

The convoy had just passed a road sign that said Concordia Sulla Secchia was nine kilometers ahead—about six miles—when Lucas heard the whistle of a mortar off to his right. He grabbed Smoky's arm instinctively and leapt from the truck.

"Take cover!" he bellowed and dove off the road, rolling into the ditch that ran alongside the road. "Diego!"

Diego jumped off the bumper and scrambled toward the same ditch just as the mortar struck.

The blast landed at the rear of the convoy, about twenty-five yards behind them, hitting one jeep, and scattering the men riding in the truck following it. A second shell landed five yards closer to Lucas's position than the first one had.

The driver of the truck on which the trio had been hitching a ride gunned the engine and took off on a jarring path to safety, steering the truck off the road and onto the narrow shoulder. Other drivers followed his lead. All the vehicles in the convoy suddenly surged forward along any path available.

That left the soldiers on foot behind to fend for themselves. It was up to them to fight back.

As more German mortar shells flew, they landed in front of Lucas and the other soldiers who had abandoned their rides and

Ice and Granite: The Snow Soldiers of Riva Ridge 221

taken cover. Two trucks were hit and exploded in flames.

"What do we do?" Lucas asked.

Smoky pointed to one of the ubiquitous stone fences nearby. "Take cover over there and shoot back!"

The three friends plus four other guys all hunched behind a three-foot-tall ancient stone wall and watched two German tanks roll toward the convoy, firing as they came. The men took turns launching their supply of grenades in its path but the small ordnances had no effect on the reinforced tank.

"We should retreat with the convoy," Lucas declared. "We don't want to get caught."

The seven men crouched and ran behind the low wall until they reached a point where the mortars had not yet landed. There they vaulted over the fence and bolted across the wide grassy shoulder onto the road.

Rumbling back down the convoy toward them was a huge howitzer. The self-propelled gun was clearly intended to meet the tanks' attacks—providing it wasn't hit first.

"Form a firing line!" One of the first lieutenants from B Company waved his arms and shouted again. "Everyone! Over here!"

A staff sergeant, also from B Company, was helping to round up scattered soldiers from the First Battalion companies. Lucas, Smoky, and Diego took cover behind a destroyed personnel carrier, along with half-a-dozen other guys.

"Let 'em have it!" the first lieutenant bellowed.

A chest-pounding and ear-shattering burst of submachine gun fire erupted from the newly formed line. As always, Lucas aimed at anything that moved.

The howitzer rolled to a stop ten yards in front of the firing line and launched an attack on the German tanks. Howitzers, however, shoot upwards so their ordnance arcs toward its target—they aren't aimed in a line-of-sight manner like tanks are. Consequently the blasts were missing the defensively-moving

German tanks, in spite of the gunners launching multiple rounds.

The tanks were still firing on the scattering convoy while the German infantry blasted the Tenth soldiers. Though their numbers were smaller, the Mountain Division guys fought back valiantly and gave no ground.

Two hours after the first German attack, D Company, which had been traveling with their weapons at the front of the stretched-out convoy—expecting to encounter the enemy in front of them, not behind them—was finally able to fight their way back through the convoy to the line of battle. They quickly established their positions and set up their mortars.

Within five minutes of setting up, the guys aimed the launchers and started firing. Because the mortars were faster and easier to move and aim than mechanized guns, their attack was more effective than the howitzer's had been.

For a moment Lucas watched the three mortar teams move with impressive synchronization.

Those weapons guys sure know their stuff.

But even though American mortars were flying with deadly consistency, the German riflemen still returned heavy fire. First Battalion's machine guns answered back in unrelenting ferocity.

Lucas had emptied the rounds in his submachine gun so he crouched behind the personnel carrier to remove the empty box magazine and reload. The concussive blast from a nearby explosion knocked him off balance and he instinctively curled on his side on the ground, his heart pounding against his ribs.

A bellow of pain made him open his eyes.

Diego had been hit.

Chapter Twenty-Four

Lucas scrambled to his friend's side and immediately saw the damage. A shard of hot metal protruded from Diego's upper right chest.

Thank God it's not his heart.

Diego shouted and writhed in pain. He lifted a shaking hand toward the jagged splinter.

Lucas grabbed his hand to stop him and pulled it away. "Leave it, Xavier. Don't try to pull it out."

Lucas heard Smoky shouting repeatedly for a medic.

"Damn it hurts!" Diego groaned. His voice was gravelly and his chest heaved. "I can't breathe…"

"I think one of your lungs is punctured," Lucas said as calmly as he could. "But you're going to be fine. Try to slow down your breaths."

Diego's eyelids fluttered as he focused on Lucas. His eyes were bloodshot with pain. "Tell Sofia I love her."

"Shut up, asshole!" Lucas barked. "You're gonna be *fine!*"

Whether that was true or not, Lucas knew that was exactly what his friend needed to hear. He heard Smoky still shouting for a medic.

What's taking them so damn long?

"Just try to relax, Xavier. It'll be easier to breathe. And the medics will be here any minute." Lucas squeezed the hand he still held. "Don't even *think* about leaving Sofia alone with your son."

Diego's brow flinched. "You think it's a boy?"

"Without a doubt." Lucas forced a shaky smile. He needed to keep his friend hopeful and not let him think about dying. "You can name him Lucas. After me."

Behind him Smoky shouted, "Over here!"

Thank God.

"You realize you'll be there when he's born now, right?" Lucas tried to keep his tone positive. "With a punctured lung, they'll send you home."

Diego struggled to draw a wheezing breath. "They will?"

"Yep. And you'll get a Purple Heart medal to go with your Bronze Star." Lucas's smile was less forced now. "You're a war hero, Xavier. And I'm proud to know you."

The pair of medics arrived on a jeep. They climbed out and pushed Lucas out of the way, so he let go of Diego's hand. He was still kneeling on the ground behind the overturned personnel carrier with Smoky now kneeling beside him.

"Is he going to be okay?" Smoky ventured.

"Yeah. Sure." Lucas pulled a studdering breath. "I think so."

The two medics unrolled a stretcher and, on the count of three, shifted Diego onto it. Then each one grabbed the poles at opposite ends and together they loaded Diego onto the back of their jeep. One guy jumped into the driver's seat and the other sat in the back with Diego.

As the medics raced away with the jeep bouncing over the shell-damaged highway, Lucas couldn't help but wonder if he'd ever see his friend again. Hopefully he was right about the severity of the wound, but there was no way for him to be certain at this point.

And lots of things could still happen. Like another German attack. Or the jostling jeep ride could dislodge the cauterizing metal shard and Diego could bleed to death. Or the wound could become infected.

Lucas sighed and tried to shake those thoughts out if his head.

God be with you, brother.

*****

Captain Niedner grabbed Lucas's arm and handed him the company's radio pack. "Our radio guy's been hit—not badly, he'll be back—but right now I need you to listen to the chatter and write down what's going on."

Lucas froze. This sudden nightmare felt much worse that the battle. "I can't—I mean—what about—"

Where was Smoky?

Niedner glared at him. "That's an order, Private!"

"Y—yes, sir." Lucas accepted the pack, drowning in dread.

"Find some cover. NOW!"

Lucas turned around and spotted a ramshackle fieldstone outbuilding which still had half a roof on it. He sprinted the twenty-five yards, tucked inside, and opened the radio pack. He pulled out the radio, switched it on, then pulled out the ragged notebook and opened it to the next blank page.

How the hell am I going to do this?

The radio crackled to life with men shouting where they were, how many Germans were attacking, and with what artillery. They were talking so fast that there was no way Lucas was going to be able to write down anything they said.

He squeezed his eyes shut in frustration and broke into a panicked sweat.

Damn it.

Shit shit shit!

The voices continued. But after a couple minutes, Lucas realized he was listening. And in his mind, he knew exactly where in the area that the voices were coming from.

Draw a map.

Lucas's eyes flew open and he grabbed the pencil. He pictured the map which they had all examined during their recent briefings and began to recreate it across two pages of the notebook.

Here was the highway. There was the advancing line. Across that field was a rugged hill. Whenever a report barked through the radio, Lucas marked the unit's location on his map, and then drew the tank or mortar launcher if one was identified.

And when that unit moved, he drew an arrow to the next spot.

He concentrated on listening to the reports, keeping the various voices straight, and not bothering to answer back. His map expanded while his arrows grew in length. He risked identifying the units with numbers, knowing that in general he got those ciphers facing the right direction.

Then he drew little swastikas for the Germans, figuring no one would notice or care if he got those backwards.

Besides there's a fifty-percent chance they're facing the right way.

The Krauts' tanks kept pummeling the Americans with unrelentingly intensity for two more hours before they finally withdrew. Lucas guessed that they had run out of ammunition. That was the only reason he could come up with for them to stop battering the ragged group of stubbornly resisting Americans.

Through all of the attack and retaliation, the undamaged portion of the battalion's convoy had continued to move north with its still-functioning vehicles.

According to radio reports, which Lucas had now mapped, First Battalion was stretched in a thin line over the six miles from

Ice and Granite: The Snow Soldiers of Riva Ridge 227

the battle site to their objective in Concordia Sulla Secchia.

Captain Niedner appeared in the opening of the little shelter with—*thank, God*—the patched-up radio guy in tow. "How are we doing?"

Lucas handed Niedner the map.

The captain looked at the notebook pages and opened his mouth as if to say something, then snapped it shut.

Lucas moved out of the way and let the radioman take over. His heart thudded as he waited for a reaction—*any* kind of reaction—from their A Company captain.

Niedner finally looked at him. "This is—I've never seen—what made you do this?"

Lucas swallowed without any spit to soothe his constricted throat. "I was listening, sir, and it seemed to be most helpful to map everyone's movements as they were reported."

Niedner nodded and returned his frowning attention to the pencil-sketched map.

The radio guy completely ignored Niedner and Lucas. He squatted, dug out another notebook, and began transcribing the ongoing chatter.

Lucas nervously shifted his backpack to even out the heavy load. That movement reclaimed the captain's attention and he looked at Lucas again.

"This is brilliant."

Relief like a wave flushed through Lucas's frame. "Thank—thank you, sir."

Niedner tore the pages from the notebook, folded them in half, and handed the notebook back to the radioman.

"Let's move out, men. The Germans are retreating."

"Are we going to chase them down and take 'em?" Lucas asked, expecting the answer to be *hell yeah*.

Surprisingly Captain Niedner said no. "Fifth Army is behind us, remember. We've let them know where we were attacked and with what weaponry. They'll handle any units still fighting when they come through."

Lucas kept his disappointment to himself. "So what now?"

Niedner tilted his head to the north. "We catch up."

*****

All of the soldiers who stayed back to fight began the six-mile march under Captain Niedner's leadership. The partially-clouded sky was now hazy with the smoke of the battle. The air stunk of gunpowder, hot metal, and gasoline.

Along the way the soldiers marched past dozens of vehicles which were reduced to smoldering piles of hot, twisted metal. Thankfully they didn't come across any dead Americans. The sun was moving toward the mountains which guarded the west side of the Po valley when Lucas could thankfully see the outskirts of their target city.

"How're you doing?" Smoky asked him.

"One of my best friends has been wounded, badly, and my feet are on fire," Lucas replied. "You?"

Smoky snorted a sardonic laugh. "Same."

Lucas made a decision. "If we get a chance, I'm going to have the medics redress my blisters."

Smoky nodded. "That's a good idea. You don't want them to get infected."

When the six dozen or so stragglers entered Concordia Sulla Secchia they were informed that the bridge over the Fiume Secchia River had been partly blown up.

"The retreating Germans tried to destroy the bridge to stop our pursuit, but they were moving too fast to get the job done properly," a sergeant major from Battalion Command told Captain Niedner. "When the first part of the convoy arrived only jeeps could cross, not trucks."

"And now?" Niedner asked.

"Engineers are working on shoring the whole thing up. We

expect to be able to safely drive everything across the bridge by sundown."

"Is the town secure?" Captain Niedner pressed.

The sergeant nodded. "Quiet as a church. The townspeople said the Krauts came through last night then tried to blow up the bridge after they crossed."

"Bivouac's on the other side then?"

The sergeant shook his head. "Not quite, we're all supposed to head to Moglia and settle in there." He pointed to the northwest. "Straight up the road six miles after you cross the bridge."

"Thanks." Niedner faced the hodgepodge of Tenth Mountain soldiers who earlier had stood firm and fought valiantly together. "If jeeps can cross, so can we. Let's head out. We can cover those last six miles in just over an hour if we want to."

April 23, 1945

Yesterday First Battalion fought their way along thirteen miles to their target and then moved north six more miles to Moglia. Once they finally reached the end of their grueling march, Lucas sought out the medics.

Both of his heels were a bloody mess.

"We can take you off the line," the medic who was treating him offered. "Send you back to the field hospital."

"Nope. No way." Lucas was adamant. "I'm staying with my company. Just do what you can."

The medic cleaned the raw skin with a stinging antiseptic so strong that it made Lucas's jaw and fists clench and his eyes water. Then the medic applied sulfur powder liberally, covered the wounds with gauze, and wrapped Lucas's heels with wide adhesive tape.

"I'm going to give you a shot of penicillin, just in case." The man rummaged in a leather pack for a vial of medicine and a glass syringe. He attached a needle to the syringe and drew the thick liquid into it.

Then he grinned at Lucas. "Pull down your pants. This goes in your ass."

This morning Lucas's ass was still sore, but his feet felt immeasurably better. Thankfully today's march was a mere nine miles, from Moglia to San Benadetto on the Po River to the north, so the pace shouldn't be as grueling as yesterday's, either before or after the battle.

"Doing okay?" Smoky asked him as the company started moving.

"Considering we're hiking on sore feet across northern Italy, existing on cold canned rations, sleeping on the ground with only a blanket to keep from freezing, and under the constant threat of German attack…" Lucas chuckled. "I'd say I'm doing great!"

Smoky sighed. "You want to hear something weird?"

"Sure."

"In one way, I'm really jealous of Xavier."

Lucas shot his friend an understanding look. "Because he's going home."

Smoky's frowned. "No! I'm glad to keep fighting."

That was not the answer Lucas expected. "Then why?"

Smoky scratched his short auburn beard. "The lucky bastard will finally get a bath."

Lucas's head fell back and he roared with laughter.

*****

Two-and-a-half hours after leaving Moglia, First Battalion of the Eighty-Sixth reached San Benadetto on the south side of the Po River. Eighty-Fifth and Eighty-Seventh regiments were already there. They had established a bridgehead across the wide river which was flowing rapidly in scampering rivulets that sparkled in the sunny spring day.

The soldiers, however, were crossing the Po in vehicles referred to as DUKWs.

"We just call them *ducks* because it's easier," Captain Niedner explained. "It's actually a code. D means they were built in nineteen-forty-two. U is for utility. K means all-wheel drive, and W means there are two rear axles."

Lucas considered the odd-looking vehicle—the first one he'd seen. It was wide, square, and flat-bottomed with an upward angled front end.

"Get aboard, men."

I thought 'aboard' was for boats.

Lucas climbed up the steps in the back of the open-topped truck and sat on one of the long benches lining each side. When the center bench was also filled and the truck fully loaded, the back gate was closed and the driver started the engine.

The truck drove out of the town and headed toward the river. But instead of driving across the narrow bridge, it drove right down the riverbank and into the water.

Lucas found this mode of transportation completely odd— and fascinating.

The truck-turned-boat crossed the east-flowing Po River with relative ease. When its tires caught purchase on the opposite bank, the driver shifted gears and drove out of the water onto solid land once again.

Lucas grinned at Smoky. "That was fun."

Smoky agreed. "Can you imagine driving one of these at home? Who'd need bridges?"

Once gathered on the north side of the river, the Eighty-Sixth guys moved half-a-mile northeast from the Po to the medieval town of Governolo, with orders to set up defensive positions around its perimeter.

Like many other towns Lucas had seen in Italy, this little city consisted of three and four storied stone building with terra cotta tiled roofs, all built surrounding a central Catholic church. This town's church boasted a large dome topped with a cupola.

After A Company was settled in, Lucas asked if there was any way to find out how Diego was.

Captain Niedner radioed Division Headquarters and requested an update. It took two hours to receive the reply, which he relayed to Lucas and Smoky.

"He's not out of the woods yet, but the doctors expect him to be well enough to travel within a couple weeks."

"Is he going back to Camp Hale?" Lucas asked.

"No, he'll be given a medical discharge and sent home."

That's a relief.

Smoky thanked the captain for checking on their friend. "Sofia will be glad to have him back, that's for sure."

After Niedner left, Lucas turned to Smoky. "I could really use a hot meal. Think we can get permission to go into town?"

Chapter Twenty-Five

April 25, 1945

The next day the Eighty-Sixth Regiment received its new assignment from the Tenth Mountain Division commander.

"Tomorrow at dawn we are spearheading the drive to attack and seize Verona, thirty miles straight north of here. We'll hold the city until the rest of the division joins us," Major Green told the gathered soldiers. "The regiment is to be completely motorized, utilizing captured German vehicles."

No marching on foot.

Lucas blew a sigh of relief.

"Capturing that town will cut the major escape route for any German troops still in Italy," Green continued. "So we do expect resistance and plenty of it. Be prepared."

The next morning as A Company trucked into the ancient walled city of Verona, Lucas held his Tommy gun at the ready, tensed and listening for the whistle of a mortar round heading his way.

He heard nothing.

The convoy of trucks carrying the Eighty-Sixth guys pulled into the center of town and stopped in front of a huge Roman coliseum, glowing white in the bright sunshine. Built by slave labor in the first century, the enormous amphitheater was made out of cut limestone blocks, each one as heavy as a truck.

"Did Shakespeare mention this coliseum in *Romeo and Juliet?*" Smoky asked as his eyes scanned the impressive stone arches towering over them. "You'd think I'd remember something as impressive as this if he did."

Lucas gave him a crooked look. "I don't know. I never read it."

Smoky flashed a sheepish expression. "Sorry. I forgot."

April 26, 1945

After securing Verona without any of the expected German resistance, the three battalions of the Eighty-Sixth Regiment were each given different objectives. First Battalion was assigned to seize the town of Bussolengo, ten miles northwest of Verona and close to Lake Garda.

Major Green loaded his men onto tanks, and along with tank destroyers and artillery, First Battalion pushed into Bussolengo.

Once again, Lucas rode with his Tommy gun at the ready and listening for the whistle of a mortar round heading toward him. He half expected to ride into the city as easily as they rode into Verona, but kept reminding himself not to get complacent.

It was a good thing that he didn't, because they were only half a mile into the city when a grenade exploded twenty feet in front of the first tank.

The soldiers jumped from their vehicles and started shooting in the direction of the launched grenade. Answering fire was sporadic and Lucas had a hard time determining where it was coming from.

The gunner in the tank didn't seem to have that problem—or he was just guessing. Either way he fired on a house that did not have all of its shutters pulled closed. The shell bashed through an outer wall and exploded inside the house. Acrid smoke poured from the open windows and even from fifty yards away Lucas could smell the burning powder.

The front door of the house was flung open and five German soldiers staggered into the street. Their uniforms were scorched and smoking and they all threw their hands in the air as they coughed violently.

Lucas and Smoky approached with their guns pointed at the Germans.

"Is anyone else inside?" Smoky shouted.

One man answered in thickly accent English, "Not alive."

The Germans appeared to be unarmed. They walked slowly toward the tank.

"We capitulate. *Aufgeben*."

Lucas reached the men first. He handed Smoky his Tommy gun and pulled out his pistol. He pointed it at the first German's head while he patted the man down, looking for weapons.

He pulled a knife from a sheath strapped to the man's leg and tossed it away. Then he pushed that man toward the tanks and moved to the next one.

All the while, Smoky pointed both Tommy guns at the waiting prisoners. "Anyone speak English?"

"I do," one answered.

"Where are the others?"

The man paused and held still while Lucas searched him with the pistol pressed against his temple. When Lucas moved to the last man, he spoke again.

"There is Czech colonel in city court building," he said, his hands still in the air. "And maybe German officer in church."

Lucas nodded. "Let's go."

He and Smoky followed the prisoners to the tanks where they

were loaded into a truck to be taken back to Verona. He told Major Green what the informant said, and the major dispatched B and C Companies to capture the hiding Germans.

Soon after the colonel and his staff were captured by B Company and brought to the truck, C Company returned with a German lieutenant and two privates. The new prisoners joined the others in the truck, and four armed soldiers boarded to guard them. The driver turned the truck around and headed back where they'd come from.

Major Green looked at his watch. It was barely noon. With Bussolengo now secured and the Germans evidently in headlong flight, there was no reason to stop their momentum.

"Search the city and report back to me at the church in the center of town," he ordered. "Once we're sure all the Krauts are gone, we'll move on to our next objective, the town of Garda."

April 28, 1945

Lake Garda was the largest lake in Italy. Thirty-two miles in length and ranging from ten miles wide at its shallow southern end, to merely two miles wide in the northern part where the water was over a thousand feet deep. The town of Garda was on the southeastern shore, at the foot of the majestic Italian Alps.

Lucas hadn't realized how much he missed the mountains during the advances and battles across the enormous Po Valley until they were marching through the foothills between towering pine-covered slopes. He caught glimpses of jagged peaks between the trees and he felt like he was coming home.

That was odd and unexpected—the farms in the Po Valley were virtually indistinguishable from the fertile fields of Kansas, his real home. Except for the far off rim of hazy blue mountains surrounding the Po, of course. Kansas was all flat.

I really, really don't want to go back.

Whenever thoughts surfaced about what he would do when the war ended, Lucas tamped them down. He told himself he'd think about them when the time came. The problem was that this particular thought, once again, would not be squelched.

For the second time since deploying to Italy, Lucas found the idea of returning to work his family's farm unappealing. More than unappealing, it was repugnant. Now that he'd traveled outside of Kansas—hell, outside of the United States—he had seen too much and done too much to ever be satisfied in tiny Sabetha again.

Parker's home was in Denver, a fairly large city at the base of the beautiful and unforgiving Rocky Mountains. The answer was obvious to Lucas.

We can live in Denver.

He was certain that decision would make Parker happy. And Colorado was right next to Kansas, so his parents couldn't accuse him of moving too far away.

But what would he do for a living?

Not farming.

Thankfully that question, placated by his new decision to live in Parker's home town, allowed itself to once again be hushed for the time being.

A Company hadn't had mail call for two weeks—since the start of the relentless push north—but as soon as they did, Lucas would send Parker a letter telling her to plan on them living in Denver when they were married. And that their wedding would happen as soon as the war ended.

He'd make sure of it.

*****

From Garda, Second and Third Battalions were headed twenty-seven miles up the German-controlled road to Torbole-Nago, the last German stronghold in Italy.

The two-lane road ran snuggly along the eastern shore of Lake Garda. Above the road soared sheer cliffs, hundreds of feet high. The tallest peak, Mount Baldo, ascended directly out of the water and reached upward to seventy-three-hundred feet. So, out of necessity, the road passed through eight tunnels carved through the cliffs.

According to radioed reports, what was left of the German Army was scrambling through the Alps toward the Austrian border. The Tenth Mountain Division was in rapid pursuit. Third Battalion of the Eighty-Sixth Regiment was given the task of clearing the booby-trapped tunnels and, after a brutal and bloody day, Tunnels One, Two, Three, and Four were clear.

The Germans had blown up the road between Tunnels Four and Five but Second Battalion moved around the blockade and attacked Tunnel Five. The Germans had evidently intended to blow up Tunnel Five, but the charge exploded prematurely killing at least two dozen Krauts. But Tunnel Five was now cleared.

Against the constant backdrop of mortar explosions, grenades, and machine-gun fire, First Battalion spent the day preparing for their own assignment—one that made Lucas very glad to be in Italy. First Battalion was going to climb into the Alps above Lake Garda and traverse their way north to the town of Nago, remaining out of the German Army's sight.

When they descended into Nago, they would enter the town from the opposite side of the rest of the battalion, once again using their skills to create the element of surprise. Together the three battalions would wipe out the German's final Italian stronghold.

As soon he was informed of their task, Major Green radioed Division Headquarters for ropes, pitons, and carabiners.

"I don't believe we'll encounter snow, but if we do I doubt there will be enough this late in the spring for us to need our snow equipment," he explained during the First Battalion briefing. "We'll be traversing ridges and peaks that average five-thousand feet so expect some breathlessness at first. Any questions?"

April 29, 1945

The First Battalion mountain troopers began their climb at five o'clock the next morning, advancing by company. A Company took the initial lead with Captain Niedner in front. The pre-dawn weather was windy and chilly but the sky was clear. Lucas and Smoky fell into step side-by-side and walked in silent comradeship

The first ten miles consisted of hiking down the sides of ravines and then back up again, each time gaining altitude on the rising slopes. Lucas was out of breath, but not from the relatively low altitude.

"Down and up, down and up," he grumbled to Smoky. "Which do you think is worse: on foot or on skis?"

"Going down is worse on foot, that's for sure," Smoky replied, wiping sweat from his brow. "Going up's a coin flip."

Lucas looked up at Mount Baldo, ahead and above them, its rocky peak bathed in mid-morning light.

"I bet the going gets rougher the closer we get," Lucas opined as A Company halted and waited for B Company to pass them and take the next lead. "This is a lot like some of the ridges we've crossed in Italy before."

"Only higher," Smoky replied. "A lot higher."

True.

Once they were moving again Lucas pulled a deep breath of the thinning air. It had been so long since they had been at any significant altitude that none of the Tenth soldiers retained their once incredible ability to function on minute amounts of oxygen.

After climbing another two hours, the line of soldiers stopped moving. The reason was passed down from soldier to soldier. "Fifty-five degree shale slope ahead. The guys in front are stringing ropes."

That's a new one.

The Tenth guys at Camp Hale never encountered a shale slope, so crossing this one was going to be an adventure. A dangerous one at that.

When Lucas and Smoky reached the slippery, gray slope they saw that two climbing ropes had been stretched across the forty-yard expanse of shale. The ropes on this side and the far side were tied to the bases of sturdy pine trees, and then secured to the rock face at two points along the way with pitons and carabiners.

The men in B Company who were ahead of them were struggling to keep their footing in the gusting wind. They all crossed facing uphill and sidestepped across the fragile plates.

Lucas and Smoky pulled their newly-supplied ropes and carabiners from their rucksacks and tied the ropes around their waists with a figure eight loop at the running end. Then they each hooked two carabiners on the loop and waited for their turns to cross.

This part was easy. They'd strapped on to a guide rope a hundred times or more when climbing at Camp Hale.

While he waited, Lucas considered the lake far below. Only the width of the two-lane road separated the foot of the mountain from the deep blue water of Lake Garda.

Diego would hate this.

Lucas donned his green glasses as protection against the sun's glaring reflection off the shale. From this vantage point the men could see what was happening at the bottom of the mountains. Supplies, ammunition, and artillery were being moved north on DUKWs, in spite of the rough, wind-blown waters of Lake Garda.

German eighty-eight millimeter canons fired a constant barrage from the opposite side of the lake and their shells threw up geysers of water fifty feet high. Even this high up the canons' explosions boomed with surprising power.

Lucas felt vulnerable on the exposed slope and wondered if the Germans could see the First Battalion soldiers way up here.

"Do you think the Krauts have noticed us?" Smoky asked suddenly.

Lucas snorted "You reading my mind?"

Smoky shrugged one shoulder, his eyes still focused on the lake. "I bet their eighty-eights could shoot this far."

"Don't temp fate," Lucas warned. "We aren't even halfway to Nago yet."

Smoky stepped forward and clipped his carabiners to the fixed guide ropes. As he moved to the left toward the opposite side of the two-hundred-yard-wide slope, Lucas clipped on next.

The going was slow. Lucas's thighs burned as he kept his weight against the pull of the sling rope around his waist so his feet wouldn't slip down the steep shale and throw him on his face. He reached the first anchor and moved one of his carabiners to the other side, then the other.

He continued his painstaking path, sweat rolling down his forehead and back in spite of the buffeting wind, deliberately not thinking about what would happen if the rope came loose.

It took Lucas over half-an-hour to safely reach the other side of the slope. He said a silent prayer of thanks as he untied himself and stowed the ropes and carabiners back in his pack.

Captain Niedner waited until all of A Company completed traversing the shale pitch and then they moved on. Somewhere below, Lucas could still hear the booming blasts of German canons.

Chapter Twenty-Six

The long line of five hundred First Battalion soldiers moved steadily, inching north through the rugged Italian Alps in painstaking increments. In order to maneuver across the many steep ridges that formed the western rise of Mount Baldo, Major Green had to lead his troops in a zig-zag pattern, often going in the wrong direction for a considerable distance before being able to progress forward once again.

And all the while the sporadic sounds of fierce warfare echoed up the side of the mountain. Lucas wondered how the other two Eighty-Sixth battalions were faring in their push toward Torbole-Nago. It was impossible to be sure, but from the occasional glimpses they got through the trees it seemed that the Americans on the ground were still advancing, moving at about the same rate as their brothers up on the mountain.

According to Captain Niedner, once they moved off of Mount Baldo and onto the next, and lower, ridgeline they would be two-thirds of the way to Nago.

Lucas considered the position of the sun and figured it was about two o'clock in the afternoon. They had been hiking and

Ice and Granite: The Snow Soldiers of Riva Ridge 243

climbing for eight hours so far. Thick snow patches in shadowed dips became increasingly common as the mountain troops doggedly kept moving across the windy face of Mount Baldo.

If we're up here when the sun sets, the temperature will drop well below freezing.

It took almost two more hours to descend off Mount Baldo and scale the next ridge on a path which took the soldiers west. The sun continued its slow journey until it finally slipped behind the mountains on the opposite side of Lake Garda.

Captain Niedner called a halt. "Take a break, men. We'll descend from here."

From their high point, the mountain troopers could see the lights of Nago coming on in the shadows below them. First Battalion had been moving for fourteen straight hours and covered twenty-five miles through the rugged Alps.

"As the crow flies." Lucas was so tired he could barely stand. He lowered himself to the ground and slipped his rucksack off his aching shoulders. "At *least* thirty, the way we kept switching back."

Smoky dropped next to him. "No wonder I'm beat."

Lucas cast an evaluative glance over the rest of the men and concluded that not a single one of them was in any better shape than he was.

He shivered when a cold blast of wind ruffled the needles on the pine trees around him. "I hope we'll get off the mountain tonight. It's going to be freezing up here."

*****

The only way down the ridge and into Nago from their high position was to hike through a long, narrow pass in the rocks. Major Green didn't sugar-coat the soldiers' precarious situation.

"The enemy has multiple twenty-millimeter and self-propelled guns down there," he said slowly. "And a tank."

"It's a tight path." Smoky's tone was somber. "No place to run if the Krauts catch wind that we're here."

Lucas didn't want to think about that.

"Make a silent descent when we go," Green warned. "Be as quiet as you were when you climbed Riva Ridge, and we'll sneak up on them again."

Well after dark and by the light of the nearly full moon, the weapons guys in D Company launched a fifteen-minute artillery barrage to make sure the pass through the rocks was cleared. When they were finished, the worn and weary soldiers of First Battalion cautiously moved forward.

Company B went first, stepping carefully through the ravine single-file. A Company followed with C Company close behind them. As the column wound its way down through the rocks, Lucas heard the grinding drone of a plane approaching.

Shit.

He immediately dropped into a defensive position, curling tightly against the rock wall, and praying he wasn't about to die. A sickening realization hit him—and if he had any food in his belly he'd probably be heaving it up right now.

D Company's artillery barrage, rather than clear the pass, had actually alerted the Germans of the mountain troops' presence—and their location.

SHIT!

Overhead the German plane, backlit by silver moonlight, dipped toward the soldiers and dropped a series of eight personnel bombs on their weapons guys at the end of the column. The bombs' explosions were painfully deafening as their sharp booms were channeled through the tight rock-walled path.

The explosions were followed by a cacophony of panicked screams and shouts.

"Medic!"

"Help!"

"*Medic!*"

Lucas looked at Smoky who was crouched beside him. They were stopped only two hundred yards from their objective. Two football fields.

So close.

The men in B Company who led the column were already heading back up.

"That's it. We're done. We are in no shape to continue," their captain growled. "None of *my* guys are going to die tonight."

Smoky leaned close to Lucas and grumbled, "I can't argue with him there."

Lucas's heart clenched in his chest. From the sounds above them, their weapons company couldn't say the same. Not by a long shot.

He stood as the A Company soldiers all turned around and he followed Smoky back up the narrow cut. When they reached the point where they started, the C Company captain told them all that nine of their D Company comrades were killed by the bombs.

Nine?

Lucas felt punched in the gut. That was a fourth of the platoon. What if he lost a fourth of his buddies? What if he was one of that number who died?

God please take me home to Parker.

Alive.

There was no place to take the dead soldiers' bodies except forward and down, so the medics were wrapping them in their drab green Army blankets and winding their climbing ropes around them to keep the blankets in place.

God rest their souls.

It was nearly midnight and Lucas was so tired he was beginning to see things he didn't think were actually there. He and Smoky found a hollow and crawled into it together, laying back-to-back for warmth, and covering themselves with both of their wool blankets.

The wind blew colder.
The shells down below grew louder.
Lucas had never felt so defeated in his life.
Or scared.

April 30, 1945

Lucas opened his eyes. He knew he slept because he was awakening from a dream, but how much he actually slept during that night was debatable. As he watched the sky lighten in increments of indigo, purple, lavender, and pink he realized that something inside of him had shifted.

When he laid down last night, fresh from the horror of losing the nine men in his company, more exhausted than he ever was during the Homestake maneuvers, inexplicably colder than he felt during the D-Series test, and wondering if there was any hope of coming out of combat alive, Lucas was at the lowest point he had ever been in his entire twenty-seven years.

But this morning, he was renewed with his awakening. And he knew he had triumphed.

The farm boy from Sabetha, Kansas had learned to ski. And rock climb. And he was good at both.

He came back from both Homestake and the D-Series having successfully conquered their unsympathetic and unrelenting challenges.

He climbed Riva Ridge in silence, in the dark. And through the forty-eight subsequent hours of continuous fighting he'd helped hold off two units of their vicious enemy—and even chased one of them off the mountain.

And when it became unexpectedly necessary, he found a way around his difficulties with reading and writing to give an accurate report to his captain about the movements of the rest of their battalion.

To top it off, he had a bright, beautiful, and strong woman waiting to marry him when he returned home to her.

Because I will return home to her.

Alive.

Lucas sat up and considered the sky, now easing from orange into yellow. He was as changed as the morning sky. He felt it in his bones and in his soul.

Nothing in his life was going to be insurmountable.

Not after this.

*****

The First Battalion guys, with Company C in the lead this time and all personnel weapons at the ready, climbed back down the rocky pass and reached Nago around eleven o'clock the next morning. Looking to viciously avenge their nine fallen brothers, the First Battalion soldiers found themselves denied that opportunity.

Last night the Germans fought fanatically and bitterly for Torbole and Nago—and this morning, they appeared to be gone. As Company A moved into the eerily quiet town, a bubbling rage turned Lucas's vision red.

"If they were going to turn tail and run like fucking cowards, why didn't they just do it?" he bellowed. "Those nine guys didn't have to die up there!"

Smoky stepped in front of him and stared intensely into his eyes. "Because the Krauts are running scared, Thunder. They're scared of *us*."

Before Lucas could respond a German armored vehicle skidded around a corner and sped down the street straight at the gathered soldiers.

Lucas spun toward the vehicle and responded with a deafening burst of submachine gun fire. He was not alone. The quickly disabled car skidded to a stop, and four German officers pushed open the bullet-riddled doors. All four bolted for the nearest ditch.

Not one of them made it that far alive.

"Take that, you filthy Nazi assholes," Lucas growled. He shot another couple rounds into the bodies which lay sprawled and bleeding on the cobble-stone street. "That's for D Company."

Then he spat on them.

Captain Niedner pulled A Company back together and pointed north. "We've been assigned to clear that sector of Nago. Let's get it done."

Lucas's anger was somewhat assuaged by the satisfying attack on the German officers, so with a deep breath and determination, he and Smoky joined a couple other guys and began their methodical search through every building on the west side of their assigned street. So far either the buildings were empty, or huddled Italians met their presence with fear-widened eyes. Once the Italians recognized the American uniforms, however, their expressions universally shifted from fright to overwhelming joy.

"*Siamo salvati!*" The men jumped up and ran forward to shake the soldiers' hands. "We saved!"

The women would disappear and return with loaves of bread.

Lucas put his hands up. "No. Thank you. You eat." He motioned as he spoke, hoping someone in the family understood.

When wine came out, however, Smoky stepped up and accepted the straw-covered round-bottomed bottle.

"*Grazie! Grazie mille!*" he said, smiling broadly.

When A Company rejoined the rest of First Battalion Lucas saw several other guys carrying bread and wine. One guy had a small wheel of cheese.

"Must have hidden that from the Krauts," Lucas said to Smoky. "Lucky bastard."

Major Green stood on the steps of the city hall to address

First Battalion. "We are bivouacking here in Nago. Second Battalion is moving into Riva del Garda. Third Battalion is staying in Torbole, where the Eighty-Sixth Regimental Command Post is setting up."

Then he smiled. "Colonel Cook's command for the Eighty-Sixth is to rest for the moment. We fought some damned bloody battles in Nago, Torbole, and the Lake Garda tunnels, and by God we deserve it."

The men broke into a loud, raw-voiced cheer.

Lucas back-handed Smoky's arm. "Let's go scope out a place to sleep first off, and then open that wine. What do ya say?"

Chapter Twenty-Seven

May 1, 1945

Many of the First Battalion soldiers hung out in battered bars and war-torn restaurants with the liberated and grateful Italians well into the night. At one point yesterday afternoon, a group of men from the Italian Resistance led the American soldiers to a huge German warehouse. It was filled with gray-green turtleneck sweaters and German blankets, among other more mundane items like socks and underwear, all abandoned when the Krauts bolted.

The grateful Americans re-equipped themselves generously, making up for battle losses and gear left behind when this push began. Lucas stocked up on blankets and socks, and threw his bloodied ones in a fire.

After that, he just wanted to sleep.

This morning he sought out the office building which the medics had claimed as a hospital of sorts and asked them to tend to his blisters. While he was there, he listened to the stories the other soldiers seeking treatment were sharing with each other.

"The Italians all say that peace will happen any minute," one guy stated while a medic dressed his bullet-grazed flesh wound. "Now that the Tenth Mountain Division has made it this far north, the Germans are fleeing the country as fast as they can."

Lucas met the eye of the medic rewrapping his wounds.

The medic shrugged. "I'll believe it when I hear it on the radio for myself."

The captain from B Company burst into the building. Wide-eyed and with an expression of incredulous excitement he shouted, "Hitler's dead!"

Every soldier in the room froze and stared at him in sudden silence.

"Men! I am *serious!*" he hollered. "Division Headquarters just sent the word down."

"Who got to him?" Lucas demanded.

The captain's expression shifted to true surprise. "No one. He took cyanide and then shot himself."

"What?" Lucas blurted. "That can't be right!"

"That little shit doesn't have the balls to do that," another man growled.

"And he's too proud," another added.

The captain lifted his palms and shrugged. "It's true. They heard it on German radio broadcasts. Says he killed his supposed wife, Eva Braun, too. And their dogs."

For some reason, that last part really hit Lucas hard. "They killed their *dogs?* Only a monster would do that!"

He heard his words as they came out of his mouth and put up his hands as well. "I get it. He is—*was*—a living monster."

"The war'll have to end now, right?" ventured the medic working on the bullet wound. "I mean, their leader—their *Führer*—is dead."

"I hope so." His wounded heels now redressed, Lucas pulled on his new woolen socks. "But he has some pretty determined lieutenants who might fight to take his place and keep going."

"With what army?" the medic pressed.

Lucas flashed a crooked smile. The man made a good point. *What army indeed.*

*****

Later that morning General Hays, the Tenth Mountain Division commander, ordered the Eighty-Sixth Regiment to establish roadblocks to the north of Nago and Riva del Garda.

"He wants us to send out patrols to determine if the enemy has established any lines of resistance, or if they are still retreating," Major Green informed First Battalion. "That means Second Battalion out of Riva and us here, out of Nago."

A Company drew the short straw. They were to march along the twisting Highway Two-forty up and out of Nago and through the mountains on the village's western border. When they descended the other side they would cross farmland to the Sarca River. The main highway north, Two-forty-nine, was on the other side of the river and ran through the narrow Sarca River valley.

"And that's where we're assigned to set up the roadblock." Captain Niedner folded his well-worn map. "Total distance is easy. It's less than two miles to the river, then maybe another quarter mile or so to the objective."

The not-completely-rested and footsore A Company soldiers shouldered their packs and resignedly set out on the uphill western path.

Along the way it was obvious that the fleeing Germans had blown up anything they could in order to slow down the American's pursuit, so large portions of the road were already impassable for large vehicles.

"The Krauts built their own roadblocks," Smoky grumbled as A Company searched for a way across the Sarca River next to a crumbling bridge. "The Army doesn't need us to do it."

Ice and Granite: The Snow Soldiers of Riva Ridge 253

"Looks like we'll be wading across." Lucas grunted. "At least we all stocked up on socks."

Smoky stared at the fast-flowing pale blue water. "The good news is it's shallow."

Lucas strode forward. "Might as well get this over with."

Several A Company guys were already on their way. When Lucas waded into the water, holding his gun and rucksack over his head, he sucked a shocked breath.

Glacier water.

Damn it was cold. Lucas's legs went numb before he was halfway across the small river. Thankfully the water did not reach higher than his lower thighs. He stumbled up the opposite bank and sat on one of the many boulders lining the river. He untied his boots and pulled off the wet socks to check the bandages on his blisters.

They were secure. And the cold water felt good on his battered feet.

Lucas wrung out the wool socks and stuffed them into an outside pocket on his pack. After donning clean, dry socks, he put his boots back on and tied the wet laces.

Smoky was next to him, mimicking his actions. "Ready?"

"Yep." Lucas stood. "Let's go."

The intersection of Highways Two-forty and Two-forty-nine was about two hundred yards west of the river. A Company went north a quarter mile and established a defensible checkpoint between two stone walls that were connected by a cattle guard across the highway,

"Look sharp," Smoky warned. "Someone's approaching and he's armed."

"Looks like a German rifle, but he's in civilian clothes. Hard to know what he's about." Lucas stood next to Smoky and held his Tommy gun in front of his chest, his finger next to the trigger.

Smoky put up one hand. "*Arrestarsi!* Stop!"

The man put both hands up, holding the rifle over his head as he walked forward slowly. "I am Resistance *Italiana*. I come for help."

"Stop where you are," Lucas barked. "What sort of help?"

He stopped as ordered this time and smiled. "I am Lorenzo, from Arco. Four miles north or so. The Germans are there."

Hearing his startling claim, Captain Niedner stepped forward. "How many Germans?"

The man shrugged. "Many hundreds. They look to be making ready for to attack."

"Attack where?" Niedner prodded.

Lorenzo looked confused. "Nago, of course. They want it back."

*****

After hearing Lorenzo's story, Captain Niedner got on the radio and reported the situation to Colonel Cook at the Eighty-Sixth Regimental Command Post.

"I asked for artillery support since our weapons company was hit, and an infantry detachment because we're spread thin right now. He's sending over troops from Second Battalion in Riva del Garda immediately."

"Do you know which companies?" Lucas asked.

"H Company—their weapons guys—and F Company. They're the ones who climbed Riva Ridge with us."

Lucas grinned. That meant Franklin, Knowlton, and Seibert if they were all three still alive and unhurt.

A Company rested at the checkpoint and waited for their reinforcements. The day was thankfully mild and the sky was hazy. Lucas lay on his back in the field west of the highway, closed his eyes, and allowed himself to imagine that there were no Germans, no guns, no dead comrades.

The damp smell of rich soil filled his sinuses. He heard farm sounds all around him: roosters crowing, sheep bleating, the rumble of tractors. Crops and animals were oblivious to war, and their keepers needed to care for them no matter who was marching through their property and blowing things up.

Two hours later, F Company approached the roadblock.

"H Company's about half-an-hour behind us," F Company's Captain Carpenter told Niedner.

He wasn't the captain Lucas remembered, so he stepped off to the side to look at the rest of the company. His gaze swept over the hundred and twenty men gathered behind Carpenter in search of familiar faces.

Franklin looked back at him and smiled. Then he backhanded the arm of the man standing next to him and pointed.

Knowlton looked in Lucas's direction and grinned broadly.

Carpenter addressed his company. "Stand down. We'll wait for the other guys."

Lucas grabbed Smoky and they went to talk to Franklin and Knowlton.

The four men shook hands, then Lucas pulled a steadying breath and asked, "Seibert?"

"Alive, but badly injured," Franklin said soberly. "They sent him stateside."

"Martinez?" Knowlton countered, his brows lowered with concern.

"Same," Smoky said. "But he's got a kid on the way, so it's a blessing."

Franklin nodded. "It would be, then."

*****

H Company caught up with the rest of the guys and, after a brief break to get organized, the combined companies began their five-mile march, heading north on Highway Two-forty-nine toward the German occupied town of Arco. Lorenzo led the way, alternating between expressing giddy relief at the nearly four hundred men and their artillery that marched behind him, and somber talk about the village that was about to be devastated when the Tenth guys attacked.

As the sun set, the column halted on farmland less than a mile outside the medieval town.

"Set up the artillery," Niedner ordered. "We'll fire when ready."

H Company was at the head of the column and their mortars were now in range of the town's center. The weapons guys went to work, setting up and steadying the big guns for the attack.

A and F Companies were told to hold back until the mortar attack was finished. So Lucas and Smoky hunkered down with Franklin and Knowlton and waited.

Captains Niedner and Carpenter walked through the groups of soldiers, telling them what the plan was. "We're going to randomly fire on them all night to keep them awake and guessing. Then we'll enter the town at sunrise. So get some rest."

When the first mortar round launched, Lucas felt the concussive blast of air against his chest, and his ears began to ring.

"No sleep for us tonight, unless we dig deep foxholes in the rear and get under the sound." He looked at the other three guys. "What do you think?"

"I'm game." Franklin stood. "Let's go."

The four men moved as far back from the artillery fire as they could while still remaining in close proximity to the other soldiers. Lucas suggested they dig in behind a stone fence.

"That should help dampen the sound."

Half an hour later, the four guys crouched in a four-foot deep hole behind the ancient three-foot tall fence. Walls of fertile, pungent soil of the Sarca River valley surrounded them and mixed with the acrid smell of gunpowder from the mortars. Pale bluish light from a three-quarter moon illuminated their hidey hole between lightning-like flashes from the mortar launches.

The booming blasts of the mortar fires were still audible, but at least now the men could hold a conversation and hear each other.

"What are you guys going to do after the war?" Knowlton asked from his corner of the foxhole.

Lucas figured out long ago that the always-smiling Knowlton was an optimist. And the idea of focusing on the future was certainly preferable to ruminating over what their fate might be when the sun rose this morning.

"I'll go back to Tennessee," Smoky said slowly. "Knoxville's been my home since I was born."

"What will you do there?" Knowlton asked.

"We own a chain of hardware stores. I'll run them with my dad until he retires, then I'll take over." His voice lifted. "But I think we'll expand into ski equipment."

Franklin laughed. "Good one."

"What about you?" Lucas asked him.

"It's college for me, boys. GI Bill. I'll be the first college grad in my family." Franklin hooked a thumb at Knowlton. "This guy's already been to a fancy eastern college and skied competitively."

Knowlton waved away the comment, his hand visible but not his face. "Just two years. Then I enlisted."

Lucas's curiosity was piqued. "Where'd you go?"

"University of New Hampshire." He forestalled Lucas's next question with, "But I'm from Pennsylvania."

"Will you go back?" Lucas pressed.

"College? I don't think so."

"I meant Pennsylvania," Lucas clarified.

Knowlton paused a minute before answering. "No. I think I'll go back to Colorado instead."

Lucas's lips quirked, wondering if Knowlton had a plan he might be able to join in on. "What will you do there?"

"Ski."

Lucas blinked. "I mean, for a living."

"Ski. Train. Compete." Knowlton sounded confident. "I'll do it while I'm still young enough to be good at it."

"What about you, Thunder?" Franklin asked. "What will you do?"

Lucas sighed. "Not sure. I do know I'm not going back to Kansas. I don't think I could stand working on our farm after all I've experienced since enlisting."

"He's got a gal back home, a WAC," Smoky offered. "They're planning to get married as soon as we're back."

"She's from Denver, so I expect we'll settle there." Lucas faced Knowlton. "I don't think I could be happy if I couldn't ski again."

He nodded. "I think all us Tenth Mountain guys probably feel that way."

"But…" Lucas sighed as the weight of his reading and writing difficulties pushed him into a deeper hole than the one he was sheltering in. "I have no idea what I'll do for a living there."

"Teach skiing," Knowlton said as if this was the most normal suggestion in the world. "And who knows, maybe you can compete now and then."

Lucas didn't know which suggestion to respond to first. "I—well, I never skied before. Not until I enlisted."

"But you're damned good at it," Franklin stated. "And with your experience, you surely could teach anyone *else* to ski."

Lucas was stunned. "Where?"

Knowlton laughed. "There are ski slopes all over Colorado."

"And with all those Tenth Mountain films and newsreels being shown across the country," Smoky added. "A lot of people are going to want to try it."

"I was a ski instructor before the war. At Sugar Bowl in California."

That was the second time someone mentioned skiing at Sugar

Bowl in California. Lucas made a mental note to tell Xavier while he stared pensively at Franklin. "Do you really think I could make money doing that?"

"Not a lot at first," he admitted. "But with twelve thousand guys who skied at Hale, there are bound to be *some* customers."

"And I'll be there, remember." Again Knowlton sounded confident. "Maybe we can start a ski school together."

Lucas sat silently, working through the startling possibility. Teaching skiing would make use of his strongest asset—his physical prowess—and require minimal amounts of reading and writing in the process.

"Parker could do the paperwork…" he murmured.

"Yes, she could." Smoky knew Lucas well enough to understand what path his thoughts had followed to that particular point. "I think you should seriously consider doing this."

A loud boom from a mortar launch punctuated the idea and brought Lucas's mind back to the foxhole.

"I will. But *before* any of that…" He pulled a deep breath and flashed a wry smile that he wasn't sure any of the guys could see. "We have to annihilate the Germans and get the hell home."

Chapter Twenty-Eight

May 2, 1945

The next morning, as the sun lightened the sky behind the mountains on the east side of the Sarca River valley, the combined companies moved into Arco.

A single tank with half the weapons guys from H Company led the way, followed by the A and F Company soldiers on foot. All of them were armed with their Tommy submachine guns and pockets of grenades. The rest of H Company followed behind them with their artillery, and was prepared to launch the mortars again if needed.

Damage from the night-long random mortar attacks was clear. Fresh potholes in the cobbled streets, smoking timbers in burned-out houses, and innumerable shattered clay tiles which littered the streets proved the ferocity of their bombardment.

The only thing missing, once again, was the Germans.

"Gone," one man said when Lorenzo asked. "In the night. Gone."

Lucas rolled his eyes and looked at Smoky. "Why don't they

just surrender? It'd be easier on all of us."

Smoky agreed and scratched his red beard. "And maybe then we could get a shower and sleep in a bed for once."

Captain Niedner looked at Captain Carpenter. "Let's radio Division Command. See what they want us to do next."

The answer was to comb the surrounding area for enclaves of hidden German soldiers.

"If we don't find any, then F Company is heading to Tenno, two miles due west over that mountain ridge," Niedner told the A Company guys. "And we are staying in Arco for the moment."

Lucas was fine with staying put. He and Smoky spent the next five hours walking through the countryside with Lieutenant Loose and their platoon, poking guns into every hole, opening every outbuilding door, and interrogating every farmer's family.

If there were any Germans left in the area, they were already ghosts.

The search platoons from both companies reconvened in the center of Arco in the middle of the afternoon. Captain Niedner radioed Division Command and reported their mission accomplished and the territory secured. F Company was told to move on to their next objective.

Niedner shook Carpenter's hand. "Thanks for the back-up."

Carpenter huffed a laugh. "Hopefully we'll find that the Germans have cleared out of Tenno, too."

Knowlton searched out Lucas. "If I don't see you when we ship out, look me up in Colorado after."

Lucas nodded. "I will."

"Be sure that you do." Knowlton grinned. "I really look forward to skiing with you."

The men shook hands before Knowlton trotted off after his departing company.

Please keep him safe, and get him home safe, Lucas prayed silently as he watched the big affable man depart.

And me, too.

*****

Late that afternoon, all of the church bells of Arco started ringing for no reason that Lucas could think of. The clanging sound of brass came from every direction and was accompanied by undecipherable commotion and lots and lots of Italian yelling.

"What's going on?" Lucas bellowed. "Are we being attacked?"

Smoky held his Tommy gun close to his chest while his gaze swept up and down the empty street that he and Lucas were patrolling.

"I don't know!" he shouted back. "What do we do?"

"Listen for bombs." Luke checked the magazine in his own gun. "And be ready to take cover!"

Minutes of rapidly increasing chaos ticked by. Whatever was causing the uproar was definitely moving closer to Lucas and Smoky.

A few brave Italian men cautiously came out of the buildings on the quiet street, looking up and down its length for an explanation of the noise. They appeared as confused as Lucas felt.

As the cacophony of bells, sirens, and now gunshots filled the air, Lorenzo rounded the corner at the end of the street and ran straight toward them.

Lucas pointed his gun at the armed man.

Just in case.

"My friends!" Lorenzo's face split into the widest grin Lucas could imagine. "It is over!"

"What's over?" Smoky shouted back. His gun was also trained on Lorenzo's chest.

"Our war!" Lorenzo slowed to a panting stop about five yards in front of the two American soldiers. He raised his rifle over his head with one hand. "We intercepted British broadcast! German armies in Italy have surrendered unconditionally!"

Ice and Granite: The Snow Soldiers of Riva Ridge

Lucas looked at Smoky.

Smoky looked at Lucas. "Do you think it's true?"

"Yes!" Lorenzo exclaimed. "It's true!"

A dozen more Italians came out into the street. One portly middle-aged man strode over to Lorenzo and addressed him in urgent Italian.

Lorenzo grabbed the man's arms. "*Sì! Si è vero!*"

The man whooped and threw his hat in the air. Then his attention shifted to Lucas and Smoky. Disregarding their weapons he walked right up to them.

"*Grazie! Grazie mille!*" He gripped Lucas's shoulders and pulled him forward, planting a solid kiss on each of Lucas's bearded cheeks.

Lucas leapt backwards, stunned into silence, while Smoky received the same sentiment. Neither one of them recovered quickly enough to respond before the grateful man picked up his hat and ran back down the street, cheering like a madman.

*****

At seven o'clock that evening the official announcement came down from Fifth Army Headquarters that the war in Italy was, indeed, finished.

"There's to be no further firing of any weapons except in defense against an attack." Captain Niedner gave every man in the assembled company a stern look. "And especially not in any kind of celebration. I can *not* make that more clear."

"What are our orders, sir?" Smoky asked for all of them.

"We'll maintain patrols to keep a lid on the celebrations in town. When it's your shift, show up sober. That's a *direct* order," he replied sternly. "It would be a shame to arrest or court-martial any of you at this late date."

Lucas raised his hand.

"Thunder?"

"I'd like to volunteer for the first shift sir."

"Me, too!" Smoky barked.

Niedner nodded. "Fine. The rest of you check in with Staff Sergeant Howard for your shift assignments. Dismissed."

Lucas and Smoky, along with four other quick-thinking soldiers, shouldered their weapons and decided which of the three pairs would patrol which sections of the village for the next two hours.

Lucas and Smoky set off in the direction of their assigned sector while the church bells in Arco continued to ring wildly. Blackout regulations had apparently disappeared along with the enemy, so for the first time in five years the residents of Arco threw open their windows to the mild spring evening. Lamps and candles blazed inside, and flares lit up the darkness outside.

Bars, no matter their condition, opened on every street. Wine and liquor—which the Italians openly bragged they'd kept deep in hiding throughout the German occupation—was brought out and served to the American soldiers for free. Lucas and Smoky politely declined offer after offer, each time pointing to their watches and indicating the ten o'clock position.

"You come back!" the proprietors urged. "*Sì?*"

The two men smiled. "*Sì!*"

"We fought the war for four months," Lucas observed. "They fought for over five years. No wonder they're celebrating the end of it with so much passion."

"Their war is over, but ours isn't." Smoky poked his gun into a dark entryway, scaring a young couple out of it. The girl buttoned her blouse as they hurried away from the soldiers.

Lucas watched them depart, envious and wishing he could share this moment with Parker. "Hitler is dead, and the Germans surrendered in Italy—"

"And possibly Austria," Smoky interjected. "I heard that rumor just before we went on duty."

Lucas felt a surge of optimism. "Then they're done. It's just a

Ice and Granite: The Snow Soldiers of Riva Ridge

matter of time. In a couple weeks this should all be finished."

Smoky grunted. "Don't forget we still have the Japs to contend with."

Lucas hadn't considered that unpleasant possibility. "They wouldn't send a Mountain Division to the south Pacific. Would they?"

Smoky shrugged. "They tried to send us to Louisiana, remember?"

He did.

Damn.

The Italians continued their exuberant revelry far into the night without any sign of slowing down. They sang in raucous and spontaneous groups outside of bars and restaurants, they danced in the streets to accordion and fiddle music, and they kissed each other with happy abandon.

Smoky looked at his watch. "Time to head back. Our shift's almost over." He turned his attention to Lucas and smiled mischievously. "Now it's our turn to celebrate."

May 3, 1945

In the late morning following the German surrender, the village of Arco was beginning to show signs of life once again. Their night-long party hadn't slowed until the first streaks of dawn shot over the mountains and the townspeople finally began to wander home.

The streets in the center of town were littered with empty bottles and confetti made from torn-up newspapers. Brass shells from innumerable victory shots gleamed in the sun from between the streets' cobbles. A few hardy souls sat outside cafés, some drinking 'the hair of the dog' while others fortified with strong black coffee.

Lucas and Smoky had enjoyed the Italians' hospitality for a

few hours last night after their patrol ended, staying out until about one in the morning. That was when the activities of the last four days hit Lucas like a cannonball.

"I have to go to bed," he told Smoky. "I can hardly stay on my feet."

Smoky's eyes were slightly unfocused. "Yeah. Me, too."

The men made their way to the church where they were billeting and Lucas stretched out on a pew.

He slept for ten straight hours.

Chapter Twenty-Nine

May 4, 1945

After the surrender of the German armies, it was the American soldiers' job to round up any Krauts still in northern Italy and confiscate their equipment. And—the weapons of the Italian Resistance. The last thing any of them needed was Partisans looking to take revenge on random Germans for their years of abuse and mistreatment.

Surrender was admitting defeat. That was the most retribution the Partisans were entitled to.

Major Green was ordered to send a detachment from First Battalion to occupy the town of Rovereto, and clean up the two German battalions waiting there. Because Arco was secured, he decided to send A Company.

Rovereto was fifteen miles south and east of Arco, and this time the tired soldiers would be riding, not marching.

"Thank God," Lucas said as the men climbed into the back of the personnel truck. "I think my blisters are just about healed up and I want them to stay that way."

Once the truck rumbled to life and drove out of Arco, one of the soldiers at the back asked if any of the guys knew where the Tenth soldiers would be headed next.

"I heard Camp Carson," another said.

Lucas was puzzled. "Why Carson? Why not Hale?"

"A guy from F Company told me they're dismantling it."

Lucas looked at Smoky. "How do you dismantle an entire camp built for twelve thousand men?"

He shrugged. "Beats me."

"You ship everyone out," the first guy said. "Then you move anything that *can* be moved to someplace else."

"And you tear down what's left. That's why they're sending us to Carson."

Lucas felt an unexpected shard of grief pierce his chest. Camp Hale was where his life took so many new and irrevocable turns. He learned to ski and to rock climb there. He learned to fight Germans there. He met Parker Williams and fell in love there.

Sure, life was hard there as well. Nothing about the two years he trained at Hale was easy. Completing maneuvers while freezing his ass off at thirteen thousand feet, and living for unbroken weeks in eight feet of snow, was extraordinarily demanding. But it made a man out of him, and every other soldier riding in this truck.

"We wouldn't be who we are if it wasn't for Hale," he said sadly. "If it's gone, how will anyone know about us?"

No one answered him.

*****

Company A arrived in Rovereto mid-morning. One platoon was assigned to set up roadblocks on all six roads leading in and out of the town and to disarm the Partisans. The other two platoons were each assigned to disarm one of the German

Battalions.

Lucas and the rest followed Lieutenant Loose through the streets to the school where the Germans were gathered. The enemy soldiers had already divided themselves up by the German Army's levels of command.

"We'll start with the highest ranking officers and have them order their men forward," Loose explained. "They're humiliated by their defeat and surrender—which they might not all agree with—so it saves a little face for them. As long as they cooperate, we don't engage."

"And if they don't cooperate?" one man asked.

"You pull your weapon." Loose's expression grew stern. "And be prepared to use it."

May 7, 1945

Two days after disarming the German battalions in Rovereto, Company A was on the move again—this time to the German-held city of Trento, fifteen miles straight north on the badly damaged Highway E-Forty-Five. Their assignments yesterday were the same as in Rovereto: establish roadblocks, and then disarm both Italian Partisans and German officers and soldiers.

No one resisted and they accomplished the task quickly.

At loose ends on this early afternoon, Lucas picked through a pile of confiscated German Lugers. "How many should I take, do you think?"

Smoky dropped three in his pack. "I'm taking one for me, one for my dad, and one for my brother."

"Next month I'll have another brother-in-law," Lucas said as he chose four of the German handguns that looked to be in pretty good shape. "So me, Dad, and my two sisters' husbands. That ought to do it."

Lucas and Smoky returned to their bivouac area with their

souvenirs. When they got there, they saw that all the company officers were crowded into the A Company command tent. A growing group of soldiers and non-commissioned officers stood outside a short distance away.

"Something's happened." Smoky's tone was somber. "Let's see if those guys know what's going on."

Lucas walked up to the closest man and asked, "What's happening?"

He frowned a little but kept his eyes fixed on the tent. "We're not sure. And no one wants to guess."

The gathering soldiers stood quietly, waiting to find out what was transpiring, and how they were going to be impacted by whatever held the officers' attention so intently.

Lucas could see the radio man in the center of the group writing furiously and nodding as he did so. Then he quietly read back what he'd written down. When he finished, the officers smiled.

The radio man handed Captain Niedner the paper he'd written on. Niedner walked out from under the tarp and faced the assembled company.

"Gentlemen, I have news." He then read from the paper, "General Alfred Jodl, representing the German High Command, just signed the unconditional surrender of all German forces—"

A roar that was far louder than Lucas thought four dozen men could make erupted from the ecstatic soldiers and interrupted the captain's announcement.

Niedner held up one hand. "Wait! There's more!"

He waited until the soldiers quieted and then continued reading. "—signed the unconditional surrender of all German forces east and west, at General Eisenhower's headquarters in Reims, France."

Another round of whooping cheers broke out as the men pounded each other on the back. Lucas noticed that Captain Niedner was still holding the paper and hadn't moved.

"Hold on guys!" he shouted. "I don't think the captain's finished!"

Niedner smiled his thanks to Lucas and waited again until he had his men's attention. "General Jodl also signed three additional surrender documents, one for Great Britain, one for Russia, and one for France."

Niedner's hands fell and he grinned like a hyena at the assembled company. "Gentlemen, the war in Europe officially ends at one minute past midnight tonight!"

August 7, 1945

The Eighty-Sixth Regiment was stationed in eastern Italy along the borders of Yugoslavia and Austria as a peace-keeping force while all of the Tenth Mountain Division soldiers waited impatiently to be sent back home.

Finally, in mid-July, the entire regiment was trucked back across northern Italy to the western port city of Livorno—the same place where their Italian deployment began. They disembarked at that very same dock on Christmas Eve, almost eight months ago.

The regiment set sail on July twenty-sixth, and today the *SS Westbrook Victory* was arriving at Newport News, Virginia. Three months to the day after the war in Europe ended.

Once they stepped off their ships, the Tenth Mountain Division soldiers all were given a thirty-day furlough before they needed to report to Camp Carson in Colorado.

Lucas figured that thirty days was enough time to get married if he set his mind to it. His first stop once he was off the ship would be Camp Crowder in Missouri.

Chapter Thirty

August 8, 1945

Today was another miserably hot and humid day at Camp Crowder. Missouri summers were a force to be reckoned with on a sunny day, but on this oppressive and breezeless day, overcast with clouds that stubbornly refused to rain, Parker was melting.

The fan in the censor's office did little more than push the heavy air toward her and the other WACs, making straight hair frizz and curled hair hang limp. Parker pulled the front of her blouse away from her chest and fanned it in and out, trying to cool herself off.

It didn't work.

She pushed herself away from her table and the small stack of letters yet to be read. "I'm going to go wash my face with cold water," she told Emily. "Do you want to come along?"

"Sure." Emily set down the letter she was reading. "Let me grab my comb."

Parker waited for her friend. She was not in any hurry. Their workload here had been much lighter than when they were stationed at Camp Hale along with twelve thousand soldiers. Since Germany's unconditional surrender back in May, the letters they were reading and redacting now mainly were concerned with the war with Japan.

Even adding in the guys trickling back from Europe, there were far fewer letters overall. Parker preferred to assume that was because the men had been discharged and were back at home now. Not because a large number of them had died.

I wonder when we'll be discharged.

"Not until the war in Japan is over, that's for sure," Emily stated when Parker asked.

Parker sighed. "I wonder how much longer that will be."

Emily's eyes twinkled impishly. "Hard to say."

That was odd.

Emily looked up and down the empty hallway to the ladies room, and then whispered, "Have you read anything interesting about the atomic bombs that were dropped on Hiroshima and Nagasaki three days ago?"

As censors it was the WACs job to make certain no sensitive war information was broadcast outside the Army. But first they had to read that information to judge it.

Parker watched Emily lift her hair off her neck, thin tendrils clinging damply to her skin, and was glad she chose to keep hers short. "Not really. Just that everyone hopes Japan will surrender because of them."

"Same here." Emily looked meaningfully at Parker. "It can't be long now."

"Just because they surrender, doesn't mean the guys will all come home right away." Parker cleared the lump from her throat. "People don't realize that."

She wondered again when she would hear from Lucas. His last letter was sent almost a month ago, and that worried her. Parker knew there weren't any actual battles being fought in

Italy, but there were border skirmishes between the Yugoslavians and the Italians. Lucas's regiment was responsible for stopping them.

What if he got shot? How would she know? Surely his mom would tell her. Even though Parker never said she and Lucas were engaged, his mother saw the family ring on Parker's finger. She had to have figured it out.

Emily opened the door to the ladies' bathroom. "Maybe we'll hear something about it today…"

Parker was more grateful than she could express that Emily was walking this path with her. Letters from either Lucas or David were comforting to both women, because it meant that both men were still alive and unhurt.

"It's been nearly a month since Lucas wrote," Parker lamented as she walked into one of the stalls. "I just want to know what's going on."

Hearing from Sofia that Xavier was injured and was sent home shook Parker's core. With that news, the war and its imminent dangers suddenly intersected with her life in a personal and terrifying way. Even knowing Xavier was recovered and enjoying his new fatherhood didn't ease the sting.

After Parker washed her face with cold water and patted it dry with the rough paper towels that the ladies lounge was supplied with, she leaned on the white porcelain sink and considered her reflection in the mirror. She didn't mess with make-up here at Camp Crowder, just a touch of lipstick occasionally, depending on her mood. Why bother? It would just melt off in the daily heat and humidity.

Besides, the man she loved and planned to marry was on another continent. Parker straightened and waited while Emily combed and patted her sagging blonde bob. She sighed and made a face in the mirror.

"I should just cut it all off like yours," she grumbled.

Parker had heard that sentiment more times than she could

count. "Then do it," was her normal response.

Emily's eyes met Parker's in the mirror. "You look cute because your hair is dark."

"And you're afraid you'd look bald. I know."

Emily stuck her comb in her pocket. "We won't be here for long. This too shall pass, I suppose."

The women left the stuffy restroom and walked back to the censors' office. Parker hoped Emily's words proved true. She loved the weather in Denver, even if did occasionally snow in May. That wasn't a big deal. The late snow always melted as soon as the sun came back out.

Parker missed Colorado. She was surprised and glad when Lucas wrote to her that he wanted to live in Denver after they were married. She had been trying to imagine herself living in Sabetha, Kansas on the Hansen family farm, but the prospect wasn't very appealing.

Denver was a great choice, and Lucas could continue skiing. Maybe even teach skiing if things with that soldier he met—Knowlton?—ended up working out.

And of course, having Parker stay in Denver would make her parents very happy.

After she told them that she was engaged, of course.

*****

The hands on the clock had to be stuck. The last time Parker checked it was four-fifteen. Now it was only four-twenty. The clouds outside the opened window had darkened and lowered, but still held back the relief that she and the other women in the censors' office so desperately waited for.

Parker rested her chin in her hand and drummed her fingernails on the tabletop. She finished her stack of letters a quarter hour ago and had nothing to do.

Maybe the captain will let us go early.

The door to the censor's office was open in the hopes of catching a cross breeze, so she wasn't aware anyone had entered the room until a man cleared his throat.

Parker looked sideways out of curiosity. With a startled gasp she whirled to face their visitor.

Her heart lurched.

Her eyes widened.

Lucas?

He smiled shyly. "Hello, Parker."

The battle-clad soldier who greeted her was very different from the one who left her almost eight months ago. There were no traces of boyhood left on this man, only a hard-planed and clean shaven face under buzzed blond hair, and a taller-than-she-remembered frame that had grown even more lean and muscular.

Parker rose on shaking legs. "Is it really you?"

He nodded, looking as though he might cry. Then he opened his arms.

With a rough sob, she launched herself into his embrace.

August 9, 1945

Parker immediately asked for—and received—seven days of leave.

"Of course you can't stay in my barracks past curfew, so…" Parker paused and drummed up the courage to make a rather outrageous suggestion. "How about if you check into a hotel and then we spend our time catching up there for as long as we want?"

Lucas's brows lifted. "Just… talking?"

"Yes." Parker's stern tone softened. "Well. There will probably be some kissing involved."

Lucas laughed. "Yes, ma'am. Consider it done."

After staying up all night in the little hotel room leaning

against the double headboard, fully dressed, and talking, Parker was more in love with Lucas than she was when he left Camp Hale over a year ago. He shared his heart with her that night, telling her about all of the battles he was in, the horrors he had seen, and admitting to her about the men he knew he had killed.

"It's war, Lucas," she said softly and wiped away the tears his own anguish prompted. "And it's over."

"Is it?" His face twisted. "There is still a possibility that we'll be sent to the Pacific Theater from Camp Carson."

Parker refused to think about that. "If that happens, we'll deal with it. For now, we're finally together and I don't want anything depressing to ruin what little time we have."

Lucas pulled her into his arms and kissed her deeply then, and for a very long time.

When the sun lightened the curtains in the hotel room, Parker left Lucas to make his way to the bus station and secure their tickets. She hurried back to her barracks and packed a week's worth of clothes in her duffle bag before she met Lucas at the bus station.

"Are you ready for this?" he asked, grinning.

"More than you're ready for Denver, I'll wager. At least I've met your family already." Parker handed over her duffle. "Let's go, soldier."

Lucas hefted both of their duffle bags. "Yes, ma'am."

August 13, 1945

Lucas and Parker spent two boisterous days with his enlarged family before taking an overnight train to Denver to spend time with her parents.

"I only have three days of leave left," Parker moaned as the train pulled into Denver Union Station. "I hope we can get our wedding plans started."

"First things first," Lucas cautioned. "I need to ask your father for his blessing."

Parker's gut clenched. She hadn't told Lucas that her parents had no idea Parker and he were engaged.

I suppose that will *help soften the news...*

"Whatever he says, though, I want you to know that I'm still marrying you," she stated firmly. "And the sooner the better as far as I'm concerned."

Lucas gave her a thoughtful look, but said nothing.

Parker had called home from Lucas's house—reversing the charges, of course—to let her parents know she was coming home on a short leave and bringing a guest. As the train squealed to a stop in the Denver Union train station, she could see her dad waiting on the platform, his eyes scanning the windows presumably for her.

Here we go.

Parker climbed down the train car steps first with Lucas right behind her carrying both of their Army duffle bags. She reached back for his arm and pulled him toward her father.

Her father's brow lifted in surprise.

Before he could speak, Parker said, "Dad, this is Lucas Hansen. He was at Camp Hale with me."

Lucas dropped one of the bags on the train platform and held out his hand. "It's a pleasure to meet you, sir."

A clearly confused Fred Williams shook it but he spoke to his daughter. "I thought—but—is *this* your guest?"

Parker opened her mouth to explain, but Lucas cut her off.

"Yes sir." Lucas flashed an engaging smile that made Parker's knees go weak. "And before we go any further, sir, I've come to ask for your blessing. I plan to marry your daughter."

Parker's jaw fell momentarily slack. "Lucas!"

He looked down at her, his blue eyes twinkling. "As you said, we only have three days."

August 15, 1945

Lucas and Parker both wore their uniforms to the church for their early afternoon wedding. After Lucas shocked her—and her parents—by immediately asking for their blessing, neither she nor he could think of a reason to postpone their wedding any longer.

"Mom, you can throw a big reception when we're both discharged," Parker suggested yesterday as she grabbed the keys to the family car. She and Lucas were headed to the courthouse to get their wedding license. "Just call Pastor McKinley and see when he'll have time to perform the ceremony tomorrow."

"What if he doesn't have time tomorrow?"

Mom was clearly stalling.

Parker flashed an unconcerned smile. "Then we'll get married at the courthouse instead."

That had done the trick.

And in the last twenty-four hours her mom managed to put together flowers, a cake, a photographer, and a small group of guests, plus some things old, new, borrowed, and blue.

Now Lucas waited at the altar while the church organist began the traditional *Wedding March*. The church secretary opened the doors from the narthex with a dramatic flourish, and Parker started down the aisle flanked by both of her parents. Lucas beamed at her from the front of the church.

Parker smiled back and her tummy fluttered in a very pleasant way.

Damn, but he's handsome.

When Pastor McKinley asked who gave this woman, Fred Williams answered a little too loudly, "I do."

Then he took his wife's elbow and the pair settled in the front left pew.

Parker and Lucas stood side-by-side in front of Pastor McKinley and repeated their vows. Parker stumbled over hers out of nerves, but Lucas said his flawlessly, making Parker wonder if he had practiced.

Maybe I should have.

When the pastor declared the couple man and wife and told Lucas he could kiss his bride, he made such good work of it that Parker nearly swooned.

*****

Back at the Williams house, the newly wedded pair only had two hours before they needed to head to the train station.

"A honeymoon on a train," Parker's mother grumbled as she packed up food for the couple's overnight journey to Kansas City. "Whoever heard of such nonsense."

Parker swiped her finger through a pink frosting rose on their white wedding cake causing her mother to smack the back of her daughter's hand.

"Stop that," she chided. Parker laughed, too happy to let anything dampen her mood, even her mother's grumbling.

"An overnight train with a private sleeping compartment," Parker clarified before popping the finger loaded with sweetness into her mouth. "I'm sure other couples have made do with far less."

"Well, take this." Mom opened a cabinet and handed her a bottle of champagne. "It will keep the mood festive at least."

"Thanks, Mom." Parker kissed her mother's powdered and perfumed cheek. "For everything."

*****

Lucas and Parker were running through the train station when the headlines at the newsstand stopped them cold.

WAR ENDS AS JAPAN QUITS

JAPANESE SURRENDER

"It's over!" Lucas yelped. "All of it!"

He dropped their bags and picked up Parker. He swung her in a jubilant circle before he set her back down and kissed her soundly.

"Let's catch our train, wife," he said happily. "Our new life has just begun."

Epilogue:

The US Army's Tenth Mountain Division was deactivated on November 30, 1945. Camp Hale was subsequently dismantled.

Nearly forty years later on February 13, 1985 the Tenth Mountain Division (Light Infantry) was reactivated at Fort Drum in upstate New York.

In accordance with the "Reorganization Objective Army Divisions" plan, the Tenth no longer consisted of three regiments. Two brigades were activated in the Division instead.

The Camp Hale Trilogy:

Sempre Avanti:
ALWAYS FORWARD
The 10th Mountain Division
in World War II

Ice and Granite:
The Snow Soldiers of Riva Ridge

Viking Spy:
The 99th Battalion and the OSS

Viking Spy

Chapter One

December 7, 1941
Berlin, Wisconsin

Holten Hansen got the call before the sun came up, which at this time of year meant he was able to sleep until six-thirty. After years of practice he was able to roll out of bed, pull on his cold-weather gear, gulp down a steaming cup of strong black coffee, and be ready to go before seven.

"What have we got?" he asked the Search and Rescue team captain.

Jan Ramstad handed him a photo. "Fritz Samelsted, age fifteen, went hunting in the White River Marsh yesterday afternoon. Didn't come home."

Holt frowned and passed the high school photo to the next man. "He went alone?"

"Apparently."

Holt blew an exasperated sigh while he strapped on his cross-country skis. Hunting alone was never a good idea, but it was especially dangerous in the wilds of northern Wisconsin during their brutal winters.

After he got the call this morning Holt checked the

temperature outside. The gauge read ten degrees below zero.

"I'll follow County D into the marsh." Holt straightened and pulled on his insulated mittens. "Hopefully he didn't stray too far."

*****

Holt skied along the single-lane unplowed county road, pulling down his scarf and shouting Fritz's name every few minutes. His breath formed brief icy clouds that the wind carried away while Holt listened for any response.

The day had dawned quiet, clear, and cold. The slanting morning sun washed the snow-covered landscape in pale pink and all the shadows were blue like the sky. The scene was beautiful and serene.

And deadly.

Holt shaded his eyes against the growing glare reflecting off the snow. He methodically scanned the terrain outside the road's marked path, looking for snowshoe or ski tracks. Though he knew that their constant winds drifted the snow in open areas and soon blew those signs away, he didn't want to miss anything. The boy's life depended on it.

The fact that he and the Search and Rescue team even had to come looking for the boy made Holt angry. Fritz should have known better than to go hunting alone. Every young man living in Wisconsin should know better. What was he thinking?

Risks will find you—you don't need to go looking for them.

Holt stopped to catch his breath and take a drink of icy water from his canteen. Standing still in the frigid cold, he felt a familiar and deep ache above his left hip where his pelvis had been shattered in the car accident. Hit broadside by a drunk driver, Holt was lucky to even be alive.

Though the truth be told, he wished he'd been the one who died and not his wife. He always believed she was the strong one, not him.

Holt capped his canteen and shouted again. "Fritz! Fritz, can you hear me?"

A shot rang out from the woods whose edge was about a hundred yards to Holt's left.

Hoping that was Fritz and not another hunter, Holt hollered, "I'm coming!"

He skied off the road's path and crossed the pristine and snow-covered meadow toward the pine trees. Once he reached the trees he scanned the protected ground for tracks.

Nothing.

"Where are you?" he bellowed.

The faint sound of wood-on-wood came from his right now. Holt turned his skis in that direction. "Keep hitting the tree, Fritz!"

Skiing over the forest's uneven floor was much harder than in the open meadow so his pace slowed. Even though snow-covered obstacles like fallen branches and rocks grabbed at his skis, Holt was able to keep his balance and move steadily toward the rhythmic beat.

When he reached Fritz, it was obvious that the boy was hurt. The dried blood on his face was gruesome to look at, but the fact that it was dried blood meant his head wound wasn't still bleeding.

Holt took off his skis and knelt beside the teen. "What happened, Fritz?"

Fritz struggled to sit up. "I was charged by a buck. I tripped when I was running and I guess I went headfirst into this tree. That's all I remember."

Holt was glad to see that Fritz was dressed well enough to survive the cold and told him so. "Otherwise, we'd be hauling out your frozen corpse." He pulled his walkie-talkie out of his pocket. "This is Holt. Can you hear me?"

His device emitted a loud pop and a voice replied. "Loud and clear."

"I found Fritz. He's injured but coherent."

"That's great news! Where are you?" the static-altered voice asked.

"Head down County D about a mile. If you hurry you should still see my tracks heading to the trees on the left." Holt waited for an affirmative reply before continuing. "We're a half a mile into the forest. If you can't find my tracks, send up a shot and I'll answer."

"You got it."

Holt glanced at the teen. "And bring the sled. He can't walk out."

HANSEN FAMLY TREE

Sveyn Hansen* (b. 1035 ~ Arendal, Norway)

***

Rydar Hansen (b. 1324 ~ Arendal, Norway)
Grier MacInnes (b. 1328 ~ Durness, Scotland)

Eryndal Bell Hansen (b. 1327 ~ Bedford, England)
Andrew Drummond (b. 1325 ~ Falkirk, Scotland)

***

Jakob Petter Hansen (b. 1485 ~ Arendal, Norway)
Avery Galaviz de Mendoza (b. 1483 ~ Madrid, Spain)

***

Brander Hansen (b. 1689 ~ Arendal, Norway)
Regin Kildahl (b. 1693 ~ Hamar, Norway)

    Symon Karlsen (b. 1705 ~ Christiania, Norway)

    Skagi Karlsen (b. 1707 ~ Christiania, Norway)

***

Martin Hansen (b. 1721 ~ Arendal, Norway)
Dagne Sivertsen (b. 1725 ~ Ljan, Norway)

    Reidar Hansen (b. 1750 ~ Boston, Massachusetts)
    Kristen Sven (b. 1754 ~ Philadelphia, Pennsylvania)

        Nicolas Hansen (b. 1787 ~ Cheltenham, Missouri Territory)
        Siobhan Sydney Bell (b. 1789 ~ Shelbyville, Kentucky)

            Stefan Hansen (b. 1813 ~ Cheltenham, Missouri)
            Blake Sommersby (b. 1818 ~ Kansas City, Missouri)

            Kirsten Hansen (b. 1820 ~ Cheltenham, Missouri)
            Twain Kensington (b. 1822 ~ Cheltenham, Missouri)

            Leif Fredericksen Hansen (b. 1809 ~ Norway)
            Chenoa (b. 1821 ~ Unknown)

***

Holten Hansen (b. 1904 ~ Oshkosh, Wisconsin)
Raleigh Burns (b. 1912 ~ Berlin, Wisconsin)

Tor Hansen (b. 1913 ~ Arendal, Norway)
Kyle Solberg (b. 1919 ~ Viking, Minnesota)

Teigen Hansen (b. 1915 ~ Arendal, Norway)
Selby Hovland (b. 1914 ~ Trondheim, Norway)

Lucas Thor Hansen (b. 1918 ~ Sabetha Kansas)
Parker Williamson (b. 1917 ~ Denver, Colorado)

***

*Hollis McKenna Hansen (b. Sparta, Wisconsin)

Kris Tualla is a dynamic, award-winning, and internationally published author of historical romance and suspense. She started in 2006 with nothing but a nugget of a character in mind, and has created a dynasty with The Hansen Series. Find out more at: www.KrisTualla.com

Kris is an active PAN member of Romance Writers of America, the Historical Novel Society, and Sisters in Crime, and was invited to be a guest instructor at the Piper Writing Center at Arizona State University.

"In the Historical Romance genre, there have been countless kilted warrior stories told. I say it's time for a new breed of heroes. Come along with me and find out why: **Norway IS the new Scotland!***"*

*****

Colorado resident Colonel Thomas Duhs, USMC Retired, brought his passion for the largely unknown story of the founding of the Army's Tenth Mountain Division and their triumphant battles in Italy to this project—along with three-hundred pages of research and information.

During his decorated career, Tom served as a Mountain Warfare instructor in California and Alaska, and he deployed to Norway in the winter for a total of five NATO exercises. His actual on-the-ground experience gave him the in-depth knowledge of the training the Tenth soldiers experienced at Camp Hale, Camp Swift, and the Apennine Mountains of Italy.

41189011R00177

Made in the USA
Middletown, DE
05 April 2019